I0760902

for Sadie, my first reader for life; our children Oliver, Abigail, and Martin, whose names you may see later....

This book is a work of fiction.

The characters, incidents, and dialogue are products of the author's imagination and are not intended to bear any resemblance to actual events, persons (living, dead, or otherwise) or to be thought of as real.

For more information, please contact:

www.ascendentpublishing.com

ISBN: 978-1-963-97010-4

"The people that Sit in Darkness are getting to be too scarce – too scarce and too shy.

And such darkness as is now left is really of but an indifferent quality, and not dark enough for the game.

The most of those people that Sit in Darkness have been furnished with more light than was good for them..."

- Mark Twain

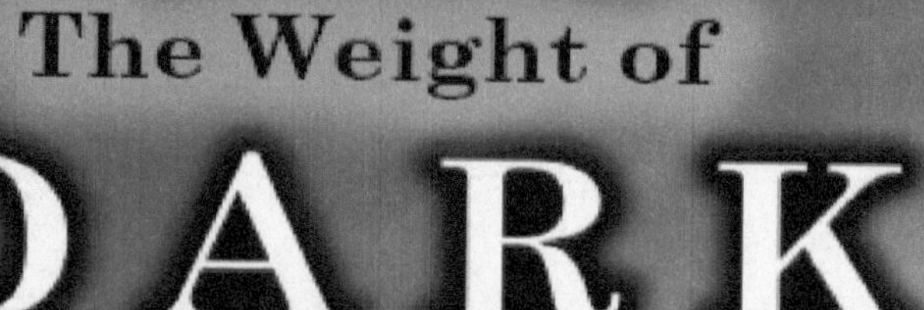
The Weight of
DARK

NESS

John A. McColley

CHAPTER ONE

Abigail readjusted her black cloth hair band adorned with deep blue silk flowers to capture stray blond locks and peered into the hallway. Thick, flower-patterned carpet she knew from memory was predominantly burgundy, though it was too dark to see color, was bounded on the far side by balusters and a railing looking out over a foyer. At the near side stood a number of vases and statues on pedestals. Between them, not a whisker flicked, not an eye watched, for now. House servants worked downstairs. Dishes clicked against one another and tile counter tops. This was her moment.

Crouching, heart racing, she ran, stocking feet sinking into the carpet's deep pile, but making no sound. The grand staircase and main foyer of the lavish house stood as empty as her ears had told her. Grasping a metal doorknob engraved with flowers on twisting vines, she looked around once more and then pulled the door open, slid around it and pulled the door closed, all in a single, practiced, motion. The last glow of dusk flooded the tiny room, illuminating dozens of boxes full of files, ledgers, records of the home owners' business dealings on overtaxed shelves. “Beckett Mining” each said in bold lettering. But these weren't what she was after.

"Took you long enough. They're not going to wait for us, you know!" a voice hissed from the darkness on a blast of cheese-scented, moist air. Her accomplice had been snacking again. He was uncomfortably close, his shoulder pressing into hers.

"Keep your hair on!" the teen girl spat back, pulling on her Wellingtons. "Go! You're the one holding us up now, always complaining." She shoved and the other rocked away. A papered window creaked as it opened. "You were supposed to oil the window. If that noise gets us caught..."

"Relax and get over here. I've tied off the rope. Hurry!" the other whispered and vanished through the window. She could hear him shimmying along the brick wall and waited until his boot scraped the slate roof before following. In seconds, they were running along the shallow slope, up a convenient tree and over the outer wall of the estate.

"Freedom!" Abigail exulted, looking out over the valley crammed with houses, tenements, and shops.

"Shush and come on!" The boy grabbed her hand and ran again toward a long building, a block of shadow that rose before them to square the mountain's jagged edge against a darkening sky. Firelight reflected on the trees across the clearing. Low laughter and the sound of tin spoons on bowls, scraping the last of a meal, told of a gathering.

At the end of the building, they ducked down behind a row of bushes to one side of the stairs up to the door. They crept to a place they had hollowed out as a hiding spot years before, a place for the hearing of stories. One of the larger trunks of the bushes had a triangle of initials cut into the bark, AB, MB, and DS. A flash of sadness came over Abigail that Daniel wouldn't come to listen with them anymore. She traced the letters with a finger.

"Well, here we are!" a man bellowed. Abigail's stomach flip-flopped. A thrill ran down her arms.

"Another day done," the man continued. Peter Smalls, foreman of the mine that provided work for the whole town in one way another, "Bellies are full and the mine is tomorrow's nightmare. Time for a tale to set your teeth on edge, get our minds clear of the black! Who's got a meaty one for us?"

"Aww, Pete, you sure have a way with words! You should have been a ringmaster in a circus or sommat!" one of the miners hollered. Laughter ran through the group of over fifty miners who lived in the bunkhouse rather than one of the tenements down in the valley town of Silver Hill proper. Faces of every color and description awaited Peter Smalls' response. He was a tall, broad shouldered black man with close-cropped hair just starting to hint at going gray over his ears.

"What do you call this outfit if not a circus?" Laughter. "We got clowns like you, Jeremiah!" Bigger laughs. "Even a trapeze artist in ol' Mira over here! How would we ever get our ore moved if not for her swinging out on that wire and getting each load hooked up? And all the rest of you, what's a circus without animals?" The laughter exploded. A shadow of a man rose against the background of trees as he stepped before the fire, waving his hands in the air to calm his audience. After a few seconds, a modicum of quiet resumed.

"I- I saw somethin' the other day," another man volunteered.

"Well get on up here, Henry!" Pete clapped, inciting the group to do the same. As the gray-bearded miner stood and advanced to take his place beside the fire, Pete moved to sit at the end of the row, attention on the new speaker.

"Well, ok," Henry said, hesitant. "You know that the Paiute have a lot of stories about the mountains, the woods. Flame-haired giants and terrifyin' huge birds and such, but this... I ain't never heard before of this thing what I saw, and I never want to see it again. I'm still chilled to ma core. I can hardly stand to think about goin' back into the woods. Gonna be a thin winter if I don't get some huntin' in..."

"Get to the story!" someone from the crowd yelled.

"What did you see, old man?" Pete urged.

"There I was, trackin' somethin', not quite sure what. The tracks were all weird, irregular like, seemed like one foot was bigger 'an the others, maybe it was caught in a trap but carryin' on... Anyway, I turned away from the river, passed a weird stack o' boulders that made me think twice about the Indians' giant stories,-"

"I seen them! I know just where you was!" someone called out.

"Did you see a giant, Henry?" someone else asked.

"Naw, but smite me if what I saw wasn't even more horrifyin'. There I was, rifle in the crook of ma arm, keepin' an eye peeled for movement, when I found myself at the edge of it." Henry paused for dramatic effect.

"The bear graveyard?"

"An Indian burial ground?"

"The giant's camp?"

"Already said wasn't no giant, Alfie, jees!"

"I call it the 'twisted grove.'" Henry said the name in a wavering voice. "Forty or fifty trees bare of leaves, stone gray, weird, lumpy branches, not so skinny as these uns here."

"Trees? You was scared by trees? Man, you had me goin' for a minute there. Couldn't you just make it a giant instead? Big ol' cookpot on the fire, tried to throw you in a stew?"

"Shut yer trap, Alfie! Let Henry tell 'is story!"

"All right, ladies and gentlemen," Pete said, standing, turning toward the crowd, hands raised before him again, palms out, fingers splayed. Laughter erupted again. "Let's just allow Henry his time. Go ahead, Henry." Pete retreated, but again, kept his focus on the storyteller. Somewhere in the distance, a wolf howled, settling the miners back into the mood to listen to a spooky tale.

"It was sheer unnatural, is what it was. Not a blade o' grass, not a shrub, just these kinda shiny gray, almost like birds feet stickin' up outta the groun'. The whole place was dead quiet. I didn't see no more tracks, but I went on, anyway, thinkin' they might come back up on the other side..."

"Did they?" someone asked after a moment.

"Never did find out. I went to step over an exposed root and I swear to heaven, it rose up and tripped me. Rifle tumbled out o' ma hands." The crowd gasped. A couple of the listeners laughed, but when no one else joined, they quieted. "Ma rifle was a good five feet in front of me now, right up next to another tree. I tried to get it back and another root swept my feet out from under me. Near t' pissin' myself now, I crawled as fast as I could. Before I lay hand on wood or metal, though, a branch dipped down and scooped me up. Another one slammed down on my side and spun me through the air."

"Never thought you'd make a good angel. You can't fly for-" The heckler was silenced by those around him.

"I thought I was done for. I was so dazed, I couldn't 'a' told you which way was up, let alone the way home. Another branch came across then, and swept my rifle and me right out of there like a housewife sweepin' out in the spring. I woke up a few hours later, with the sun on the other side of the sky, a headache like the day after St. Paddy's and this." Henry lifted the right side of his shirt. Abigail could just see from the edge of their hideout. Martin tried to squeeze in beside her to see as well. Across the man's ribs lay a black and purple bruise the size of a frying pan. She gasped. The nearer miners turned, jumping up, wide eyed, one surprise followed by another.

A miner threw a tin cup in the direction of the bushes where Abigail and her brother hid. She did her best to remain quiet as the cup fell down through the branches and bounced off her headband, but must have let out some sound. "What was that?" a miner cried. A murmur of panic rolled across the crowd of weary workers. Someone grabbed a flaming stick from the edge of the bonfire.

Martin grabbed Abigail's hand and pulled her back along their hidden passage. The bushes scratched at her arms like claws. She stumbled and a flaming stick shot through the foliage, inches from her face. She smelled smoke and felt heat on her skin. Digging in, she pushed herself to scramble harder as something else crashed down through the branches, thudding to the dirt just behind her heels. The pair made the stairs, past them to open ground, and sprinted around the side of the bunkhouse.

"That way!" a man yelled behind them. Another rock whizzed through the air over their heads. The siblings had a lot of adventures together, and kept fit, but they had geared their attire to climbing and hiding in the bushes, not running. Their boots were clunky and heavy, slowing them down. For a moment, Abigail thought they should stop and try to explain themselves to the miners. A rifle shot rang out, killing that idea dead.

"Hold your fire until you get a clear shot!" Peter Smalls ordered.

"What is it?" a miner asked.

"Can't tell. Lost it in the trees!" another responded. Abigail heaved a sigh of relief, mentally, anyway. Her actual breaths were coming ragged now. Scared miners, it turned out, were quick on their feet, if not good shots.

Hearts pounding, Abigail and Martin huddled in the

brush at the base of one of the trees they'd used many times to reenter the estate.

Voices grew more numerous. Torches waved. Abigail leaned close to her brother, whispering, "What should we do? If we stay here, they'll find us and rat us out to Mother and Father."

"We can't climb up, or we'll get stoned, or stabbed with a stick," Martin replied.

"Or burned with a torch. Already had that close call. And now someone has a rifle? When did they start bringing guns to story hour?" she asked.

"I don't know, but-" All too close, something growled. Martin's eyes opened wider. Abigail felt in the dark for his arm and slid her hand down to his, gripping it tightly.

"Here!" a woman yelled, not five feet away. The rumble grew louder, smashed into a series of harsh, sharp, barks, then settled back into a throaty growl. The ground trembled with approaching boots.

"Get back from it, Henrietta," Peter Smalls said. The growling increased again.

"I- I can't. It's got its eye on me. You're gonna have ta shoot it."

"Just stay calm. Back up toward the bushes if you can." The leaves around the twins shifted, leaning toward them as the woman pressed up against the plants. Abigail could smell her sweat, hear her shallow breathing. Then Abigail spotted the creature at the edge of the torchlight. It was like a wolf, but one of its ears was larger than the other, and its head stood at an angle as if maybe the whole creature was bigger on one side. Abigail pushed back into her brother.

"There's no more room," he breathed in her ear. "My back's against brick." The wolf's head turned suddenly. It stared past Henrietta into the leaves. Abigail was certain the creature saw her.

"Give me your hand," one of the miners whispered to Henrietta.

Abigail turned to look.

The wolf lunged, a blur of dark fur and yellow fangs.

Henrietta screamed.

The bushes shook.

Abigail raised an arm defensively inn front of her.

A cold, wet, nose brushed her hand, teeth as a mouth twisted, finding its target.

A rifle shot rang out, stunning Abigail and keeping her from screaming too, as the wolf's deformed head fell back through the foliage. The creature whimpered and stumbled back on two feet a few steps before dropping clumsily to all four feet, wheeling around and making for the undeveloped area north of town. Another shot roared through the night. Bark exploded off a tree.

"You're all right," Peter Smalls said.

"Thank you, Pete, thank you."

"Don't mention it. Gonna have to sweep the north forest tomorrow. Nothing that big should be inside the palisade. Mariah, you got any bullets left?"

"I surely do, Señor Smalls."

"Good. I'll gather a few more hands and make sure you get reimbursed for the ammunition."

"Gracias," the woman said, settling the butt of the weapon on her hip. A cool wind blew, a reminder that summer itself was dying, even if no one else did tonight. It broke the spell of the moment.

Abigail and Martin waited a few more minutes for the crowd to disperse, staring at the splatter of blood in the dirt.

It looked black in the moonlight. Abigail leaned forward, eyes narrowing. Had it moved just then? A little twitch? Before she could ask Martin, her brother lay a hand on her shoulder and pointed up. They climbed the tree and out onto a sturdy branch to drop down into their mother's flower garden.

A lantern, unshuttered, shed sudden light on them amid the columbine and day lilies. Abigail gasped.

CHAPTER TWO

"Abigail Evangeline Beckett! Martin Schuster Beckett! You two have no idea how worried your mother and I have been since bringing today's reports to the filing closet and finding a *rope!* Hanging from the window! We thought you had been kidnapped! You know the state of this town! The lawless elements salivating at the chance to get back at this family... to ransom you or..." Michael Beckett, Father, stood, a tall rail of a man, the wash from the lantern giving his angular features an otherworldly look.

"We're not *that* rich... are we?" Martin asked, bringing a hand up to shield his eyes from the glare of the lantern. To Abigail, the fact that they were standing inside their own brick castle complete with private gardens, well, and iron gate looking over a valley full of ramshackle wooden buildings huddled together and leaning like drunks answered the question with absolute certainty.

"Actually..." Father said thoughtfully before snapping back to the matter at hand. "*That* is besides the point, young man! There are! Ahem..." Father readjusted his voice to a lower, still stern, register. "There are other motivators out there besides money. We employ a great number of people in this town, and they're not always happy, no one is, but some peoples' idea of righting wrongs is..."

"Michael!" Another voice, sharp, sudden, cut through Father's, then also fell back to a nearly conversational tone. "Let us not frighten them so much that they daren't go outside these walls even in the day."

"I don't know that's such a bad idea, Mother. The elements out there, in the street, the less than reputable shops... Dens of thieves..." Father said, as if toying with the idea of restricting them to the estate.

"I sincerely doubt our little scholar and future debutante would allow their own reputations to be sullied by association with *those* kinds of characters and places. We've raised them a far-sight better than that." As much as the idea of being a debutante turned Abigail's stomach, she knew Mother and Father were playing games, taunting the twins with what they saw as reformative punishment.

"And yet... here we are, holding this discussion over your crushed crocus and trampled pansies... no, I can do better than that... err. Trampled..." Father turned in thought while Mother waved them toward the rectangle of light that was the kitchen doorway.

"We've got them!" Mother shouted into the dark. "You may all return to your work or beds, as appropriate!"

"Tulips," Abigail whispered to Father as she passed. His focus on the moment returned with a jolt, his head snapping up.

"Tulips! Trampled tulips!" He called out.

"Yes, yes, very clever. The moment's passed," Mother said, an ushering hand on his shoulder.

Reconvening around the island counter in the midst of the kitchen, each Beckett sat on a stool at one side of the rectangle slab of wood.

"What are we going to do about you? We simply cannot have you running off into the dark like this. It really is dangerous out there. You don't know what kind of man Rudy Swindon is. We had to let him him go for stealing equipment and then I hear he's started up some kind of gang that robs coaches to Carson City. If he's willing to point a pistol at simple travelers and our guards on shipments, what would he do to you, children of the man who fired him?" Abigail looked to Mother, expecting the round-faced woman to pooh pooh the idea.

"I'm with Father on this matter. Despite what I said out there for the servants' benefit, I know you have been seen around town talking with Swindon's son. That must simply stop, if it hasn't already. You don't know what danger you could be letting yourselves in for."

"But Mother! Do you know how hard it is to make friends when you're cooped up in this brick hen house every day? And when we do get out, everyone walks on eggshells so that we can't have a decent conversation. All because of you and that mine and all that damned money!" Abigail rose from her seat, both hands slapping the heavy wood counter.

"'All that damned money,' as you say, is what allows your brother Oliver to attend school in Europe, and Martin to take correspondence courses, expanding their minds and granting them a far greater future than your father or I ever dreamed of when we were your age! 'All that damned money' buys you those silly books you get your head lost in, the clothes on your back, the ribbons in your hair!" Mother reminded her, rising to her full height, still outstripping her daughter, if only just. It wasn't an advantage she'd have much longer, but she used it to good effect now. Abigail wilted back into her seat, and she and her brother both stared down at blond wood, nicked and dented as it was from years of knives and tenderizing mallets.

Back in her room, Abigail sat at her desk, not studying forces and reactions, but staring at a flat, round, stone. She picked it up and was transported some years back...

Summer in full swing, Abigail, Martin, and Daniel stood

on the rough pebbled beach at the edge of Mile Lake. They called it that because it was said to be a mile deep, but Abigail didn't know if it was true.

"You say you've *never* skipped a rock?" Daniel said with disbelief. Martin shrugged.

"It's not something that's ever come up. We've taken swimming lessons, Father insisted, but we always swam in pools."

"Well, this here ain't no pool, that's for sure," Daniel said, hefting a flat rock about the size of his palm. He held it up for Martin to see. "Gotta be kinda flat or it'll tumble. Hold it like this," he said, laying a finger along the edge, "then give it a little extra spin as you let it go." Abigail was intrigued by the concept immediately, did the spinning provide son advantage? What was the nature of that advantage? She was certain someone had studied the idea in a laboratory somewhere, perhaps Europe, or China. Martin loosed his rock, which struck the water once, popping up, then striking but only once more, vanishing quickly into the dark depths.

"That was pretty good for a first shot. Angle has a lot to do with it, too," Daniel said. "If it hits with the front down, it kind of slides into the water like a bird after a fish, but then it just sinks. If the front is a bit, it bounces... Like this." Daniel launched his stone with only marginally more force, but far greater technique. The stone left a trail of expanding ripples ten or more strikes long. He turned to Abigail. "You want to try?" He handed her a smooth, sun-warmed stone and then picked another for himself.

The next morning found Abigail reading and taking notes on Martin's engineering texts.

"Dynamical Illustrations of The Magnetic and Helicoidal Rotary Effects of Transparent Bodies on Polarised Light," Martin read over her shoulder with some difficulty.

"Yes, it's fascinating. I should visit the glassworker at some point and order some equipment to replicate the experiment."

"You mean *I'll* have to go down to that blazing hot, choking workshop and try to translate your inane descriptions to Mr. Verne."

"That was one time. I've given you precise, direct instructions, veritable schematics, every time since. All you need to do is remind him who you are, hand him the papers and ask how much money he'll need." Martin sighed at this. "Experimentation is the heart of science. If you don't have some equipment around, Mother and Father will realize you're not taking your courses seriously."

"And?"

"And then *I* will be left to languish in the company of 'Lady' Bradbury and her infinite supply of pink pillows and rose hip tea."

"Fine, whatever, I don't know what your problem with her is, anyway. She's nice."

"She's insipid."

"Does it count as an insult if the person you're talking to doesn't understand what you're saying?" Martin asked.

"You're insipid, too, sometimes..." Abigail shook her head.

"Put the pen down. We've got a shopping trip with Liza." Abigail raised and eyebrow at this. She set her ribbon bookmark and stood.

"A constitutional would go well at the moment, lead on." They headed out from the house with the purpose of retrieving a short list of goods, including the mail and the latest edition of The Voice of Silver Hill, the local newspaper, under the watchful eye of Liza, Mother's most trusted household servant.

While Liza waited for the grocer to fill the household order, Abigail and Martin slipped behind a tall set of shelves. Martin tilted his head toward the door. He pantomimed pulling a watch from his vest pocket and consulting it. *Let's give Liza the slip,* Abigail knew he was thinking, *We have plenty of time before she'll be ready to head home.* She pointed to the tin bell on its little wire, ready to tattle on them.

Martin took a step toward the door just as it opened, setting off the bell. The shopkeep, Mr. Williamson, glanced up to note another youth enter, tall and thin like Father, but with seemingly permanent dirt smudges marring his face and ill-fitting, worn, clothes. The clerk dismissed him and went back to assembling the Becketts' order.

"Daniel!" Abigail said, surprised by the boy's appearance after Mother had just mentioned him the night before. "How have you been? You've made yourself scarce of late."

"Hi, Abigail, Marty, yeah, things have been... different since..." Daniel looked at the worn floorboards.

"Yeah, sorry about..." Martin said, his own gaze drifting away.

Eyes shifting to Mr. Williamson, Daniel moved into one of the aisles. He grabbed a few long strips of jerked meat and stuffed them into his pocket.

"You don't have to do that," Martin said, keeping his tone low. "We can buy those for you."

"I don't know what you're talking about." Daniel didn't look at the twins, but moved along, pilfering more food.

"Seriously, we don't want you to get in trouble. Let us help you," Abigail pleaded.

"You two don't *know* trouble. Swindons don't take no charity." Abigail bit her lip to keep from correcting the double negative and shot her brother a look to urge him to try again.

"Children! Time to go. Mr. Williamson has agreed to send along the rest, as it's a large order, but we need this parcel immediately. It's too heavy for me to tote it all myself." Martin turned and Daniel shoved him toward the counter and ran for the door. The bell rang and the shopkeep called out after him, but Liza and her package and Martin getting his balance held him up so that by the time he reached the door, Daniel was long gone.

"Who was that? I saw you talking to him. You must know his name, his parents?" The shopkeep demanded.

"I thought he was a friend when he came in, but I guess I was mistaken," Martin hedged. "He wasn't who I thought he was."

As they walked to their next destination, Abigail was drawn back to another time Daniel had stolen food...

"Danny Swindon, you sit up here with our new students where I can keep an eye on you. We don't want the kind of trouble you caused last year," Mrs Marquez had said. The boy was half a head taller than Abigail and her brother, probably older, but also dirty, as most of the rest of the class. Abigail felt self conscious at being the cleanest in room, with nicer clothes and trimmed nails, alongside her brother.

As the day progressed, Abigail and Martin sailed through the lessons. Mrs. Marquez was impressed, but no one else seemed to care, or if they did, it was in the form of sneers and nasty whispers.

At the start of lunch, Martin and Abigail talked with Mrs. Marquez, whose husband, like most of the folk in Silver Hill, worked for their parents. When they went to fetch their lunch pails, they noticed both vessels were lighter than when they'd arrived. Martin spotted Daniel slipping out the front door, arms laden and started after him, but Abigail stopped him with a hand on the arm.

"If he's that hungry, let him have it."

"I'm hungry, too," Martin had replied, his stomach growling to reinforce the claim.

"Would you steal one of their lunches?"

"No..."

"Me either, but I think that just shows how little we'll really miss ours. We can eat when we get home." Martin deflated, shoulder falling, and nodded.

"I guess..."

The Voice of Silver Hill
ISSUED EVERY SUNDAY
by
C. Valente and S. McGuire

Terms of Subscription:
One copy, one year........................45 cents
One copy, six months........................23 cents
Single copies........................1 cent
Contact purveyors for advertising rates.

The Silver°

Vol XIX - No.40 • SILVER HILL, NEVADA

GIANT INSECTS

SILVER HILL- Local miners have reported sightings of outsized animals, including otters the size of wolves, and rams to match the largest draft horses which hail from the stories passed on by Paiute Indian tribes who used to inhabit this area.

When the white man first settled the valley, he took such legends to be the superstitions of simple folk, unworldly, and innocent. But these tales turn out to be one hundred percent valid!

The Voice staff has been hearing whispered rumors for some time, but little could be substantiated or corroborated... Until now!

This reporter is shocked to have been brought not one or two, but five different accounts of these strange creatures in the last week from mine workers scouting the hills for new shaft locations and in their off time, hunting and foraging.

Descriptions varied wildly, but were generally of shadowy creatures, strange faces in the gloom of the dense forest, or simply so disturbing we dare not include full description.

ESCAPED AGAIN- - Pastey Marley of Swindon's Bandit Crew, convicted of stage robbery and sentenced to the State prison, has gained his freedom by leaping from the train that was taking him to his future home at Carson. Search was made for him, but without success.

Voice
f Hill

Weather

Mid-week showers to bring much-needed rain.
Temperatures drift down like autumn leaves.

SUNDAY, SEPTEMBER 27, 1874 · 1 cent

HARASS MINERS

Sheriff Hornsby was unavailable for comment on how the current situation may impact the town's safety, or whether he was planning on increasing the number of deputies patrolling these streets against dangers natural and supernatural. At least one sighting within the walls has been reported, however, of a creature like unto a wolf, but traveling alone and being of startling proportions.

Are these monsters shape-shifters? A creature one minute, a kindly old man the next? Are they predators, disguising themselves to devour the unwary? Perhaps it's time to invest in old world remedies, and carry wolf's bane and garlic with one, especially while traveling at night! Beware, Silver Hillians!

* * *

The headline was clear, enticing. The article sucked Martin in. As they walked home, his excitement grew. The stories they'd heard from the miners, strange creatures that could be the same ones reported by local tribes for generations, could really be true. It was in the newspaper, after all.

"We should go up the mountain," Martin said, leaning over the kitchen island. Now, it was just Abigail and himself, dining as they often did. Mother and Father worked late at the mine offices, trying to solve some problem or other with finding a new place to dig a shaft. They might well be out until after midnight.

"Not now," Abigail whispered, her eyes widening and rolling toward the servants. Louder, for Liza and Herman's benefit,"You need help studying for your next exam, Brother? Of course I'll help you." Martin nodded and slipped her an exaggerated wink while the servants went about their business of checking the bread baking in the oven and folding linens that had been flapping in the wind all afternoon.

"You know, these newspaper men have important jobs, making sure everyone knows about... *Current events,*" Martin said. "I wonder how Mother and Father would feel about my becoming a reporter. It seems like fascinating work, listening to peoples' stories, asking probing questions..."

"You *are* becoming quite the word smith, Brother," Abigail agreed. "Don't I recall you saying you had even written to Mark Twain for advice?"

"Oh yes, Sister, I told him about our little mining town and asked for advice on a number of topics regarding writing to engage. I read that he was a miner himself for a while, and helped to run the newspaper in Virginia City. He told me he had friends in Carson City, just up the road. I eagerly await a reply to my last post." All of this was strictly true, though Abigail had heard it before. They were merely passing words that would sound reasonable to the servants after Abigail had pointed out a desire to keep the older pair in the dark regarding the twins' plans.

"This note," Liza said, suddenly appearing beside the island, "from Mrs. Beckett arrived while you were cleaning up for dinner. My instructions were not to bother you until you had finished eating." The young woman, between their age and their parents', held a pale yellow paper flower blossom, pleated into a near-circle and sealed with silver wax impressed with the signet of a stylized 'B,' after their family crest, which Father had commissioned.

"Thank you, Liza," Abigail said, taking the note. She used her dinner knife to pry open the seal. The amorphous round of wax broke and scattered across the butcher block counter top. "That never did seem very wise of a message. Why place one's symbol on a seal that will be so easily broken, and won't really keep anyone out?" Martin shrugged at his sister's question.

"What does it say?"

"One moment, let me finish opening it." Abigail pulled a pair of opposing folds, allowing the flower to bloom. Their mother had always had a flair for the dramatic. Abigail saw a strong streak of the same energy carry over to her brother. "'Dearest Abigail and Martin,' Mother's hand, no doubt. Have you seen Father's scrawl of late? I swear the lamps in his side of the office aren't bright enough and he's hurting his eyes working in such dim conditions."

"I heard 'Dearest Martin, blah blah blah.' Get on with it," Martin urged.

"Rude. Maybe I'll just read it to myself and then put it away, or maybe just leave it out. You can barely read any-oh..." Abigail stopped, her eyes having strayed to the creased paper and read some of the words as she argued with her brother.

"What?" Martin asked, color starting to fill his cheeks. "Just re-." But Abigail *was* reading, quickly, silently, focus zipping across the page. When she was done, she handed him the note.

"What?" Martin held the paper up and began to read himself. "So? They're searching for a new place to dig along the ridge? The whole range belongs to us. It's not like they're going to have to go far to stake a claim or anything."

"One, it's quite a few more dinner duets for us. But that's not the core of my worry." Martin read on, searching for the source of his sister's consternation.

"Aunt Helen?"

"Aunt Helen. Apparently our foray to the campfire has left Mother and Father with no confidence in our growing maturity. She'll be here in three days. We're not to leave the house, even to retrieve the mail or the paper. Liza is to go alone."

"I may not know much, but I know *that's* not happening," Martin said, dropping the note on the counter between their plates. "Father's not wrong about Daniel's father causing trouble. I hear his men have been waylaying travelers outside of town and even mugging folk on their way to the market."

"Mrs. Beckett knows what she's about, Young Master," Liza said. "I'll be fine. I may just have to bring your little blue wagon."

"You're welcome to that old thing. It's a child's toy and I'm nearly seventeen."

"*We* are nearly seventeen, you mean. I'm no less keen to allow Miss Liza to take to the potentially dangerous streets on her own."

"It's agreed then, two to one. We'll be your honor guard. See you in the morning, Miss Liza." Martin bowed, one hand sweeping back up behind him.

"Um... Good night, children," Liza said with a small smile.

CHAPTER THREE

After dinner, Abigail retired to her bedroom to study the books Martin was meant to read but had no interest in. Mother had always gone on about the importance of her son getting a strong education, but expected her daughter to find a man to whom to cleave rather than finding her own place. It was pure hypocrisy in Abigail's mind, given that her mother and father had met as independent prospectors and only later joined forces to open a proper mine upon finding a pair of closely-linked silver lodes.

She'd argued the case, in her head, with Mother's image, many times. Would she ever truly stand up to the woman instead of letting herself be knocked down a peg every time she gave the slightest hint of wanting something different? A bit too energetically, she flipped through pages of a weighty tome of engineering formulas and machine diagrams, trying to muster focus.

"Hey!" A hollow, haunting voice called from behind her. She jumped in her velvet-seated white wooden chair, then turned to stare into a brass bell like that of a trombone. This trombone, however, produced not music from buzzing lips, but carried her brother's voice from his room into hers, and vice-versa.

The device was simple enough, derived from the communication system on a large ship. A long brass tube branched as it came from the wall, one line running along the floor and up the wall beside her bed, flaring to the right of her pillow, the other up to the side of her desk. In her brother's room, it was very similar, so they could speak into the horn and be heard by the other while either was laying in bed or sitting at their desk, working. It satisfied decorum in them having separate rooms, but allowed them to be in each others' presences.

"What do you want? I'm studying. Maybe you should try it sometime."

"If I did that, the books would be over here and you'd have nothing to do but practice putting on make-up and brushing your hair."

"Touché," Abigail said, sighing. "Not that you would be able to get through a chapter of this engineering book without a tutor."

"Ouch, do you want to know what's up on the mountain or not?"

"Oh, are we doing that tonight? It doesn't seem very wise. It's dark and cold."

"Tomorrow, first thing. It's got to be before Helen arrives. Should only take a few hours to get up there. I'll record what we see in my journal."

"We'll need a lunch, at the least, and canteens for water."

"There's plenty of water on the way. No need to carry more. Water's heavy."

"Only at the river. I know it's going to be our main landmark, but who knows when we'll be drawn away from it by Providence?" Abigail pointed out.

"Fine, you can bring water if you want. I'll look for the compass I got for my birthday a few years ago."

"That heavy brass thing meant to be mounted in the bridge of a ship? And you complain about the weight of water?"

"Do you have another?" Martin asked.

"Of course not. Mother and Father would never allow me to have anything so...useful. But we could make one."

"What? How one Earth would we do that?"

"If the Chinese can invent a compass two thousand years ago, I'm sure we can find a needle and a magnet to rub it on to make our own in a reasonably short time."

"How do you...know these things?"

"Once again, books, dear brother. While you fantasize about bushwhacking through the jungle like an explorer in deepest Africa, some of us focus on practical matters."

"Building a compass is a practical matter for a princess-in-waiting?" Martin sniped.

"If she wants to free herself without waiting for Prince Charming, it is. Besides, there's no royalty in the United States. The Founding Fathers saw to it. And Nevada has been a state for nearly ten years."

"I knew that. How could I miss it? There was such a to do."

"It is rather a big deal, being incorporated into the United States. At any rate, unless there's something else, find what you think we'll need for the trip and I'll do likewise. Goodnight, Martin."

"Goodnight, Abigail."

Abigail read for another hour, then prepared herself for bed, brushing out her hair, though she hated that her brother was right about it. She arranged her clothing and what equipment she had in her room for the trip before turning in and blowing out the lamp.

Somewhere in the dark, something howled. It was long, drawn out, and after a few seconds, joined by additional voices. Many sounded far away, high up on the wooded slopes that hid so much silver, but others sounded terribly close. Abigail shivered, pulling her arms in tight, hands balled into fists by her chin, imagining the cold nose on her, the brush of teeth before the creature had been knocked back. The window rattled in the breeze and she jumped.

"Silly girl," she whispered to herself, "that's a thirty foot drop out there. Nothing's jumping up." Still, she reached up and pulled the silver hat pin from her favorite hat and clenched it in her fist until sleep crept up on her.

"That's the rope you're bringing? You look like a fisherman or something." Abigail gawked at her brother's get up, from the rope spooled across his torso over one shoulder and down to his opposite hip to a cowboy hat. The compass, a massive affair of a 5 inch diameter brass circle housing with flanges for attaching to a pedestal or panel on a large, seagoing ship, hung from a thick length of twine through the screw-holes and over his neck.

"Well, what have you got then? Sandwiches? Water?" Martin prodded.

"Yes, I have. Both are a far sight more practical than your choices," Abigail shot back. She held up the picnic basket, a red and black checked blanket rolled up and fed through the wood handles.

They set out for the front door, thinking it the least likely one at which the servants, buzzing about the kitchen and laundry last they saw, would catch them. Also, Abigail didn't relish the idea of carrying the wicker basket up over the ten foot brick wall her parents had had erected when they first began to make headway on the mine. Once upon a time, the whole town was within these premises. Now, it sprawled down the valley, protected by a palisade of pointed wood poles and the brick compound was their home, mansion, gardens, sports corner, carriage house. The original wood buildings of Silver Hill had all been moved. A tenth of the town's current population might fit within the estate's confines.

Abigail mused on the evolution of a tiny pocket of civilization, seeding itself in one spot and expanding outward toward resources, the silver in the mines, the river for water, the flat areas for limited farming, the high plains for sheep and cattle.

"Where do you think you're going?" A voice, sharp as the cavalry saber Father kept over the hearth in his study, slashed through her thoughts. She and her brother turned to see Liza, hands on hips, glaring at them. "No more adventures, no trouble. The Lady and Master said. They were quite clear in their note. You are to stay here. Hiding under bushes, listening to rowdy, rough miners tell horrifying stories. You two are above all that, or *should be*." These last words, Liza thrust like the aforementioned blade. Abigail's enthusiasm cooled. "Learning your place in life means taking responsibility for yourselves, your family, the future of the mine, and the town. The town doesn't exist without the mine. If it were a plant, the mine would be the root." The woman wasn't wrong. Abigail hung her head, ready to return to her room, and the refuge of Martin's books. Someday, they would get her out of this town, to a proper city where expectations for young ladies were more egalitarian.

"That's a poetic comparison. Have you been *reading*, Liza?" Martin asked in his "I'm trying to be manly" voice.

"Everyone down there," Liza pointed past them out the gate at the cram of slanted rooftops, steeple of the church and water tower standing as giants above the masses. "Is counting on you, or will, someday, sooner than you think. You've got to keep to your studies and make good examples of young lord and lady of yourselves."

Abigail had no intent of living the life set out for her by

her parents, but she couldn't deny they *did* have a responsibility to use their wealth, their position, to help the people. And they would do that, she realized, by investigating the strange events on the mountain and convincing their parents to take real action, hire more deputies, more guards for the miners, something.

"Dear Liza, we're simply going for a picnic. If this is to be our prison for the foreseeable future, with Helen on the way to sit on us like moppets, we need to go soak in freedom for a few hours. The river is perfectly safe and well-traveled by miners." Liza's brown eyes narrowed.

"What do you need the rope for?" Martin grasped for an answer, but Abigail's mind was primed now.

"You know Martin, always reading his adventure books when he's not studying. One of his books mentioned hammocks, these hanging beds made from ropes."

"I know what a hammock is."

"Then you know they're supposed to be very enjoyable. He hopes to find a couple of trees the right distance apart where he can tie off and try it out for himself." Liza looked anything but convinced.

"We have trees right here, inside the walls. A number of them are older than yourselves and capable of carrying your weight. If you want a hammock, tie off here, else you may find yourself in a hammock on a working ship, bereft of your parents' money. How far do you think you would get in life without that?"

They were hard blows, but true, Abigail knew. They as good as chained her to the floor. Martin looked ready to make a run for it, but she took his hand. After a moment, he pulled away.

"Fine, I'll make the hammock here..." He turned back to

the door. As soon as they were through and the heavy wooden panel shut behind them, though, his demeanor changed. "I can't do it. I can't just sit and read and play with gadgets. I am a man of adventure!"

"A what of what?" Abigail asked, almost bursting out laughing right in his face. She certainly didn't feel like a brave woman after Liza's berating. Perhaps she had taken lessons from Mother. "We've got to stay. Liza all but threatened you with being sold off to a merchant ship."

"She couldn't if she dared," Martin scoffed.

"And Mother? Has she not waved that same stick at you previously?"

"And yet, I am here," Martin pushed back. "Are you with me? Or with them?" Such a choice. Martin began walking for the front gate of the compound. Abigail stood for a long moment, arms crossed, half a mind to open the door to the house and call Liza to gather up the gardener and others to capture her brother. But with the mood he was in, someone might get hurt. She sighed heavily and lifted the picnic basket.

In minutes, they were past the East Gate which most of the miners trudged or rode out every morning and back every evening. The forest was a presence, looming, brooding. Trees they were used to, the apple and pear on the estate, and the small stand of pines, were tame, kept.

This forest was a chaotic mass of living force, with a jumble of species and varieties, from red oaks and white, to firs from bluish to so dark green they were almost black. Brush, berry bushes, wildflowers, creeping vines, took up every inch of space. The only bare spots were the dual tracks carved by cart wheels, the road up to the mines, an almost unbearable scar Martin's eye was drawn to even while feeling he should look away.

He loved nature, and truly his desire to follow in the footsteps of the great explorers was deeply rooted in his awe and love for the natural world. The reminder that his parents cut a swath through this paradise in order to access their hole in the ground made him a little sick. If this was the meaning of becoming an engineer, he wanted it even less.

Passing up the rutted path, grasses growing defiantly from the center ridge, Martin kept his eyes peeled for anything unusual. The river burbled nearby, visible in places, but blocked off by a dense row of ancient trees left in place to keep the river from wandering. Birds sang, insects thrummed and chirped. Every step, he felt as though something was tracking their progress, noting their location, perhaps waiting for its chance to strike.

"How long would you say is it to the mine opening?" Abigail asked. Martin started, roused from his hypnotic connection to the green and black and blue and brown.

"The Landing? That's what they call the current hub. I guess there's a couple of buildings for offices and equipment, some stamp mills to crush the ore, a refinery to smelt it into ingots... There must be a place for the wagons to get loaded up... Uh, an hour? The first shafts were a lot closer. We already passed the first one-that overgrown track on the left back there-but as we expanded, they ranged farther from town. They bring workers up in the ore wagons pulled by horses. They used to be able to walk, but now that would eat a large chunk of the day. If the shafts lasted longer, maybe they would put in a train. Wouldn't that be something?"

"I'm sure, but then a lot of this would have to be knocked

back," Abigail said, looking around. "And I'm not sure it would allow such intrusion."

"I get that feeling, too, like it's..." Martin peered at a bush that seemed to be slowly twisting rather than rustling in the wind.

"Watching us?" Abigail suggested.

"Exactly. I really wish I could say that's crazy," Martin said, clutching the bundle of rope at his chest. The compass had migrated to the knapsack on his back after the first mile. He was sure there would be bruises even from that short time of bumping and gouging. "Let's just keep on. When the path turns left again the Landing can't be much farther."

"What's that?" Abigail pointed at the leaf litter at the side of the trail. Something like a sausage as long as one of their arms lay, ruddy pink and glistening. As Martin slipped off his pack and stepped closer, one end of the creature whipped around to face him. From it sprouted a small bird's head, perhaps a robin. It seemed alert, eyes blinking, beak slightly open.

Eyes wide, Martin leapt back, stumbling over his feet and landing hard between his pack and Abigail. In a flurry of flailing teenage limbs and damp leaves, he regained his feet and looked around for a stick to fend the thing off. As they watched, the long, segmented, body flopped back over and let out a sad little cheep before snuggling out of sight in the leaf litter.

"Not to repeat myself, but what *was* that?"

"Some kind of blind snake, a burrowing creature I have read about."

"But its head..." Abigail shuddered.

"I have to assume it came up from the ground and happened upon an unwary bird, struck poorly-snakes usually eat their prey head first-and hadn't finished swallowing."

"It didn't look wider at that end, like it had a bird inside, and look, slime. That was definitely a giant worm with a bird's head. Is that enough weird for you? Do you really need to see this 'Twisted Grove' place? We're not even to the Landing yet and I'm uncomfortable, tired, and ready to go home."

"Not a chance. Let me write down my impressions, try to sketch this creature. Then we can get to the ridge above the Landing and have lunch. Tell me you packed more than one meal."

"What do you take me for? I've been adventuring with you before. You remember the high plains standing stone debacle? I always pack for at least two meals, so I can get some before you devour it all."

"Heh, sorry about that."

"You realize that's your first actual apology after nearly two years?"

"I said I was sorry. You can eat first."

"I'll believe that when I see it."

CHAPTER FOUR

Up and up they hiked, ancient, gnarled trees and the burbling river their constant companions.

"Look! A butterfly. I'm sure I've never seen one quite like it." Abigail held out a finger to the fluttering green creature and to her surprise, it wheeled around her and alit on the back of her hand. "Ugh, oh, how odd!" She said, getting a much better look at the creature. "Shoo!" She flicker her wrist, encouraging it to take flight once more.

"What was that all about? You wanted it to come to you," Martin said.

"That was when I thought it was a beautiful butterfly of some unknown species. It wasn't that at all. It was a grotesque, unmetamorphosed, caterpillar with 'wings' of green maple leaves! I think it scratched me with its little pointy legs." Abigail shivered with disgust, determined not to assume anything was what it looked like in this forest. In contrast, Martin took out his notebook again and sketched the creature from her description. The resulting abomination of squirming segmented worm with claw-like legs, bulbous eyes and grasping mandibles, leaves crudely erupted from its back, turned Abigail's stomach.

The Landing far below them, beyond the maintained road, they picked their own way, slower, along disused paths frequented only by hunters, foragers, and the men and women the twins' parents sent out in search of likely spots for new shafts.

"How much farther is this upper landing or whatever nonsense you've written down to substitute for proper directions?" Abigail pressed. Her feet were beginning to hurt and while they had a small tent, she didn't relish the idea of sleeping in the woods. The creeping things they'd found in broad daylight were more than enough. She daren't consider what might lurk in the night, attracted by Martin's snoring, which was bad enough from the next room. She'd tried stuffing stockings into the brass communication horn, but the sounds simply reverberated through the walls.

They stopped to eat again as the sun moved past its apex. Abigail bit her apple, awaiting a response.

"Not far at all, actually. I've just checked my compass and we're still headed due east."

"Please. We're following the river and you know it. But there's supposed to be a turn off. We won't see it in the dark, I expect. We should have brought a lantern, but by the time we got all the things we should have for this, we'd be a party of five- hey! Where'd you go?" Abigail stopped, eyes darting back and forth for a sign of her brother.

"I'm right here, the turn. It's here." Martin stepped back around a massive sequoia Abigail thought they could live inside comfortably. The notion got her thinking of old faerie tales that she'd read before Martin started engineering school and gave her more worldly, scientific, things to learn about. If there was something this strange place with its dense, dark canopy, immensely-trunked trees, and strange creatures apparently seen nowhere else reminded her of, it was that primordial forest of lore. She shouldn't be surprised to see a witch's hut made of gingerbread and candy on the other side of the gargantuan tree. The dreamlike feeling didn't diminish as they strode away from the river, letting the forest engulf them.

"Do you hear that?" Martin asked, his tone hushed, eyes wide and flicking to focus on nothing as he turned his attention to his ears.

"I don't, and if this is your idea of a joke, it's far from funny. I'm already feeling... enchanted by this place. I might believe anything could walk around the next tree, a satyr, a minotaur, Cernunnos..."

"Shh!" Martin insisted, holding up a hand. And then Abigail heard it, too. It reminded her of playing pirates with her brother years before, wood swords carved by the local woodworker, Mr. Higgins, rapping and popping in the yard, the sound echoing off the brick wall. Then Martin was running, crouched, one hand flapping at her to follow. Abigail sighed and, not really seeing an option, sped up. "There!" Martin said in an excited whisper.

Abigail peered into the gloom, expecting a falcon with a chipmunk head or some such, but then stopped when she spotted a herd worth of antlers arrayed across a single head, neck and back of an overlarge, well, she supposed it was a deer. As it ducked its head down to browse some leaves, the antlers splayed out. Hearing a noise, its head rose quickly, causing a chain reaction of hard clacks which ran down its spine and back up, like the Newton's Cradle she had on her desk.

Without a conscious decision, Abigail spun on her heel to run, but Martin caught her hand.

"It's all right. It's just a deer. They're not dangerous."

"Regular deer may not usually be aggressive in the summer, but THAT," she stopped herself, closing her eyes and jabbing a thumb in the direction of the continued sound. Resuming at a lower volume, "That is *not* a regular deer. We have no idea what its demeanor is. I've seen enough. We're going."

"Aww, but it's so close, it's right-" The rest of Martin's argument was cut off by a catastrophic explosion. They both jumped, the picnic basket striking the ground and the compass in Martin's bag clanging off something else. Gripping one another, they huddled in the knees of another great sequoia tree, searching the sea of dark green for detonation's source.

The miner they knew as “Alfie” came running through the brush, spotting the twins immediately for their light clothing and generally standing out from the scene.

"The Beckett twins? What are you two doing here? These woods is dangerous! Did you see my deer? Did I hit him?" Martin extended a wavering finger in the direction they had seen the deer. "Well, come on, then. I can't just leave you out here, but I need to get that beast! Think of the meat! It'll last months by itself!" Alfie waved his hand at them as Martin had done with Abigail moments before. "Move it!" The older miner insisted, holding his rifle across his chest, brushing the tip of his gray beard as he spoke.

The chase was on! Alfie led them on a surprisingly energetic spree through the brush after his prize. From ahead, constantly over the rush of brambles and leaves sliding by or catching their clothing, came the clack of too many antlers. Abigail did not relish the talking to they would get from Liza, then Mother and Father when they saw the state of their outfits. She could see a number of green streaks on Martin's shirt and vest that weren't likely to come out via conventional cleaning methods. She began to giggle at the absurdity of chasing a clear aberration of nature through the dark woods rather than running from it home as fast as she could.

"Isn't this great?" Martin misinterpreted her giddiness. "Ohhh!" He gaped as the creature crested a bald crown of stone before them, majestic in its own way standing in the golden light, the next, higher peak majestic behind it. The creature bore a grand rack of antlers full up on its head and a dozen pair trailing down its neck and back. Many of the protuberances were distorted and twisted from their normal shape, lacking the symmetry that often lent such things beauty. Blood flowed from its shoulder, sleeving its left front leg in red.

"No! It's not 'great' at all! Mother and Father are going to switch us for this insanity, perhaps even put us away. Maybe they'd even be right to..." Abigail scratched absently at her hand.

"Oh come now, sister. Is this not our grandest adventure? Pursuing a creature fit for the age of legend, matching the Lernaean Hydra, Jörmungandr the World Serpent, with a trusty hunter at our side?" Martin gestured grandly.

"Jörmungandr? Don't you think that's-" Abigail began to object.

"Quiet down now, you young uns. It's tired and growing calm. If I can line up another shot, we'll grab it and drag it back down to town. Might even get there by true dark," Alfie admonished. "That would be better. Don' wan' to see what roams up here at night."

"Like what?" Martin asked eagerly. He certainly did want to see just that.

"Creatures that defy description, like in Rev'lations."

"The end of the world in the Bible?"

"Sure 'nough, now shush." The older man brought his weapon to bear once more, taking sight down the barrel. A few yards away, a flock of birds they hadn't noticed took to the air as one, startled by something. Likewise, they startled the deer and it was off again, leaving only a small pool of blood on the gray stone.

"Damn!" Alfie swore and started on again. "Nothin's easy."

He continued to mutter to himself as they stalked the injured deer through another half mile of woods before coming to something that wasn't quite a clearing. The space stood devoid of ground cover, and filled with dozens of what one could only assume were trees. They looked unlike any species Martin had ever seen. This must be Henry's "Twisted Grove."

The "trees" were a hazy silver, so that when the deer moved close to the first, it cast a blurred reflection like a fogged up mirror. The area being clear, Alfie took aim once again.

Martin and Abigail, anticipating another deafening blast, crammed their eyes closed and covered their ears with their hands. When no such sound issued within a few seconds, Martin opened on eye, turning back to see Alfie, frozen with his finger hovering over the trigger, eyes wide as full moons.

Tracing his line of sight, Martin spotted the horror which held the elder transfixed. True to the story they had heard from Henry at the campfire, the trees within the grove swayed wildly as though beaten by a gale. There was barely a breeze in the still wood where they stood. At the fore of this motion was the deer, staggered to its knees by even more violent motion from the "trees." Martin had heard tales of anemones in tropical waters, with bulbous arms battering away and pressing prey into a central mouth. With the exception of the lack of a mouth, this looked just like those stories, with branched arms and trunks bending in concert to bludgeon the creature.

When he first looked, the thing seemed dazed. It leaned to one side, but in seconds, additional arms struck, battering the great animal around as though it was as small as a shaking-legged newborn. Finally, the pewter tendrils of two different "trees" took hold of either end, wrapping around ankles and tugged back and forth, the head flailing, the clacking of antlers so violent they cracked and shattered against one another and the ground.

With a sickening sound like a wet grocery bag giving loose, gore flew in every direction, with intestines looping over branches of the not-trees and trailing like streamers even as the not-trees continued their work, slamming the sections of corpse over and over again.

Something struck Martin in the foot and he jumped back. A section of skull, with the pelt partially torn away and a blood-shot eye stared blindly up at him. He felt the sandwiches Abigail had packed rising and turned to retch even as Abigail herself hauled on his elbow.

When his stomach had finished emptying, the not-trees stood still, silent, painted red, strung with entrails. The halves of deer were nowhere to be seen. "What happened to the..." he tried to ask, but seeing that he was done losing his lunch, Alfie joined Abigail and threw an arm around the boy's back, guiding him away from the scene.

The going was rough, and Martin stumbled, coming face to face with a four inch section of antler. In a moment of clarity or insanity, he snapped it up, slipping it into the side pocket of his knapsack before his sister pulled at his sleeve again.

Alfie in the lead, they fled. Exhausted by the pursuit of the deer creature, they ran out of steam quickly.

"Hurf, I think, hurf, that's as hurf, far as I can make it," Alfie wheezed, leaning against a tree for a moment before realizing what he was doing and withdrawing his forearm from the bark.

"No argument here," Martin agreed. "I don't think those things move from their spots, but I don't want to find out if I'm wrong."

"They ate..." Abigail said, still trying to process, digging at her hand with her nails. "The trunks just split open... so many... were they even teeth? Clusters of spines like some kind of... inside out cactus, you know the desert plants?"

"You're babbling," Martin barked.

"She's not. I saw them, too. Hurf. They kind of unrolled like a map curling at both ends, and then wrapped around the mashed up deer... Hurf. My deer. Months of meat..." Alfie lamented.

"I'm not certain I would be comfortable consuming such an animal. Why are these strange creatures so abundant here? I have to wonder..." Abigail said, seeming clearer of mind now that she had gained some distance from the threat.

"Ye may be right, girl. The Paiute moved on from this area ages ago, and still tell their tales of strange creatures roaming these woods." Aflie sounded better, with fewer wheezes interrupting his speech. "We should head for the prospector's cabin."

"We need to get home. We're already pushing being late for dinner. Liza will have our heads," Abigail said. "Where... where's the trail?"

"Off that way," Alfie waved to his right as he started pushing his way through the scrub. "But shelter is this way and a heck of a lot closer. I don't think you'll make it down before nightfall."

"I agree," Martin said, setting his pack down and pulling

forth his compass. It caught a stray beam of light from the setting sun on the flange just above his fingers. "North is that way, so the trail, and town must be that way." He pointed behind him, then toward the setting sun to his right. "But with how dense the canopy is, we'll be traveling in real dark quicker than I expected. Maybe we should go with Alfie."

"I don't like it, but am forced to concur. We can deal with Liza tomorrow when we've survived this ordeal," Abigail said, starting off after Alfie. Distant creatures hooted and howled and croaked to one another. Abigail tried her best not to picture what kind of hybrids or monstrosities they might be, but every wolf grew lizard scales, every frog an extra pair of legs and compound eyes. She shivered in the dark.

"Are you getting cold? I have an extra shirt in my pack. I know you don't think I plan, but it's there, along with another pair of pants and socks."

"While that's surprising and admirable, it's not the temperature that shakes me. Those sounds. I know that in normal woods, they would be simple owls and such, but I can't help thinking of how they would be twisted here, like the deer and that worm-bird thing."

"Nothing we've seen has been truly dangerous. There's at least that."

"Nothing... mobile, anyway..." Abigail agreed, "It's all just properly bizarre. I can't think that there would be so many strange creatures undocumented in the whole of the world. Where did they come from?"

"If yer lord and ladyship wouldn't mind piping down, there *are* dangerous beasts aplenty out there in the dark. I've seen some fey footprints in my time hunting up here."

"Footprints? We've seen far scarier than footprints on this trip already," Martin said.

"Not like these, I wager. Bigger'n a straw hat, so deep I put my hand down and went nearly to my elbow. Others, long and thin, like to a rabbit's foot, but long'r'n my foot and not in proper rabbit position. Can't say I ever saw the owners of either print, but to me that means they were out there when I wasn't, which was night."

"Frightening footprints of nocturnal beasts, good to know," Abigail accepted. "And how far to this cabin?"

"Not too long, quarter hour? Longer if we keep talkin' instead of walkin'." Alfie headed off in earnest again, putting pep into his pace, forcing the teens into silence to put on the speed to keep up.

CHAPTER FIVE

As predicted, after ten minutes of crashing through brush, they came to a cabin. From the front, in deepening gloom, Abigail got an uneasy feeling. "That looks like something from my Gothic novels phase. The shutters are falling off, the roof sags. From the brush and leaves piled up against the door, no one's been here in years, let alone kept it up."

"That may be so, but it was a lifesaver in its day," Alfie pointed out. "And hopefully it will be again. Your parents built the first of these huts as shelters while lookin' for the big lode. This is older than the two of you, but I don't remember it being *so* bad. I bet the inside is still cozy. There's a fireplace. We'll get a fire going and-" As he spoke, he fiddled with the door, finally pausing to put his shoulder into it to get it open.

Stumbling into the space, he let out a disappointed sigh. "Looks like it's in even worse condition from the other end. I can see a crack of sky between treetops," Alfie said. A low rumble permeated the darkness.

"There's no need to growl, Martin. We'll have to make do. A fireplace is still something," Abigail said. "Partial walls are better than none."

"That's... not me..." Martin objected as the growl grew louder and was joined by a second sound, more of a strangled gurgle. Timbers creaked. Furniture crashed over as a massive body shifted.

"Time to go," Alfie said, backing through the doorway before turning and pushing between the stunned twins at an all out run. Abigail and Martin looked at one another and gave chase, dodging between thick trees that had never bordered a trail.

Behind them, the creatures roared. The sound reverberated in Abigail's chest, nearly knocking her from her feet. She caught herself on a rough bole, and shoved off, determined to outpace whatever things they had awoken. Wood shattered. Stone tumbled, heralding the death of the imagined safety of hearth and chimney. Given their focus on ledgers and survey maps, it seemed so odd to think of her parents building such a place, and it angered her that it was gone before she'd had a chance to set foot inside.

A tree behind them creaked, then splintered with such a tremendous crack that Abigail stopped, turning to see if she needed to run a different direction to avoid the falling timber. She caught motion in the distance and another treetop fall out of sight, revealing stars. The first two trees thrashed their neighbors and slammed into the ground, motivating her to run even as Martin called for her.

His face was a pale oval in the dark, his body a vague shadow of vest and dark trousers, white, ghost-like arm flailing to urge her on. She charged through the brush as best she could. The bushes had crashed back together in Martin and Alfie's wakes, obscuring whatever path they had blazed. The beasts grew closer as she fought with one wrong trail after another. This was wild country at the best of times, but now it seemed to fight against her, reaching for her, seeking to entwine her limbs at every step. Something wrapped around her wrist and she screamed despite herself.

"Hush girl!" Alfie hissed out of the darkness, now so deep she could barely make out his face from arm's length. He hauled with a gnarled old hand. Thorns pulled at her blouse with violent tearing sounds. They bit her upper arms, leaving cat scratches. The ground shook again. "We gotta find shelter. Would that we had a cave at hand, but they're back the other way, past the beast. There was a Paiute settlement out this way..." Alfie said, reaching for mental maps as Martin helped his sister to her feet. "Blasted dark... Blasted beasts..."

"What about that? It looks like a boulder. Maybe we could hide behind it," Martin said, staring into darkness Abigail's eyes couldn't penetrate.

"Better than standing here," Alfie agreed and they were off again. Abigail's arms felt streaked with fire. Her feet ached and her legs were tired. Her lungs weren't far from giving out. This was the most exercise she could remember having at once. It would either kill her, or she would be in excellent shape for meeting her new friends at the boarding school her parents would surely send her to after this...

What Martin's questing eyes had first seen through the gloom as a massive stone was in fact a modest sized hut of local materials and native design.

"It's a wickiup," Alfie informed them. "They Paiute would build 'em for to live in."

"What about teepees?" Abigail asked.

"That was mostly plains Indians, I think. They moved around a lot more and took their houses with 'em, like snails."

They huddled in the hemisphere of vertical sticks twined together with grass ropes and leather straps, bark woven in to create closed walls against the weather, shaking and praying against being found by the creatures from the cabin. They continued to hear trees being upended, but the sounds grew farther away until they danced at the edge of Abigail's consciousness and she couldn't be sure if they were really still happening or her mind was playing tricks in the dark.

She thought about asking to light a fire, as the cold had really set in, and the ground was damp, but immediately dismissed it as something the heroes of the adventure novels Martin read would never do. The smoke might well attract the creatures back, or some new horror from the cursed forest. She leaned against her brother.

"If... rrrsh..." Abigail shivered, "If we make it down in one piece, I swear I'm never stepping foot on this mountain again."

A weight fell across her back, sweeping up and down in broad, slow strokes. She snuggled against Martin more, feeling the moment of sibling closeness. They had their disagreements, but in the end, they were the closest of family, not just siblings, but twins, having traversed every step of development so far side by side. She would not be who she was without his presence in her life, nor he, she was sure, be himself lacking her.

"Uh? What you want?" Martin grumbled, at least half into Morpheus' realm. Abigail reached around to grasp his hand on her back, to give a measure of comfort in return. Her hand met only a cold, hard, sharp-ended stick about the width of a broom handle. She jolted up, trying to roll away, but found the darkness around them filled with searching tentacles like a school of octopuses. They immediately grabbed her, under her arms, around her chest, rounding her neck even as she struggled to scream.

"Wha- whazzat?" Alfie demanded of the dark, the same muzziness to his voice that Martin had. Abigail kicked, trying to keep her legs from being bound up, and connected with flesh.

"Oof!" Martin's responded, surprised, but not yet panicked.

"Wazallanoise?" Alfie demanded, annoyed at his own drowse being broken. "Ahgad!" He said a moment later, somewhat more alert. There came a metallic click and then an explosion to rival the crashing of the beasts in the dark. Thunder struck Abigail's whole body at once, as though she was being slapped by a giant. She fell to the ground in a heap, a pile of loose muscle with no control. She lay, shoulder and forehead in the dirt, rear in the air.

The passing seconds advanced like glaciers scraping out the mountain valleys of the Northeast. Something struck her back again. She tried to scream, but could scarcely release a breath. A hand, warm, slid across her back. She tried to squirm away and found herself unable to shift her weight. The muscles seemed barely to respond at all. *Is this it? Am I paralyzed? Will Martin leave me behind? Can he have the strength after this ordeal of a day to carry me out? Even drag me?*

In the next moment, she was in the air again, pressed against a larger, warm, body. Something warm and wet slid down her cheeks as she bounced along, and she realized that the thunderous calamity was the last sound she had heard. In place of footfalls crushing twigs and grass, the heavy breathing of her savior, there was only a constant ringing, now, a dull roar. She tried to move her arms, but one was pinned against whoever was carrying her, who seemed not to be Martin, after all, from the smells of rum and tobacco, and the other flailed, alarmingly unresponsive. She tried to lift her head to see where they were going, but had to rely on the chaotic bounce of Alfie's stride, with her weight unbalancing him, to let her head bob up to show variations in the darkness.

Abigail could feel Alfie's arm straining to keep her on his hip, to carry her as far as he could through the dark forest. The limb vibrated with effort, fatigue. It was hardly a surprise when she crashed to the ground, but she couldn't catch herself. She felt him fall beside her, say something that didn't make it past the ringing in her ears, and collapse entirely. She tried to reach out to him, but only managed a weak twitch. Somewhere nearby, someone else screamed, calling out for help, Abigail guessed. The sound was a dull blur against the dull roar that dominated her soundscape. Her eyes played her no better through the growing darkness.

Summoning all her will and demanding her body react, she managed to incrementally flop an arm over Alfie's back. As far as she could tell, he wasn't breathing. She couldn't feel his back rising and falling with breath, or find a pulse. Of course, she was no expert in such matters. She felt his rifle laying against the other side of his body.

What am I to do with this? I understand aiming and firing by pulling the trigger in only the most rudimentary way. No, stop that, Abigail! You're a capable young woman and your brother needs you!

Seconds... minutes? rolled by as the feeling began to return to her limbs. Abigail tested each of them, crawling over Alfie to retrieve the weapon. She rolled onto her back but held the weapon in her arms, legs still draped awkwardly across the fallen miner.

Forcing breaths out hard and fast, she demanded response from her muscles and brought the shotgun up, wide back end against her shoulder as she'd seen in woodcut prints in Martin's adventure books. Her hand naturally found its place on the body of the gun, her finger, the trigger. She moved the digit away lest she accidentally discharge the weapon early.

She had no idea how many times it would fire and no idea if Alfie carried more ammunition or how to load the killing machine.

Once, twice, she struggled to sit up, to spot Martin or whatever was chasing them now in the gloom. She could only make out the vague outline of the wickiup. Was it getting closer? Hauling one side, then the other, forward... *walking?* She didn't have much time to contemplate this stomach-wrenching turn of events as Martin was suddenly standing over her, followed by the wickiup, blotting out the few stars she could see above her. She brought one leg up, shoving Martin to the side, and found the trigger again. Without hesitation, she fired.

The second blast was nowhere near as loud, but the weapon slammed into her shoulder like a medieval army battering down a castle gate. She was sure she felt something snap, and she once again lost control of her right arm. Brow knit, mouth a rictus of fear, she fumbled for the rifle with her left hand as it fell away from her. Another hand bloomed out of the dark, grasping the nearly invisible barrel.

A face loomed close.

"Can you hear me?" Martin yelled as though from across a valley, his mouth mere inches from her ear. The world swam.

"Not really," she tried to say. What she could hear of her voice through the din was off, distorted. Another hand shot forward, offered to help her rise. She awkwardly pawed at it with her left hand.

"Both hands!" Her brother called.

"I can't. I- Something broke!" She yelled back, tears finally welling her eyes. She willed them away. It was hard enough to see already, and she couldn't hear. Her heart slammed in her chest. The ground shook, another ponderous step of...

something. With a cry, she heaved herself up while holding onto her brother's hand and they began hobble-running as best they could. They had always been good at the three legged race, being twins, but the terrain was rough, dark had fully fallen, and they were both thrust into a full panic.

A roar overrode Abigail's ringing head, filling her ears, rattling her bones. They stumbled on, constantly assaulted by entangling brush, raking thorns, every impact striking at their fear-filled minds as well as their flesh.

The wind picked up, cold and damp. Was there a storm coming? That would be a fine end to this expedition. Suddenly, Martin hauled back on her, sending pain through her injured shoulder and whipping her around, stealing what little orientation she had amassed.

"What are you doing? We can't stop now!" Abigail cried out.

"The river!" Martin returned, gesturing behind her. She looked and a bare rock wall illuminated by the moon stared back. Ten feet below, black waters rushed, set with shifting flashes of moonlight. They were trapped.

CHAPTER SIX

Another great roar tore through the twins, reverberating off the rock wall beyond them. Abigail thought briefly about jumping in the river, wondering at their chances, disoriented and injured, tired from constant flight over the last hours... Still, it would be better than being torn limb from limb by a giant bear. She pulled on Martin's arm and pointed at the water. He shook his head.

"I'd never make it!" He yelled. "Our best bet is to get down to the edge of the river and hope to find a cave!"

The wind shifted. From cool to hot, damp to downright fetid, it carried the scent of death. It gusted, then let up, gusted again. Abigail turned slowly back to the wall of black behind them. Two green disks stared back, bright like unholy lanterns the size of saucers. As she stared, unable to tear her gaze away, she noticed other lights, a smaller pair just down to the left and a fainter pair straight down from the main set. Abigail's grip on her brother's arm increased.

"Ow! Hey!" She could hear him howl as through a closed door. Then he turned. The faces advanced. The canopy stood thinner close to the river, allowing moonlight to play across mottled fur. Abigail had only seen bears in drawings and once in a zoo when she and her parents went to New York City for business. This one seemed somehow lumpier, larger on the left side. Then the second face came into view and she screamed, cramming her eyes shut. The hot wind blew in her face again even as the image haunted her mind's eye.

The second face was also that of a bear, smaller, but not standing on its own. The right side of cub was fused with what she assumed was its mother. It hung, two outer limbs thrashing, as if trying to run at Abigail and Martin, its jaws working, but producing no sound Abigail could hear with her damaged ears. Martin shook her and she opened her eyes again, only to take in the beast's full visage, greater jaws open, showing forked yellow teeth and a serpentine tongue which lashed through the night at them.

The second face mimicked its mother and the third, barely visible from between her front legs, snarled and shook, pitiful and terrible at the same time, the size of a normal bear, dwarfed by the monster. A paw the size of a mine cart came up ponderously, swiping at them.

Martin pulled her down, sending a burning lance of pain through her shoulder, but letting them keep their heads as the paw tore the air and smashed a maple tree, the trunk cracking and dirt flying up in a cloud as roots snapped like firecrackers at their feet.

The soil loosened, the ground dissolved beneath them. They tumbled in the dark, dirt pattering down around them, as the bear charged in, swiping again. It roared as they splashed into the river, the icy water engulfing them, accepting the bear's sacrifice of its meal.

Abigail's reflexive gasp pulled water into her lungs. The cold inside and out now, she was shocked to action. Where was Martin? She flailed at the water just enough to keep her head up, unable to touch the bottom with her feet. She tried to kick off her boots, but they were too securely fitted.

Something struck her alongside the head and injured shoulder. She cried out again, dipping down and taking in more water. Completely submerged, she opened her eyes and saw the moon, wavering through the filter of the water, the maple tree to one side and her brother's silhouette, hanging as though flying but showing no sign of life. *The tree must have struck him harder than it did me.* She thought. Her boot touched a boulder on the bottom and she launched off it toward her bother, kicking as hard as she could to lift him as well. Wrangling him with one leg, she grabbed onto a thick lower branch of the tree.

Relief flooded through her when Martin sputtered and reached for the branch himself. It increased as she realized they were floating downstream, away from the bear. It seemed hesitant to follow them into the water. There were blessings to be had today, after all.

The sound began as a low rumble. She couldn't tell if it was real, or if it was just the blood in her ears or her ears trying to adjust to their new state. Would ruptured eardrums fix themselves over time? Would she be permanently deafened? Would she need to carry around one of those ear horns she had seen in advertisements? But no, as they floated on, she could hear the roar more clearly, constant, a thunder that made it to her chest even through the water. The water.

"Tell me-" She tried to speak, pausing to spit out water than raced to silence her. "Tell me there are no waterfalls on this river!" She called to her brother.

"Oh lord!" Was his only response before the branch began to twist in their hands.

The damaged maple creaked and moaned as it tipped over the brink. Frigid water sprayed over Abigail's face, making it impossible to see anything. She held as tightly as she could to the branch as it rose into the air, praying it was the right course of action. The bark bit into her hand. Her shoulder screamed. Her legs and body felt numb, chilled through and slow to respond, but as the broad trunk silhouetted against the sky, she tried to wrap them around it for security. Behind her, Martin wrapped an arm around her chest just below her neck, his legs around her waist, trying to cross and trap the tree limb on the other side.

"Hold on!" He cried. The lower half of the tree finally gave way with a crack that penetrated Abigail's damaged hearing. The top half slammed back down, thrusting them under the water again. Abigail gasped, but only got a partial breath before the world was a tumult of black, fluid ice, threatening to kill her in half a dozen ways.

"Not kill, *understand*," an intrusive voice said within her mind, composed and still like a stone in the crashing tide.

And then they fell.

The sense of chaos deepened as the treetop tumbled, dragging them through the water and back out into the night air, once, twice. Then with a tremendous crash that reverberated through her hand with such force she was sure, for the next few seconds, that it, too, was broken, they struck the lower river.

The next thing Abigail was aware of, the stars shone above in a brilliantly black sky crisscrossed with a band of light she knew was called the "Milky Way." She had never really appreciated the name before that moment, drifting, teeth chattering, lying on something rough, but solid enough to be comforting in its own way.

Looking around as well as she could only moving her head, she spotted Martin's sodden curls just inches away from her face.

"Martin?" She asked in a normal voice. She could barely hear it, even in her own head, with that shift in timbre that made her wonder how other people heard her voice. There was no response. "Martin!" She tried again, the effort causing her shoulder to remind her of her many injuries.

We should have stayed home. This was so much worse an idea than I expected. Will we even get home? I doubt I could swim to shore at this point, let alone find my way back... Who knows where that... monstrosity is, or what others lurk in those woods?

"Urgh..." Martin finally responded.

"Oh, thank goodness. I couldn't have explained what happened tonight without you. If I had to try to tell them how you died... I would have ended up in an asylum. I still might, if we make it home."

"Don't..." Martin began. He sounded tired, drained. It seemed he hadn't fared any better than she. "Don't talk like that. We had a brilliant adventure, saw amazing things perhaps no other living people have seen. They'll make amazing stories."

"Stories... Poor Alfie. Surely he must have..." Abigail stopped, overcome by feelings for the old miner who had tried to do them a good turn. It seemed impossible that he was still alive.

"He was a brave man. I'll make sure Mother and Father know and his family gets looked after," Martin promised.

"That's a good idea. He deserves that much, and maybe a starring role in the story?"

"We could hardly tell the story without him," Martin agreed.

"There aren't... any more waterfalls, are there?"

"I don't think so. I lost consciousness for a while, but I think we're past the worst of it. The stars seem more beautiful tonight, don't they?" Martin said.

"They do, but I've heard of such things, food tasting more intensely, smells, colors more vibrant after one has a brush with death, and we've had a few, just today. I honestly can't tell if I'm shaking purely from cold, or from nerves." As she finished speaking, Abigail felt a bump.

The stars above spun to the right. They came almost all the way around, and there was another bump. Abigail winced at the pain in her shoulder, the scratch of the bark against her neck. Leaning over carefully, she looked right and saw what looked like humps of white water, glowing in the moonlight. "I thought you said no-" A sudden drop accompanied the third bump. She left the tree trunk, slammed back into it a second later, and then bounced to the side, straight into the icy water again.

Right arm useless, she pulled herself along with her left as well as she could, but the current was fast and wily here, pulling her first one way, then the other. Martin called out, but Abigail couldn't tell what direction his voice came from. She gasped for breath, and paddled as best she could, thankful for the swimming lessons her father had insisted upon. It was a strange thing, swimming, but a fad he had been certain would catch on.

She gathered bruises and scrapes for a minute that seemed like a month until the water calmed, turning to subtly rippled glass. She saw no sign of the maple tree, nor her brother. She wept as rounded gravel rose up under her knees. She crawled to the edge of the water and collapsed.

Abigail drifted again, but this time, at the shore of a great lake, or perhaps a sea. The stars splayed out above, and trees reached for the sky along the water's edge. She sat in a dinghy. The water lay still, a perfect mirror, except... The faint glow of the sky was punctuated not by pinpricks of light, but of motes of absolute dark. The trees, full and lush, were mirrored below by the vicious club-branched denizens of the Twisted Grove.

A bird, long of neck and leg and beak, flew across the water even as she noticed these reflections. Her chest tightened. The bird, white and flying low across the water as though fishing, made a graceful arc until it was barreling right for her. She cast around for an oar or a pole to push herself away, or defend herself, but nothing lay in the bottom of the boat. She was alone, unarmed.

The bird pulled up as it came within a few yards, and in a flurry of flapping wings, alit on the pointed prow of the tiny boat. It stood sideways to her, considering her with its nearer eye, then peered over the gunwale into the water. When Abigail remained in place, staring, the bird turned toward her, then looked pointedly over the side again. This time, she leaned forward and saw the bird's reflection.

Like the stars, its light became dark. The creature stood, silhouetted against the sheen of the water. Its head suddenly darted forward, as though trying to spear a fish. When it struck the water, though, there came a tearing sound like paper being pulled apart. An ebon crack appeared in the surface of the water. It grew by the foot, spreading and bifurcating like lightning for dozens of feet before she spotted the bird, still standing on the prow, writhing and splashing against a creeping black that spread over its beak, its feathers, dancing to a staccato beat that made her deepest inner animal recoil. There had to be some exit!

Touching the water was out, though. She was trapped. The bird shook and jerked, finally bringing its head back up, a pause in the dance? Or a struggle completed? The beak, previously yellow, was streaked with black now, and the striations shook and danced even as it settled, multiplying across the yellow and impinging on the snowy feathers, turning them dark line by needle-like line.

As the darkness overcame the light, becoming the majority of the visible creature, its form shifted as well. The eyes spread, growing larger. The feathers of the wings fell out, scattering, light and dark, across the bottom of the boat and out onto the water, where they fell into cracks or teetered on the edges. Scaled skin grew between the joints of the wings, and in a crest at the back of the head.

The crazing of the water reached from shore to horizon, a broken mirror reflecting a mad sky full of ever deeper degrees of darkness.

The bird, flapping fish-like fins now, lurched toward her. The back of her hand itched as it had... when was that? In the woods? That butterfly that was anything but a harmless, joyful creature... Had it bitten her? Scratched her? As she watched, a coin of flesh just above her wrist cracked, shattering. Flakes of skin fluttered down, falling the water and revealing nothing but shadow beneath.

The bird loomed now. Abigail tried to turn away, to hide her face, but its chest was a mass of infinite darkness that drew her eye. Despite herself, she leaned in.

"The abyss," she heard herself whisper.

"Ab-yss," a breeze hissed back. Was it the bird? Some other source she couldn't see?

CHAPTER SEVEN

Abigail awoke in her own bed. Thin, dim, light crept through her window. Was it still the same night? The approaching next? She was unmoored from the clock and the calendar, adrift in time. She looked at her hand, thinking of the bird and the leaf-winged butterfly, but it was bandaged, hiding the flesh. She reached to pull away the white cloth, but a voice, sudden, but muted, barely understandable, demanded her attention.

"Thank the saints!" Liza shouted on seeing her eyes open. "If you had died, I would have been on the road by morning, looking for a new situation! I might still, if your parents weren't so absorbed by their work. Maybe tomorrow. I should write my sister in San Francisco. Perhaps she has a room to lend me as I look for work. I've always wanted to see the Pacified Ocean..." Liza's words were like a background buzz of nonsense that Abigail could barely make out, though she could tell from the woman's tone she was being none too quiet with her rant.

"What day is it? Is it morning or night?" Abigail asked, bringing Liza up short.

"It's Saturday, of course, silly girl. You've got some bumps and bruises, but the doctor doesn't think you'll have any lasting injury. Your ears should recover fully in a few months, one eardrum busted, the other nearly so. Doctor said I'd have to speak up to be heard. I'm doing by best, such a retiring and mouse-like one am I of a normal day. Don't give me that face. Martin hasn't woken up yet, so I have no earthly idea what happened yesterday or last night, but it was clearly one hell of a time, if you'll excuse my expression. I'm glad enough that you're still alive, but your parents gave me orders not to let you off the estate and I'm kicking myself for not doing just that. I should have locked you in your rooms. Hammocks and picnics, indeed!"

"Martin's alive!" Abigail perked up, tried to sit up, but her shoulder was bound securely and she didn't have the strength to sit up without her arms to help. “Mother and Father, are they here? Can I see them?”

"Just you lay there, Miss. The young master is in no better shape than you, but not much worse. The doctor, as I said, has been and gone, bundled you both up, and prescribed a whole kit of tinctures and solutions to get you all mended." Liza gestured to her desk, where a small army of dark glass bottles stood, awaiting their duty. “I've sent a message up to your parents. I expect they'll be down on the next wagon.”

"We didn't know it would be so dangerous," Abigail said, eyebrows drooping, searching for any pity in the older woman. She found none, only disappointment and relief that one of the teens had awoken, as battered and bruised as they both were.

"Well, you should learn to listen to your parents, and old Liza. The Becketts are tough cookies. They've been around the block and fought off their share of bears, and I'm sure they wanted better for you, to never have to deal with such deadly encounters. They want you to get married and serve them up grandchildren. You should give that road serious consideration. Childbirth may not be easy, but I daresay you'd come through with fewer injuries than your 'adventure.'"

"Deadly... Alfie..."

"Pardon, Miss?"

"While we were up there, we ran across Alife, one of the miners. I don't know his last name, but surely Peter Smalls will know him. He tried to help us… but there was a… I'm afraid he didn't make it."

"I will make sure he knows."

"Alfie was brave. Tell him that. I'm not sure we would have made it back down but for him." Liza nodded at this.

"You just about didn't in any case, but I'm sure Mr. Smalls will want to have a proper talk with you at some point, a story to pass onto the man's family." Abigail's eyes filled with tears again. Twice in as many days. Maybe she *was* more suited to staying in the home. The thought frustrated her.

"Don't let me keep you away from your duties, then, Liza. I'm clearly not going anywhere right now, or attracting any bears *or* beaus. Of all the things I need right now, I could use some comforting, some food, rest, a kind embrace from my parents."

"You've got yourself into this situation, young lady, and from where I stand, bad as it is, it could be worse. Men could be searching for your body, or digging your grave by now. This gallivanting around in the woods, in the mines, listening to spooky stories from miners, these are not the activities of a proper young lady. I know your mother doesn't put much stock in femininities herself, growing up as she did and finding her way to the top, but they would certainly help a young lady who doesn't need to go scrabbling in the dirt for the tiniest glint of silver to pay for dinner attract a proper future."

"I will find my own future, thank you very much!" Abigail yelled as loudly as her abused body would allow. The servant huffed, threw down the towel from over her shoulder and stalked from the room, slamming the door and locking it from the outside.

"You can have whatever future you want. In. That. Room!"

The other yelled through the door. Doubly muffled, it took Abigail a few moments to figure out what she had said, but by that time it was too late to continue the argument as the other had stomped away angrily.

"Abigail?" Came another voice, in another tone, altogether.

"Martin!" She called back, angling her head toward the speaking horn.

"I'm so glad you survived!" They both said in unison, then fell back to their beds, laughing at themselves.

Martin lay back, content that his call to adventure hadn't resulted in his sister's demise. He couldn't imagine life without her. They had been constant companions since their first days and when decorum called for them to have separate rooms, they both fought for those rooms to be adjacent, then for the means to communicate between with the talking horns. They were unique in a home setting as far as they knew, but they seemed like the perfect solution to carry on their late night discussions, musings, and debates. Having Abigail's ear right there was comforting.

His notebook had been ruined by the dip into the river, but he had some ideas that he had to get down. He shuffled over to his desk and lit the lamp. Opening his ink and setting a clean page before him, he started making note of all he recalled, from the bird-headed giant worm to the smashing trees. The collapsed cabin led to the memory of the great bear beast, even more disturbing than the many-antlered deer, and leading to new questions as to the development of such a creature.

He thought again about Mr. Twain, and how the writer might be interested in "tall tales" about strange creatures roaming the woods. Certainly he still had chills from the events of the night before, and if one could pass such feelings on to a reader, make them so gripped with excitement and fear that they could not bear to put out the light and submit to sleep... such an achievement would be worth quite a lot in the publishing field, he was certain. Mary Shelley had done well enough with her tale of a reanimated patchwork man and the scientist who made him.

Martin sketched and noted and mused for some time before he consciously became aware of the sound. It was like a tickle at first, an insect buzzing at the far corner of the room, or a strain of music just heard through the wall. As he took a break from his scrawlings, though, it gripped his attention. Or had it been growing louder?

He set his pen down beside the ink bottle and turned slowly, trying to identify the location of the scratching. The drawer of his bedside table... He rose, slowly, and picked up the letter opener from the pen cup. He wasn't really sure why he did it. The sound was most likely a mouse. He would pull the drawer out and let the thing scamper away and that would be that.

Reassessing, he took up the lamp in his other hand, placing it atop the table before opening the drawer, to afford himself a better view. The drawer slid open easily. The local furniture makers were quite good. He wondered briefly if they got their wood from the local forest. Why wouldn't they?

He paused with his hand inches from the pull. Had the sound stopped? Or was his heart just beating so loudly he couldn't hear it anymore? His mind drifted back to the question of wood. With so many animal aberrations, why not plant as well? That one butterfly thing the Abigail saw had leaf-life wings... How would one tell? An expert would see strange patterns in the wood grain perhaps... Maple seedlings with acorn seeds... Spinning acorns with fancy hats... Musketeer Acorns! All for Oak and Oak for all! This elicited a faint smile as he turned back to the matter at hand and pulled the drawer.

Within, the light picked out a few coins, his pocket knife, a rock he remembered picking up on his trip, and the antler point... The base was jagged, sharp from where it had been smashed free of the rest of the antler, the surface rippled and bumped, but with a slight sheen to it. He pulled the drawer a few more inches, looking for the tiny fugitive he expected. The back of the drawer came into view, revealing only more pocket flotsam, some taffy wrappers, a stray rectangular-headed nail, and snail shell the size of the tip of his thumb.

Martin lifted the drawer over his head, thinking perhaps the animal had escaped over the side and was climbing down, or clinging to the bottom. No. He peered into the gap where the drawer usually rested. No. The sound returned while he crouched, the drawer laying on his bed.

He stood quickly, steadying the lantern. There, in the small wooden corral, shifted and shimmied the antler point. Its motions seemed much like a caterpillar, bunching up and stretching forward. He picked up the nail and rolled the thing over with the piece of iron.

It paused for a moment, then rejoined its behavior, reorienting its movement to push against the floor of the box even though the side of the antler which had been down now stood off at the two o'clock position. He retrieved his pen and paper and a board on which to place the paper, and sketched each phase of movement.

"Abigail's not going to believe this," he muttered to

himself as he looked around the room for an appropriate container.

"Martin!" His sister called through the brass tube.

"Yes, sister?"

"I'm bored, and vexed..."

"What vexes you now, sister? Are we not home, safe behind walls of brick and stone? Our wounds seen to and time aplenty to recover?"

"I suppose. This isn't going to turn into one of those 'our parents had it so much harder than us' sermons, is it? Because I really don't need that right now."

"Of course not. Mother and Father may have been ambitious enough for two or three generations to benefit, but I have no desire to build a company or a town."

"Good. Liza gave me the 'perhaps you should act more like a *boring old* young lady *with nothing between her ears...*' speech."

"Ha! I adore your asides. Too bad it hurts to laugh right now. Two broken ribs is what the doctor wrote in his note to Father. Possibly three, or maybe the other is just bruised. Anyway, no climbing walls for a month or so. Shame, Liza will never let us leave again, and I've got to go see more of these creatures, strictly during the day, of course."

"Are you unhinged? Did that tree knock your brain out? Maybe a rock in the rapids? We're lucky not to be dead. I don't want to be Lady of a Thousand dresses or anything, but I also don't want to go up there again in this lifetime. I'd just as soon not see another one of those scary mixed-up creatures."

"Oh, that's too bad, because I have a souvenir."

"Gods, tell me you didn't... It's not a snake-headed beetle, is it? A chipmunk with scales instead of fur?"

"Those are really interesting ideas. You're in the spirit, but no. I've got a piece of the deer's antler."

"Oh, whew, that doesn't sound so bad."

"It moves on its own, like a worm. I'm sketching it now."

"Great Caesar's Ghost!"

"You know, if you wanted to come up the mountain, all you had to do was hail one of the wagons, or get Gregory to bring the carriage up to the Landing," Father said, poking at his eggs with a fork.

"Is that all you're going to say?" Mother demanded. "They very nearly got themselves killed."

"You see? You've upset Mother," Father pointed out. "If you don't care for your own well being, what of hers?"

Martin floundered at this. Abigail had had an argument prepared, but now she was distracted by a blemish below Mother's eye. She watched the spot, certain the tiny black spot had moved, forgetting any defense she may have mounted for their actions. It had been Martin's will that brought them there, after all. She was not entirely unwitting, but certainly not the prime motivator.

"We're... sorry," Martin finally uttered. "We have so little contact with the outside world, and the folk of the town are generally... not much for conversation or enlightenment."

"This again. You want to go away? To Europe? To Africa?" Mother started building up a head of steam. Martin held up his hands before him, palms out, placating.

With you and Father at the offices so much, who are we to converse with? The servants have their work, our- *my* instructors are hundreds, even thousands of miles away, days or weeks by post. That's no way to converse."

"Perhaps we have isolated you here, and not just behind the brick walls which kept us safe for so long," Father said. "You *should* come up to the Landing. Soon. We will show you around, teach you all about our operation. Perhaps some of the engineers would provide the kind of interaction your require. And a few of them are unwed and not unhandsome, if I may gauge as another man..." Father said. Abigail's attention was drawn by this. As she focused on his face, she spotted a mark over his eye, not a bruise or cut, but like Mother's, dark, tiny, but somehow... moving. She glanced at her own hand, still bandaged.

"Oh, Michael..." Mother smiled, but looked down at her plate. Another spot there, behind her ear. Abigail reached for it, tried to bat it away. "What are you doing, Abigail?" The woman leaned away.

"I thought I saw a bit of..."

"Dust?" Father offered.

"Something..." Abigail said uncertainly. Liza stepped forward, peering at the spot. Abigail could see it, plain as day, a grouping of lines, like a haphazard pile of sticks, like a drop of ink on a heavily textured surface.

"I don't see anything, Ma'am. Must have blown away at Abigail's fluttering," Liza said. But she was wrong, and as Abigail watched, she noticed a few other, nearly imperceptibly small spots, all deepest black.

"Where do you think the oddities really come from?" Abigail asked later that day. After some "tching" and "oohing" over their wounds, Mother and Father had retired to the parlor, apparently to discuss what to do with them. Liza was on guard in the hallway, preventing them from listening in.

They were both feeling more energetic, and restless, despite lingering limitations and twinges. They sat in Martin's room while he expanded his notes into full articles on the creatures they had seen. He hoped to sell them to the local paper as part of a special series on local color, or find a publisher for a book.

"Why do they have to be oddities? There's a lot of the world we've never seen. I've seen some grotesque creatures brought up by dredge in Norway, deeper than most people thought there could be life. Rather than a compendium of monsters, let us think of this work as a field guide."

"You can't tell me that a three headed bear, more than just extra heads, extra... bodies, melted together like a box of candles set too close to the fireplace... That's not natural, by any stretch. And plants combined with animals?" Abigail shuddered.

"You mean the butterfly thing, what I've called the Western Maplewing, proposed scientific name Papilo Beckettsi? Those could just have *looked* like leaves. Many animals use camouflage to blend into their surroundings, from coloration to physical form like the stick insect," Martin said, reminding himself of his idea about hybridized wood. He made a note on his scratch pad about interviewing local woodworkers.

In his desk drawer, the chunk of antler knocked against the wood. He hadn't determined what it wanted, or where it thought it was going, but he'd tried to offer it water and various types of food over the days he'd had it under observation, and hadn't noted any decrease in said resources.

"Oh for heaven's sake, Martin, you still have that thing? What if Liza finds out? Or Mother and Father?"

"What should I do? Let it go in the garden? Maybe it will

burrow down into the soil and grow up to be an antler tree," Martin joked.

"Ugh!" Abigail recoiled at the thought. "That was completely unnecessary. You do need to get rid of it, though. Maybe in the fireplace."

"It's a living thing... I think... At any rate, I can't prove it's not, and that would be cruel. Besides, it has great scientific value. It keeps moving even though it doesn't eat, or in fact, have any outward features of an independent creature. It just slugs around in there all day and night, but what powers it? What makes it *move*? You're the one studying natural philosophy and such. Don't these questions interest you?"

"I- *we*, for your matriculation and name on the papers and my reading, calculations and brilliance, are more of engineering students than natural philosophers. We look into how machines operate, stresses of various materials for building and creating new tools, you know, like everything around you. It's fascinating. I don't understand how you aren't interested."

"Likewise for the wonders of our natural world. There's nothing better than being out there in the wilds, far away from the smoke and bustle and machinery making all kinds of grinding, clinking, clunking noises, sounding like it will all explode at any moment. Isn't that nerve wracking?"

"The steam engine is the epitome of human achievement. So many disciplines, metallurgy, mining, engineering of the machinery and tracks all to move people at unheard of speeds across endless distances with almost no demand of effort on the passengers' part. *That* is amazing. Bugs and dirt and being eaten by bears..." Abigail pulled a face. "I see your point about deep sea creatures. I remember the plates well, strange umbrella-shaped things and fish with overlarge jaws, but I wouldn't want to run into them in the middle of the night, either. And they have a certain symmetry, a rightness, even if they're frightening. The bear-"

"The bear again? I told you before. You saw it wrong. It was just a bear and its cubs. Three sets of eyes flashing in the shadows, barely any moonlight to see by... You have quite an imagination and it ran away with you that night. You were too tired to resist. That's all."

"Don't you 'That's all' me like Father. You know that's not remotely all, and you had to have seen it yourself. Perhaps your own eyes saw only what you told them, or you refuse to remember something so utterly alien. Not much of a reporter if you can't stand to see the truth!" In the drawer, the antler rattled against the wood in a quick, repetitive manner, like someone ringing a bell.

"I don't? Not see?" Martin was stymied by Abigail's attack on his faculties, that he should miss such important details, or lie about what he saw simply to disagree with her. "I think it's time you left. Go read those engineering books you're so enamored of! Maybe one will marry you!" Martin's voice rose as he spoke, rolling up a head of steam like the aforementioned train.

"Perhaps I will! I would certainly rather be wed to knowledge and advancement than to debase myself by joining with one of your species!" Abigail stomped out of the room, slamming the door behind her, then stomped to her own door and slammed her own door for good measure. She looked at the brass tube's flared end, in the stylized shape of a flower and preemptively stuffed a stocking into it. She would dwell in silence until she was ready to hear from her brother, not be cajoled into forgiving him half an hour hence when he'd cooled off.

CHAPTER EIGHT

"Constance!" The demanding bellow reverberated through the brick-walled mansion, giving both Abigail and Martin starts as they sat up from where they reclined in the library. She studied a text on fluid dynamics for an upcoming test and he had been knee deep in an African river, following a guide back to his village after a day of fighting off snakes and mandrills. The twins looked at each other.

"Helen!" they said together, setting aside their books. They hobbled together to the library door and beyond, the mezzanine, where they could look down on the entrance and see a number of large trunks, porters standing by, Liza wringing her hands, and Aunt Helen, resplendent in a shimmering violet dress and matching hat with a cloud of tulle artfully encompassing much of her head aside from her face.

"She looks like a foil plum," Martin said just barely loud enough for his sister to hear. Abigail giggled, but slapped at her brother's hand.

"Shush, be nice. We don't need to antagonize her on the first day. This could turn out to be a very long visit indeed." Abigail put on her "fill the room" voice Mother had taught her by example over the years. "Aunt Helen! It's so good to see you! Mother and Father are up at the Landing, overseeing the mine. How was your trip? Can we get you coffee? Tea? Liza, fetch some refreshments for dear Helen. She's had quite a journey from New England." As she spoke, she moved along the railing to the stairs, trying not to make it obvious she was using it for real support. Liza looked at her, then back at Helen and decided retreating to the kitchen was the better part of valor.

"Abigail, darling!" Helen projected with a nasal Mid-Atlantic accent Abigail suspected was an affectation. "It's so lovely to see you again. You've grown a foot since I visited last, and is that man at your side our Martin? Come down and give us kisses!" The pair navigated the broad stairs as best they could. "Why so slow? Put some pep in your steps! Two strapping youths like you? For shame, making an old woman wait!"

"Oh, Auntie, you're hardly old!" Abigail called across the foyer. "Martin and I may have overdone it in the gymnasium the other day. Today, our bodies betray us in return. Also, I stood too near to one of the miners firing her shotgun at a wolf and my hearing is not what it should be. You'll have to continue to speak up."

"A wolf? Shotgun? Dear, no no no, these are not things a proper young lady should associate herself with!" Helen chided. As the twins finally drew close to their aunt, they heard a warbling growl, the faintest echo of their sojourn on the mountain, but still jarring. They looked around, expectantly.

"Oh! Don't worry yourselves!" Aunt Helen waved one hand at them distractedly while turning her attention toward the overlarge sling over her other shoulder. "Hush, Rupert! Friends! Abigail and Martin are our friends! Well, my niece and nephew, but you wouldn't understand that, would you? No you wouldn't!" Helen squeaked as she lifted a wriggling mass from the bag and held it cradled in one arm while stroking its brown and white fur with her other hand.

"Rupert is a Jack Russel Terrier! I bought him from John Russel himself last year. Isn't he just the cutest?" The creature calmed, allowing Martin to approach it. It sniffed, then licked his hand and allowed him to scratch its ears and chin.

When Abigail stepped up, the creature tensed. When it sniffed her still-bandaged hand, the growling returned with bared teeth, then a sudden snap at her fingers. She yanked back her hand and stumbled away, losing her impaired balance. Arms wheeling, she struggled to catch her balance, finally landing on her rear, jarring her shoulder and a number of other tender areas painfully.

“He must not like the unguents the doctor prescribed,” Abigail laughed off her mishap, though she thought she felt a slight tingling at the back of her hand. Dogs were said to sense certain things... This was going to be a long visit...

A week later, the twins were on close-watch, with Liza and Helen marching just behind them. Rupert mostly rode in Helen's arms or purse, but occasionally he ran around the wood boardwalks or rough dirt roads, yipping at strangers or horses. Liza had filled Helen in on all the details of the twins' exploits days before, and they both hovered like hawks waiting for the youths to step out of line.

The doctor suggested a daily constitutional of at least twenty minutes and they suggested they accompany Liza on her trip to the general store and post office. The road was in decent repair for once, but carpenters were also hard at work extending the boardwalk along the frontage of main street. The spring would bring floods again, no doubt, and Mother and Father must have been convinced it was time.

Martin tried to address one of the workers, seeing his moment to discuss the wood from the mountains above, but was "tsked" back into formation beside his sister before he got a word out. "I don't see what harm talking to the workers would do," Martin whined. "I just want to know about their materials, where they get them, and what the best wood for this kind of work is."

"You're not a carpenter. Your mother would have a fit if she thought you would aim so low when you have that stack of engineering books back home," Liza snapped. "Besides, it's not all about you getting into further trouble. You're still in hot water up to your necks until your parents say elsewise."

"It's been nearly two weeks since they told us they'd be working out of the office. We barely saw them when they checked on us after... our accident... And they missed last Sunday's dinner. They always made time before. This new shaft must have them extremely vexed," Abigail said.

"Apparently. Something about a lack of surveyors willing to go up in the mountains since the miners' stories have spread through town."

"I'm sure some have gone and haven't returned," Martin said to Abigail. She had difficulty deciphering his surreptitious tone and took overlong to put what she *could* hear into order. Meanwhile, Aunt Helen perked up.

"Stories?" Rupert stopped and looked up at his mistress on hearing her voice. "I love a good bit of... community insight!"

"You mean gossip," Abigail said, drawing a sharp look from her aunt.

"They're not that kind of stories, Ms. Campbell," Liza said. "Ghost yarns and fireside tales, some quite gruesome from what I hear. And that blasted paper Martin insists on buying isn't helping, with their sensational stories blowing a few oddities out of proportion."

"Out of proportion?" Abigail wheeled on Liza. "Do you have any idea-"

"Abigail!" A new voice blended with her aunt's, breaking

the wave of her tirade before she got a chance to get herself into trouble talking back to Liza. She turned to see Daniel, eyes wide, eyebrows high, a hopeful expression on his face. "I brung you this. I saw it and thought of you right away!"

From behind his back, the lanky boy brought forth a flower on a foot-tall stem, its roots bound up in a ball of rough cloth. Its leaves stood up like blades of grass to either side of the stem, and its petals were similarly shaped, long and pointed. Superficially, it looked something like a lily, but with gentle purple coloration Abigail had never seen before.

Without thinking, she leaned in to smell it and caught the scent of pine trees. The juxtaposition made her immediately think of the strange crossed creatures of the mountain and she backed away abruptly. The flower, however, leaned to follow her, seeming to grasp at her with its petals. Liza swatted the flower from the bandit's son's hands with her bag.

"How dare you accost the young Miss! Your father is a known brigand and you are no better, Daniel Swindon!" She laid into him. "The Becketts have banned their children from interacting with any of your clan. I hope you will pass this on and we can avoid further unpleasantness in the future! Good day!"

"I-I just wanted to... Aww, l-look, it knows you are the queen it is meant to serve with its beauty. It struggles to be near you. The color purple is so beautiful, don't you think?" Daniel stammered, but then found his place in the speech he had no doubt prepared.

The words sounded rehearsed, but why would he have gone to all the trouble? Abigail had hardly spoken to him in the weeks before the misadventure on the mountain. They had been confined to the estate, seeing none of their friends since. Perhaps it was simply a token of missing her over that period, but it seemed oddly... romantic.

"I said 'good day!' I shall summon an officer of the law if I must, and see you put in jail if you do not turn around and walk away right now!" Liza came back in for a second round while Abigail looked down at the poor plant, eyes widening in horror at the fact that Daniel's words were literally true. The plant was pulling itself across the dirt toward her.

"Come now, Liza, surely he's beneath the girl's station, dressed as he is and covered in dirt, but one needn't must be cruel in one's rebuffs. Run along young man. Perhaps if you make something of yourself, you will find a young lady who will welcome your meager country attempts," Aunt Helen said, waving him off. Rupert yipped, but stood close to her skirts.

Frightened by the crawling flower no one else seemed to see, Abigail backed away another step. Between the motion and Liza's strident words, the carpenters were watching, and now stood away from their work, hammers and saws held up in a threatening manner.

Daniel held up his hands, palms forward, and Abigail noted the crisscross of dark lines there. Surely it was just dirt resting in the natural creases, the lines that palmists read to tell peoples' futures. Of course it was that. How would he have been infected? Surely he didn't make habit of going up to the mountain... Or perhaps he did?

He had been digging in the dirt to retrieve the plant, maintaining its root so it could survive. She repeated the thought to herself. *Just dirt, he was digging in the dirt. The lines don't mean anything.* She barely heard Liza's words as they continued on to the general store.

The Voice of Silver Hill
ISSUED EVERY SUNDAY
by
C. Valente and S. McGuire

✶ ✶ ✶

Terms of Subscription:

One copy, one year.......................45 cents
One copy, six months....................23 cents
Single copies....................................1 cent
Contact purveyors for advertising rates.

The Silver

Vol XIX - No. 42 • SILVER HILL, NEVADA

SIGHTINGS

SILVER HILL- In the weeks since this paper's first report on the strange goings-on along the local range, sightings of myriad unexplainable creatures have reached double digits, with fifteen verified stories, verging on one encounter per day, flooding in. Are these anomalies originating in the deep hills and high valleys betwixt the mountains? Perhaps the farther we push into the wilds, the more they are wont to push back.

✶ ✶ ✶

SILVER HILL- And surrounding areas have been afflicted with repeated loss of livestock. Shepherds and cow tenders in the high pastures have reported animals missing on a number of occasions. Corroborating this, hunters from in town have been having a harder than usual time tracking down their own prey. It seems there is something afoot in these mountains.

✶ ✶ ✶

Perhaps the Paiute, unhappy with the previous agreement ceding their lands to us have summoned these demons to drive us away so they may reclaim what they see as their rightful property.
An envoy must be sent to the local reservation to get advice on how to assuage these feelings of revenge and brings us all into peaceful alignment! I call upon the Becketts to see to this.

✶ ✶ ✶

N. DEBLANCO,

SUCCESSOR TO

M. P. FREEMAN & CO.

—— AND ——

REINHART BROTHERS

IN THE

Forwarding Business

GOODS PROMPTLY FORWARDED

From Elko to any point in Eastern Nevada

✶ ✶ ✶

Voice f Hill

SUNDAY, OCTOBER 11, 1874 • 1 cent

Weather

Sunny most of the week, some winds. Expect more leaves than usual on roofs and in streets.

CONTINUE

They are the de facto mayors of Silver Hill, having brought it up from a small camp of their own workers to a thriving town. Our being here in the path of this wave of alien creatures is on their heads and they need to take care to attend to more than the business of removing metals from the ground.

REPORTS NEEDED:
The paper is compiling a list of new dangers and threats to our community. It is clear, whatever the source or reason, we are in the midst of a terrifying moment in history most of us have not seen since the war.

We came to Silver Hill to live a peaceful, calm life, not engage the demons and monster of the invisible world.

If you have witnessed unnerving creatures, please contact one of our reporters or come to our offices directly. Forewarned is forearmed!

★ ★ ★

Martin read this last with interest. He had dreamed of publishing his writing for some time and had been conversing with authors and editors of dime novels and story collections around the country in search of someone willing to print his stories.

Now that he had the edge of having his own first hand experience, he felt certain he would be able to place a story with the paper and get more attention from publishing professionals in New York or perhaps even London.

As badly as Abigail had felt for Daniel when he was chased away by Liza and Helen, she was haunted by the marks on his hands. They were different to the ones on her hand, but undeniably similar. And how did they connect to the spots she'd seen on her parents?

"Attention!" Helen barked. Rupert threw in his two cents with a growl-yip. "A young lady does not drift away from conversation. She engages with it, and with the speaker. She looks for her means to ingratiate herself to a given man, to guide him to perform at her will."

Well, that was not where Abigail had expected her "lessons" on being a young lady to lead. She was both repulsed by the thought of manipulating people, and saddened that a young woman was expected to use all of these "wiles," as Helen called them, to do her manipulating. False promises, innuendo, flirting... None of it held any interest for her, but she could see where others could need these skills to survive the modern world. It seemed to be the prevailing consensus that the only way to get to the top was by riding a man's coattails. He job, as Helen put it, was to "find the right coattails."

"We were discussing modes of dress. If you are going to tea with a potential suitor, what kind of outfit would you wear? What dress? What shoe? What hat? Colors? Fragrances?" Abigail sighed at the barrage of questions, but reviewed what she had absorbed over the last weeks to formulate an answer.

CHAPTER NINE

Evening came with a surprise. Mother and Father showed for dinner for the first time since Aunt Helen's arrival. When Liza told the twins to follow her into the dining room, which looked like she had spent all day cleaning it, their jaws dropped. Aunt Helen was there, apparently already having taken care of greetings and worked out whatever friction might have accrued at her sister not welcoming her earlier.

Abigail rued missing that interaction, but waited for the other shoe to drop. Her hearing largely restored by time and the doctor's tinctures, she almost looked forward to the yelling over their adventures. Almost.

Their parents smiled and embraced them, not a hint that anyone's nose was out of joint. Perhaps their news was so good, it outshone the recent difficulties.

"We've been in contact with the folks who run the cog railway up Mount Washington, in New Hampshire," Mother said, eyes practically glowing with excitement. "They're working with our engineers to design a similar system to get miners and supplies back and forth, and a gravity sled to get the ore down."

"Two tracks all the way up the mountain? It's practically unprecedented!" Abigail said, surprised that Martin's daydream had so quickly turned into a prediction. She'd studied the unique railway in the granite state in Martin's courses. The line had the steepest grade in the world, addressing previously unsolved problems in everything from keeping the boilers at an angle to allow them to operate on the incline, to creating enough friction via the cog, a large toothed wheel essentially climbing the specially made trestles as though climbing a ladder.

"Ah yes, you've been reading over your brother's shoulder again, haven't you?" Her mother chided. "You know there are more proper avocations for a young lady. Perhaps needlepoint? Helen, I thought you were going to give Abigail some lessons on being a proper lady, getting along in polite society? Never mind, this *is* all very exciting, isn't it? The town will get a sister. We will have brought another set of twins into the world. The valley will grow richer as silver flows down the mountain."

Mother's speech startled Abigail. It was entirely out of character for her to be so poetic or openly hopeful. Life had been tough for her early on. She struggled for everything. It had made her tense, tight like a fist, or a coiled snake, ready to strike at every opportunity. In this, at any rate, Abigail could see the common thread through Helen's personality and her mother's. They both acted out of desperation, a poverty of choice. But no more, it seemed, at least for Constance Beckett.

Those ingrained reactions reflected deeply in her need for her children to be pushed toward education and have everything they could ever need, or want. Abigail tried to attribute it to the stress of living away from the house, her children, and working so hard over recent weeks. But they didn't look tired, or worn. If anything, the pair seemed bursting with energy. Great success might do that for one, Abigail conjectured.

"How would you like to help out with the project, Martin? Surely your studies have prepared you to at least act as an apprentice to the engineers. Being part of such a monumental project will look good on the old curriculum vitae." Martin raised an eyebrow at this, shooting a glance at Abigail. "It was good enough for Leonardo Da Vinci to create a list of accomplishments and skills. It's good enough for my son to wave as a flag to prospective investors in his future!" Father said, slapping the table.

But Abigail knew the use of the archaic letter of introduction espousing one's virtues, a vanity project if ever there was one, was not her brother's concern. He didn't know much beyond the first correspondence courses of his degree-in-progress, as he quickly grew bored with the work and frustrated with the textbooks' dense paragraphs of technical terms and illustrations that initially bore no resemblance to the real world. Abigail, on the other hand, had picked the concepts up quickly, and been engaged.

While it had been Martin who brought the concept of the talking horns to their father, they had been her idea. There were dozens of small fixes and improvements around the house their parents naturally credited him with while Abigail was the brains behind each.

"Perhaps we could both help with the designs," Abigail blurted out. Then she had to cover. "Who knows? Perhaps one of the engineers or their assistants will be interesting enough to hold my attention..." It sickened her to play Mother's, and society's, game, but it was the only way to get what she wanted: access to the plans of a unique, immense, project which would affect the lives of hundreds, even thousands of people directly if Mother's declaration of a second settlement bore out.

"Of course! You're both welcome! We'll all get a good night's sleep tonight and head back over to the office in the morning," her father said with an energetic sweep of his arm toward the presumed direction of the office. Alarm bells rang again for Abigail. This was totally out of character for the normally reserved Michael Bartholomew Beckett. "And we'll be sure to keep you away from that Swindon boy and his ilk. We don't need any proposals from the gutter in this house! Only the best son-in-law, and perhaps daughter-in-law in due course." He winked bawdily at Martin. "For this family!"

Aunt Helen looked like she wanted to protest this disruption in Abigail's training, but held her tongue. Abigail guessed it was to keep from arguing with her parents in front of the "children."

The next day, the twins rose earlier than usual, and packed a lunch and the schoolbooks Martin was meant to be studying, so Abigail could keep working if she couldn't shoulder her way into the real engineering business of the day.

They ate by lamplight before the sun made itself known, watching their parents move eggs and oatmeal around their respective dishes without consuming anything. What could they do but exchange looks and keep their eyes out for further strange behavior or the cause of it all?

Abigail noted the spots she had seen on her parents before grown since the last time she'd seen them, and others having appeared on their hands. She hadn't mentioned them to Martin, because it all seemed too odd. Was it just in her head? If so, would it go away when she was healed from their sojourn on the mountain? But what if it was real?

"You see it, right?" Martin asked, startling Abigail from her thoughts.

"You see it, too? Thank the stars!" Abigail said.

"Of course, how could I miss such changes in behavior? They're both completely different people... Not necessarily in a bad way. I wouldn't say they're possessed, not by demons, anyway... but there's something..."

"Stress, I'm sure," Abigail said, covering for her misunderstanding. He didn't see the marks. Why could she? Because she carried the mark, too? Would she start acting against her normal nature? She wondered again if she should tell her brother about the spots. Having a secret, such a potentially important secret, at that, ate at her.

"I hope so, but you know mines, all kinds of gasses, tainted water... I'm packing a canteen, in case there's something amiss with the water at the offices."

Abigail nodded. Something amiss.

The crew wagon came for them first, being the mine owners, and the four Becketts set off to the rally point near the East Gate just as a glow began to appear above the mountains.

A dozen engineers and planners joined the wagon in veritable silence. Abigail tried to greet the few men and women she'd met previously, but received only glassy-eyed smiles which showed no recognition. *It's early.* She told herself and rode beside Martin, their packs on their laps given the tight space.

The eeriness deepened as they rode up the mountain. Night sounds still echoed in the predawn wash of pale light. Hoots and howls and even a screech did nothing to pierce the riders' stupor. *They're probably just all used to these sounds, and haven't had our experiences with strange things from the forest.* Abigail reasoned. Still, their lack of any chatter, any news brought back from their foray into town after weeks at the office weighed on her.

When they debarked half an hour later at the Landing, a small cluster of buildings and a gaping maw into the side of the mountain, Martin waved her around to the side of one building.

"That was as close to riding in a funeral wagon as I'd ever hope to experience," he said.

"Then it wasn't just me? I'm relieved. But also troubled. Are we overworking them? Are they so drained that even a day off, in their own homes and with their families wasn't enough to bring them back to right?"

"It could be the work, or something... else."

"What are you thinking?"

"I don't want to jump to conclusions."

"Since when? Are the conclusions that frightful?" Abigail asked. Martin looked away.

"We should get up to the engineers' office. We need to catch up on what they're doing and how."

"*Martin,*" Abigail pressed.

"I'm sure it's just my dreams of late giving me a fanciful mind."

"Mmm, my dreams have been disturbing as well. But they seem less important in this moment than 'The Mystery of the Silent Wagon.'"

"You're so good with titles. When I get published, you're going to have to do all my titles," Martin said.

"Aww, thanks," Abigail said, then as they began to walk. "Hey! You were just distracting me, weren't you?"

"Distracting you? From what? You need to keep your focus on the task at hand, Abigail. You've told me as much yourself at least weekly since I can remember..."

"Ugh, you!" Abigail shoved him and he careened into one of the engineers, a shallow-cheeked man with a thin brown mustache and receding hairline. The man's lunch pail fell to the packed earth, its lid flipping up.

"I'm so sorry, we were just..." Martin knelt to retrieve the pail, but the man walked on without it, as if he hadn't even noticed its loss. "Sir! Your lunch!" Martin took hold of the handle and lifted the pail. Not an apple, not a napkin marred the perfect emptiness of the vessel. "Or not..." he mumbled to himself, puzzled. Abigail looked into the pail, then at the ground, which was still untouched by the rising sun, but uncluttered by anything that could hide a stray sandwich or pieces of fruit.

Martin shrugged and they followed the man into the building, placing the bucket beside the desk where he stopped and sat, his papers already arranged and awaiting him as though he had only gone away for a quick meeting.

"Oh!" The man exclaimed with great energy, his face suddenly animated. The twins jumped back, surprised. "You must be the Beckett twins! Here for the day to help us knock out this incline problem? Klin here, Thomas Klin. Nice to meet you both. Well look here..." The man pointed to the schematics before him, leaping right into a detailed explanation of their latest issue. Abigail followed along eagerly, though the man spoke with vigor and speed, technical terms shooting by so fast she didn't have time to try to explain them to Martin.

When Martin and Abigail volunteered to work on the railroad design, their restrictions vanished. Liza was aghast. Helen nearly left, storming out into the yard, but then having left her luggage and not made arrangements to get train tickets home, returned hours later and stewed in her room for days, coming out only to walk Rupert. The twins went on more regular walks, going to the general store and post office daily and the library twice a week, visiting with friends and gathering news from beyond the valley.

Martin's correspondence with Mark Twain was going well, and he even bragged the man might come for a visit, though he now lived in Connecticut. No one really believed Martin, even when they saw the letter Martin said proved his claim. For her part, Abigail had made a pen pal as well, responding to scientific articles put forth by a gentleman from Scotland about his work on the Transatlantic Cable project.

Of course, the gentleman thought he was conversing with the bright, young, Master Martin Beckett, not his sister. She didn't feel the other would understand, the world being what it was, a notion reinforced by Helen's lessons, which has slowly crept back into her schedule.

The twins found themselves once again at the bunkhouse, waiting for the lighting of the bonfire where the miners gathered to blow off steam and exchange stories. Given the chill invading the nights of late, the twins waited inside, on the upper landing looking over the mess hall which ran down the middle of the three story building. Dozens of doors stood behind railings on each tier to the left and right.

The pair contented themselves with their newest correspondence while they waited for the festivities, such as they were. Of a sudden, the door below them burst open, swung with such force that it struck the wall.

"Smalls! Smalls! You gotta see this!" A scratchy voice hollered across the space. Dozens of miners looked up from their dinner plates to see what was the matter. Abigail and Martin set down their letters and went to the railing, looking down on the scene.

"Calm your britches, Scalzi! Just what's got you so riled

up?" The mine foreman emerged into view beneath them. The first speaker held up a rough burlap sack in one hand.

"I got proof! Not just a tale! No one can deny this! I caught me one of the monsters!" Now more of the miners' attention turned to the scene. Knives and forks were set down, mugs carried along as men and women rose from their seats and closed a circle around the pair of men.

"Just what. Do. You. Have. In. The. Bag?" Peter Smalls asked slowly and steadily. He held his hands up before him, palms out.

"Look!" The man said, upending the sack with a flourish. "Straight from the mine!" Across the broad floorboards spilled what looked like a pile of gloves or maybe old, sodden leaves that had darkened through decay. Then the mass moved.

Martin whispered to Abigail. She looked at him, uncomprehending. She pointed to her ear. “Bats!” He mouthed, making a flapping motions with both hands beside one another.

"What's so strange about bats? Or should I ask?" She started to back away from the railing, unconvinced she needed to see whatever monstrosity this turned out to be. Her hand itched beneath the thin glove. Then she caught the serpentine movement. The whole thing was like a chain of bats, front to back to front to back, wings trying to lift them into the air, but their awkwardly aligned bodies resisting flight.

The creature screeched and lunged at Smalls, striking like a snake. Abigail gasped, hand over mouth, stifling the scream she felt struggling to escape. The rest of the crowd fell back a few feet.

"By the Saints, man!" Peter swore, stomping hard with

heel on the "head" bat of the strange line. Immediately, the thing fell limp. "Get this thing on the fire now. Don't bring things like this back to camp. You don't know how dangerous they might be. We've got more to think about than just making a good show of our stories or outsiders believing us!" Smalls chided Scalzi.

"Yes, sir, of course, sir," Scalzi said, his head down as he scooped the corpse up in the sack again. He headed toward the massive fireplace at the far end of the room where pots still steamed away with the tail end of the evening's meal.

"Outside, Scalzi, the bonfire. We don't want... whatever that is turning into smoke and getting in our lungs." The miner spun on his heel, almost tripping over his feet he moved so fast.

"I knew that!" He protested. The crowd tittered at the obvious lie.

"Everybody go back to your meals. Nothing here but a sick old snake too dumb to stay away from the mines when there are men stomping all over," Smalls told the crowd. They stood around looking stunned for a moment. "Get back to eatin' or get to cleanin' up!" He finally shouted, which got the first ones moving back to the long tables. Shaking his head, he turned away, vanishing beneath the landing where the twins stood.

"Well, that was exciting," Martin said, heading back to his seat and picking up his letter. "I don't suppose it will get more interesting than that tonight. Do you want to head back to the house?" Abigail, shaking, nodded, scooping up her own post from the low table between the chairs where they'd been reading.

At the top of the stairs, Peter Smalls was coming up as they approached.

"I don't think I need to tell you how important it is that scenes like that be kept to a minimum. I know that the local paper has been playing up these 'sightings' and 'encounters' to try to sell more copies, but it ain't right. Some are talking about going into the woods, into the *mine,* armed. Knives, hatchets, *pistols*... I can't have it. The miners are getting spooked by the most ridiculous things now and it has to end before it does so... badly."

"I'm sure we don't have any control over such stories, Mr. Smalls. I enjoy reading about them, sure, like my adventure books, but I don't want anyone to get hurt."

"That's just fine, then, Master Martin. You just keep that in mind when you write your articles and try to make a name with your books. There's always someone who'll get all het up over anything they read, go off half-cocked. That's not good for anyone."

"No sir," Martin nodded.

"Good night, Master Beckett, Miss Beckett," Smalls said, stepping off the last stair and letting them pass. Abigail gripped Martin's hand as they descended.

CHAPTER TEN

Inspired by the vision of the segmented bat-conglomerate Scalzi had discovered, Martin scribbled and sketched, trying to nail down his impressions of the creature from the perspective of a distant onlooker.

"This field guide will be a great introduction to the publishing world. It's exciting, engaging, look at this entry!" He held up the paper for Abigail to see. "Oh, right... It's just like you're right here with me. You'll have to see my drawing in the morning. I was too concerned with survival previously to really grasp the details, the nuances, but I got solid look at the chain bats, have the details firmly in hand."

"This... fusion of bats is a travesty of nature. No one is going to want to pay money to read about it."

"It's not just about money. I could make money a hundred ways, working at the mine as an engineer or foreman, at least some day, the newspaper, Carson City's not far up the road or rail, and the city provides ample opportunity for an enterprising young man to make his fortune. No, I... see something in this abomination of the cave bat form. It... speaks to me on a different level."

"I don't even know what that means," Abigail objected. She didn't he knew, either.

He drew the thing curled up as it had fallen from the bag, trying to fly, striking, discovering new details such as antennae on some of the heads, pincers at the front-most head, a tangle of small, seemingly useless legs along the undercarriage... The more he drew, the more disturbing the creature seemed, the more grotesque. Finally, he realized what he was looking at.

"Centipede bats! Mister Twain is certainly going to want to

hear about *this!* He's always interested in tall tales, and what makes for a better tall tale than a spooky creature lurking in the primordial, untouched forest?" He turned his head slightly to holler into the talking horn which he'd angled toward him to communicate as he worked. "It's like one of my exploration epics! Delving into the deepest jungle of Africa, to see wonders no white man has ever laid eyes upon!"

"That's excellent," Abigail said wryly, still recovering from the encounter herself. She had convinced herself she'd never have to face the "amalgamations," as Martin had dubbed the conjoined creatures, again. He had become obsessed with the idea of cataloging the creatures, and written full pages about the different types, as he saw them, the amalgamations, combinations of disparate lifeforms, fusions, which were like the bear and her cubs, and now the bats, the same species combined... Her main concern with the whole project was the danger of Martin insisting on going back up the mountain and somehow convincing her to go along, despite her best judgment.

These creatures were some kind of punishment by whatever universal forces watched over Man and his folly for the trespasses against the forest, past and imminent in the form of the railway, for which a swath of trees was already being felled...

"I hope so! I think I really captured the creature," Martin said, the broad smile on his face evident in his tone even through the brass tube and Abigail's slowly-healing ears. She shook her head, exasperated, and continued reading the account of Sylvester Marsh's development of the cog railway concept to improve on the standard model of simple friction keeping a train rolling up a track.

After a fitful night, Martin and Abigail went into town on their standard trek before heading to the Landing. The sun was still climbing, and a chill clung to the shadows of the huddled together buildings along Tanner Street.

They turned into an alley toward Main Street, where the post office and general store stood, only to come face to mask with a scrawny hooligan with a stick. As one, they turned around, only to see two more youths with bandanas covering their features. One held a rusty old shovel, the other waved a fist reinforced with iron knuckles. Martin had heard of such a weapon before, used in the recent war between the North and South, but had never seen them in person.

"Hey now, that's not very polite," the boy behind them protested. "I wasn't even given the opportunity to introduce myself. Such finely dressed, upstanding young people should carry themselves with more manners."

"But they don't need introduction, do they, boss?" One of the boys before them said, dragging the iron knuckles wrapped around his fist against the hoop of a barrel, bringing sparks. A number of barrels and crates served as obstacles that made flight all the more difficult. The twins had walked into an ambush.

"Mother did warn us about such people," Martin noted in as nonchalant a tone as he could muster. "Who would envy our position, our clothing."

"Your money, or your blood," the third miscreant threatened.

"Those too, yes," Martin agreed.

"What are you doing?" Abigail hissed through clenched teeth, looking around as subtly as she could for anything resembling a weapon. She let out a small shriek as the first boy shoved her from behind, the point of the stick putting a hole in her blouse. She reflexively leaned away from the pain, and stumbled toward the shovel wielder. He swung his weapon. The flat piece of metal swooped toward her face. She stared for a fraction of a second that seemed like minutes before turning away and cramming her eyes shut.

Without sight, the world around her shifted. She was aware of her spine in a way that she had never been before. It branched and followed what she imagined were her nerves or perhaps blood vessels, with the strongest line ending at the back of her hand. Not her spine as such, then, but the infection spreading through her body. The bundled black lines progressing across the bird's body in her dream flashed in her mind's eye. Something hauled her backward by her arm. There was another flash, of lines, making the rough shape of a body. Had Martin been infected, too? And his it from her?

Abigail opened her eyes again as the shovel passed within an inch of her face. Had she worn glasses, she would have lost them. She turned to thank her brother and found Martin on the ground. The hand just above her elbow was Daniel Swindon's. He flashed her a quick smile before spinning her around and leaping on the shovel boy before he could recover from his failed swing.

Distance closed, the shovel was useless, only keeping the other boy from defending himself with his hands. Daniel took advantage and punched him, once in a sweeping blow that turned the boy's head, and again into the exposed mandible, sending the hooligan sprawling, and the shovel to the ground with a clatter.

Daniel swiftly ducked to pick up the shovel and then jabbing it, spearlike into the iron knuckler's gut, doubling him over and then swinging upward, sending him reeling as well. Tossing the shovel toward the third assailant, he grabbed Abigail and Martin's hands as the latter stood. Daniel guided them back down the alley onto Tanner Street.

"Daniel!" Abigail cheered as they fled. "That was amazing! Where did you learn to fight like that?"

"When you live in the gutter, you gotta be light on your feet and heavy in the hand."

"That's... I would say 'truly horrifying,' but I'm afraid my capacity for that phrase has been filled by other recent events. Suffice to say, thank you for coming to our aid, Daniel!" Martin, still out of breath from the blow that felled him and the running, simply nodded at his sister's side.

"It's nothing. Honestly. I should get going, though. I hope I can talk to you again soon."

"You are very welcome to speak to me whenever you like. We have never stopped being friends, simply because my parents make certain assumptions about your character based on your father," Abigail said, then realized how unflattering her statement might be to the elder Swindon. A cloud briefly passed over Daniel's face, but then he smiled. "I mean..." She began.

"No, it's all right. I understand. I do have to go, though. Be careful," Daniel said, turning away and leaving at a trot.

"Well, that was brilliant. *And* we're still on the wrong street. We have to find a place to cross to Main without an armed guard..." Martin grumbled, holding his side.

Lights out, Martin lay in bed, drifting away toward sleep. The intermittent scratching from his drawer returned, a modicum each of terrifying and comforting that he had some piece of this phenomenon under his control. Then he heard wood slide on wood. Just a small movement, it was like someone opening a closely fitting door, or a window. But his window was closed, secured against the increasingly cold nights.

The sound came again. The light grind of wood made him turn toward the talking horn. "Abigail? Is this a trick? Are you trying to scare me? I get it, ok? The centipede bat gave you a fright for some reason. I'm sorry I brought it back up. Can we just sleep please?" There came no reply from the horn, but the sound of wood on wood came again, followed by something clattering to the floor.

"Abigail? This isn't funny, all right? I-" Something touched his throat. Eyes wide, searching the dark room for any sign of movement, he swatted past his neck and sat up. His ribs, not yet fully healed from the alley altercation, protested, but he reached for the matches. He struck one, but moved too quickly to set the flame to the wick of the lamp. It blew out with a small flare of light. His assailant scrambled across the floor, bouncing off various furniture, causing him to start each time. "Rupert? Is that you, boy?" He asked hopefully.

Finally, he got the lamp lit. He panned its light across the space, seeing the spines of his adventure books on their shelf, the globe with its brass arc showing the latitudes gleaming dully. The tone of the scratching changed and he turned to the talking horn just in time to see the jagged end of the mobile antler shard vanish into its depths. He ran to the wall between his and Abigail's rooms, pounding on the plaster with the meat of a clenched fist.

"Abigail! Wake up! It's coming down the horn! Abigail!" He paused to listen for any response that might come back, but heard nothing. He couldn't see the thing anymore, no matter how close he held the light to the flared bell of the device. Racing to his door, he hauled it open and ran to the next door down the hallway. He knocked, then pounded. After a few seconds of no sounds from within, he heard a scream and a crash.

"Ribs be damned!" Martin shouted to no one and stepped away from the door, then turned and ran at it, laying his shoulder into the wood panels. The door rattled on its hinges, but didn't give. Pain exploded across his side as the healing bones were tested. He backed up to try again and as he began forward, Abigail opened the door, face as white as her nightdress in the lamplight.

"That *thing!*" She yelled. "That thing just came through the horn and attacked me!" She held up her injured hand, still in a light bandage, but the linens were in disarray now, as though clumsily pulled away.

"Where is it now? Did you see which way it went? It's so small, it could get anywhere, under the bed, behind some books on the shelf..." Martin pushed past his sister and moved the lamp around, pouring light across the whole room by sections. His eyes scanned back and forth, up and down, but then he saw it on her window sill.

"Catch it! Smash it!" Abigail demanded. Martin started forward and the antler levered its tip under the edge of the window, lifting it to its full height of about four inches, then popped away into the night, the window slamming shut after, one of the lower panes cracking.

"Well, it's gone now! There's no way we're going to be able to find it across the whole estate, in the dark. It's too small and apparently has a will beyond doing laps in my drawer."

"It's not funny, Martin! It's loose out there! It could hurt someone!"

"All right, I'll try..." Martin threw on his jacket and

searched for the next hour before the lamp's flame grew into a low arc of dim light from lack of fuel. He had seen not a single sign of the creature after the initial divot to its impact with the lawn a few feet away from the foot of the wall below Abigail's window.

CHAPTER ELEVEN

Dear Mr. Twain,

I write to you today to again thank you for the advice you've dispensed on writing and share another terrifying bit of news. I sincerely believe that "spooky" and "spine tingling" stories have a lot of appeal, perhaps as an offshoot of adventure stories, or perhaps a progression from myths and fairy tales, which often have frightening endings or turns of events.

Allow me to describe this latest monstrosity to come from the mountains that loom over my head even now:

When first the miner deposited the creature on the floor of the cafeteria, I thought it was a collection of worn old leather gloves or perhaps wet leaf litter, darkened from age and decay. Then it moved. One of the "leaves" flapped weakly. Another, then the central spine of the serpentine beast shifted, showing how the abomination was assembled, clarified its parts in my mind's eye.

"Bats!" I cried out from my vantage on the balcony above. It was a chain of bats, with the frontmost supported at its hind end by the front of the next, and so one, for more than a dozen brown, flopping creatures. The unnatural aspect of the thing turned my stomach, but I could scarcely look away. In the next moment, it rose up, revealing yellow fangs that worked side to side like the pincers of an insect, swaying slightly as a cobra looking for its moment to strike.

I hope you enjoy my above vignette and accept that every creature I've described to you over the last weeks is not spawned purely from my imagination, but that I have laid my living eyes upon them, though they filled me with terror and revulsion.

All the Best, hope to hear from you again soon,

Martin Beckett

"Did either of you hear anything in the night?" Liza asked them as they laid into breakfast.

"What kind of thing?" Martin asked, wearing his most innocent face.

"At different times in the evening, once in the kitchen, and once in the linen closet, I heard a very distinct scratching noise. I'm afraid we may have acquired mice, or perhaps chipmunks, some kind of small vermin."

"Oh! How unsettling!" Abigail said, giving a shiver.

"I agree. Just the thought of tiny creatures crawling all over the place, perhaps watching us while we sleep, eating and ruining the grains and fruits... I know we've never had any kind of animal here as a pet, but what do you think your parents would think if we got a cat?" Abigail's eyes lit up.

"Could we?" She turned to Martin.

"I suppose." He shrugged. "I don't have much interest in little puddles of fur that laze around in sunbeams, but if we have rodents, we may not have much choice. On the other hand, it occurs to me that Jack Russells, as we've heard a number of times from Aunt Helen, were bred in part to hunt rats. Rupert might solve the problem in the short term, nipping an infestation in the bud, so to speak."

"That is an excellent point. Do you think Ms. Campbell would approve of her little treasure being set on some unknown creature? She does dote on the pup so," Liza mused.

"True, true, but he was meant for this. If dogs could have callings, this would be his. We can at least ask her," Martin said.

"Ask who what, young man?" Aunt Helen asked, made up to the T, but looking beneath the veneer as though she had gotten not a wink of sleep.

"We were wondering about Rupert helping out with a possible mouse problem. Liza tells us she's been hearing some scratchings," Martin said.

"Oh, really? We've been here for weeks and this just comes up now? Well, I suppose I could bring him in here and let him have a sniff around. He's still sleeping now. We're still on a city schedule. I'm only up so early because I wanted to go into town and visit with local artisans about having a new collar made for Rupert, perhaps something involving the silver from our very own mine."

"That sounds spectacular, Aunt Helen. I don't think you need to rise early for such things, though. Our businesses don't get very busy. Most people work up at the mine during the day. You may have to wait until evening to talk to a smith," Abigail pointed out.

"Oh, is that right? Very well then... I will see you for lunch." The older woman took an apple from the bowl at the center of the island and sailed back through the door to the foyer.

"All right, then, we can give Rupert a chance, though I know of a few families around town whose animals have recently had litters of kittens... If the matter's not resolved in the next few days, I'll check directly with your parents and then those families." Smiling broadly, Liza poured them both more juice and wandered off to see to other chores.

"You know, it might not be the best idea," Martin said,

drawing his spoon through his porridge absently.

"Oh? Why not?"

"I've never heard anything in the walls." Martin held up one finger. "Liza just mentions this today of all days." Another finger rose. "The night after..." He lowered his tone so that Liza wouldn't hear. He was convinced she spied on them for their parents. She could be just behind the door. He might have said too much already in a normal conversational voice. "The antler got away."

"Ohhh." Abigail nodded. It was a point. If it was the antler knocking around in the walls and scratching around looking for food, a small animal might not be safe. A flash of worry over Rupert passed through her mind. Her shoulders fell.

"Well, maybe someday... Did you hear that?" Martin asked, rising from his stool and stepping in one direction, listening intently, then turning another way, trying to locate the source. He pulled one door after another open, then the drawers. He turned and pointed excitedly.

Racing across the kitchen, Abigail threw open a cabinet door to find a small gray mouse perched at the edge of a box of crackers. "Aww look at him! He's so cute! We should keep him as a pet!" Before she finished the word "pet," or could react, the hand-long chunk of antler leapt out of the dark corner of the cabinet, unzipping down its length much as the trees of the Twisted Grove had done. It wrapped itself around the rodent in one motion, leaving only a drop of blood that glowed jewel red in the morning sun at the base end of the mouse's severed tail. "Uh- I-" Abigail fumbled for words.

"Did it get away?" Martin asked, oblivious to the horror she'd just witnessed.

"N-no... It definitely didn't get away... Uh... Get a bowl?"

"I don't think Liza would approve of trying to keep a

mouse as a pet, especially since she seemed so set on a cat."

"No, it's here. The antler... Thing... Is right here. I can see it."

"Ohh! Grab it!" Martin said, looking up, finally engaged by the conversation.

"Um... no. Not in a millions years. And you'd better not either. What I just saw... Just get a bowl before it runs... hops... whatever, away."

"Fine. I had it for days in my drawer and it never even mussed a notepad. I tried to feed it all kinds of stuff from fruit to steak. Nothing." Martin rose and took his sister's empty bowl in one hand, ready to turn his hand over and capture the antler against the shelf. He moved up beside his sister slowly, bringing his hand forward in what he hoped was a calm enough manner to not frighten the thing, though he wasn't sure how it sensed its surroundings, or navigated.

Breathing slow, he counted down to himself and flipped the bowl quickly, pressing it down against the pale wood of the shelf. The antler was pinned two thirds of the way out from under the bowl. It writhed and struggled, even twisting back and assaulting the glazed surface of the bowl. Instinctively, Martin reached for the creature, but Abigail caught his arm. The antler raised up toward Martin's fingers and unzipped. A thin, gray, thread of something fell out onto the shelf as the sides of the body-mouth undulated, waving hundreds of small spikes, hungry for more.

"Ugh!" Martin cried, falling back, knocking Abigail over. She ended sitting up against the island, one arm through the legs of a stool, and desperately off balance. Martin tumbled past the island entirely. The antler point seemed to appraise her from the edge of the shadows, then turned away and vanished amid boxes and tins. "Are you all right?" Martin asked, regaining his feet. Where'd it go?"

Abigail pointed with her free hand and extricated herself from the stool. "Gone again."

"That's not good. Did you see all those... I don't know if I'd call them teeth, they were all along the inside like some kind of weird natural iron maiden."

"A what?" Abigail asked.

"Never mind. What's this?" Martin leaned closer to the shelf to inspect the line of gray sediment the thing had released.

"That's what's left of the mouse," Abigail said.

"We definitely need something higher power than a cat. Like one of Mr. Colt's revolvers," Martin said.

As Martin and Abigail finished breakfast, basking in the normalcy of the sunlight beaming through the windows and trying not to worry for their parents who were still up at the offices, perhaps not eating or drinking for days on end, a series of five sharp "dings!" intruded on their thoughts.

"Who could that be?" Liza asked, wiping her hands on a towel and striding for the front room and the door. Shaken from their ruminations, Martin and Abigail followed, arriving at the entrance just as Liza opened the door to a man with a thick brown wave of hair across the top of his head and a full mustache riding his lip. His linen suit shone in the morning light like a beacon.

"Samuel Clemens, at your service, ma'am," the gentleman said, his white boater already in his hand, a bag by each foot. "Am I right in thinking I have reached my destination, the Beckett Estate?"

"Why, yes, Mr. Clemens, though I'm afraid the master of the house and the misses are both out right now, deep in mine business up the mountain. They've been keeping themselves up there for- I really shouldn't get into that. You are welcome to leave a message."

"That is most thoughtful of you, Miss...?"

"Liza, Liza Dodsworth, sir," Liza blushed at getting direct attention. She was used to serving, being a procurer of things. Only the twins ever seemed to ask after her, and she was certain that was mostly as part of their plots, distracting her in the course of one of their capers. They were wily.

"A pleasure, Miss Dodsworth,"

"Liza, please. Did you have a message for the Becketts?"

"Ever the efficient caretaker, I see. Very well done, but I must admit, I'm here to see neither the master of the house nor his wife."

"No?" Liza asked, puzzled. "I hope you're not here to sell something. The Master and Lady have not built up this estate, indeed, this entire town over the last decades being taken in by snake oil salesmen." To this, Mr. Clemens let out a hearty guffaw.

"I assure you, Miss Dodsworth, I'm glad as anyone to hear that. My guess is it's you, young Master Beckett, who I'm here to see, about your letters, and the..." Clemens glanced quickly at Liza, then back to Martin. "*Tall tales* you've been been sharing with me. Your town sounds like quite a hotbed of amazing activity and creatures."

"I am!" Martin said exuberantly, stepping up beside Liza and taking Mr. Clemens' offered hand. "Liza, if you don't mind, I think Mr. Clemens will be staying with us for a little while. Could you prepare one of the guest bedrooms?" Liza just stared at Martin. Her eyes narrowed as though she had been roped into another of the twins' schemes, but she couldn't formulate a rejection of the noted author, about whom Martin had spoken endlessly over the last year. She nodded.

"Of course, Master Martin. Do you prefer morning sun or evening, Mr. Clemens?" She asked.

"Evening, I think, Miss Dodsworth, I'm sorry, Liza. I never held with the old saw cut by Benjamin Franklin about being 'early to rise' making one 'healthy, wealthy, and wise.'" Abigail stifled a laugh, as that exact quotation was embroidered on a pillow in the drawing room and painted on a board in the other guest room, the one Mr. Clemens would not be occupying.

"Very well, then, follow me if you would," Liza said, turning on a heel. She seemed a few degrees less solicitous, on edge, even, since learning Martin circumvented protocol by inviting a guest without consulting his parents, or alerting her.

"Do I detect the delectable odor of eggs?" Mr. Clemens asked as they approached the staircase. "The train and the chefs were both rough on my stomach, but my appetite is returning with each step."

"I can certainly cook you up some eggs, Mr. Clemens. You'll just have to let me know how you like them," Liza said, gesturing to the left as she reached the top of the stairs. Clemens' charm did seem to take the edge off her attitude, though.

"Thank you most kindly, Liza. Your hospitality is everything one could expect from the finest southern home."

"I shall endeavor to take that as a compliment, sir," Liza said. The twins snickered at the foot of the stairs. Martin took his sister's hands in his own, eyes wide, smile strange and broad.

"He's here!" He whispered. "He really came! This is the most amazing day!"

CHAPTER TWELVE

"Did I hear a man's voice?" Helen asked, opening the door to the first occupied guest room a crack to peek out. Hat still in his hand while Martin and Abigail hauled his bags up behind on the stairs, Clemens bowed.

"Good morning, ma'am, Samuel Clemens. You may call me Sam." Rupert barked from within the room.

"Hush, Rupert!" Helen said. The door closed, but a few minutes later, as Liza led Sam back downstairs toward the kitchen, twins in tow, the door opened again, with Helen fully dressed as though on her way to a Broadway opening night and beaming. "Hello there! I am *so* sorry for cutting you off earlier, Mr. Clemens, was it? It seems that I've heard that name. Have you been in the papers?"

"You could say that," Sam chuckled, "You could indeed. I've done many jobs over the years, including working as a newspaper man, a miner, a riverboat hand, and I've dabbled with creative writing." Martin gave a little laugh at this, though he tried and failed to contain his mirth behind a hand over his mouth. His shoulders leapt and danced. "I did not, however, catch you name."

"Helen, Helen Campbell," Helen said, trotting forth as quickly as her restrictive dress would allow. She extended a hand to Sam. He took it and shook it lightly.

"Well, Miss Campbell, we were about to go find this weary traveler some eggs. Would you care to join us in the kitchen?" Sam offered.

"You know, I am feeling a bit peckish. I haven't had breakfast yet. I tend to be a late riser."

"Myself as well, my dear, can't abide waking in the dark, having to work a lamp before I've properly cleared the cobwebs from my brain."

"Oh! Well, you're quite, descriptive!" Helen laughed.

"I do try," Sam said with a wink to Martin as Helen joined them on the stairs, moving past the twins. "And what brings such a radiant late riser to Silver Hill, Nevada?"

"Martin and Abigail are my nephew and niece."

"That seems near to an impossibility. You could scarcely be of an age. I bet you're a cousin and your mother sent you out here to learn about frontier life. Of course, there's no real frontier here, just a blooming city ready to come into its own."

"Sir, you flatter me... Don't stop." Abigail and Martin exchanged eye rolls.

"At least they're getting along. Perhaps he'll keep her off our backs. It would be nice to have a few days off from 'ladyhood' lessons," Abigail whispered, hanging back with Martin while the rest descended.

"Go up the mountain?" Martin's enthusiasm cooled like the tiny puddles of yolk on Sam's plate. "I don't know, sir. It's dangerous. As I've been writing to you, I've been taking the lighter side, bird-headed snakes-"

"I'm certain it was a worm, the circular striations around its body, the slime trail..." Abigail interrupted.

"Fine, a bird-headed worm. Butterflies with leaf wings-"

"Ha!" Clemens barked, "A worm with the head of a bird? Perhaps the bird was too early and the worm tried to eat *it!* Can you imagine? I suppose you can. You're the ones who brought it up." Sam took another bite of fried egg and wiped at his generous mustache. "But still, what's a little danger in the face of such stories? Surely, there must be some risk in any endeavor worth undertaking?"

"That's exactly as I thought before our big adventure the other day. We came across a number of disturbing sights, trees smashing a deer to pieces, a wickiup that had arms like an octopus or a jelly fish in its undersides..."

"Smashing...? Deer? Surely you two don't think such is proper mealtime discourse. We shall have to accelerate your training regarding small talk. I can't stay forever, and in fact, should really head out before winter sets in," Helen said, dabbing at the corner of her mouth with a napkin.

"A wickiup? Like one of those domed homes the Indians build?" Sam drawled, disbelief thick in his voice. "I would never have taken one for dangerous."

"I'm sure they're not usually. Something truly strange is happening, or has been happening for ages... Up there..." Martin said, turning toward the mountain that loomed over the mining town even as the denizens of said town delved into its belly to pull forth riches. Perhaps it resented the trespass...

"Then that's where we need to go," Clemens declared. "Can't report on a fire from the station, can you? No sir!"

"No, sir..." Martin agreed. The man had the same fire he himself had felt before facing off against the bear fusion.

They packed even more food than the first time, knowing they could be trapped on the mountain, though that was the least of their worries. They also packed heavy kitchen knives and Martin stowed a few of his secret treasures, including a small pack of Coston flares which he'd picked up in the city expecting them to be fireworks.

All the while, Liza flitted around, demanding they put things back, and where did they think they were going? She threatened to send one of the other servants to summon the police to eject Mr. Clemens and other servants to block the doors from the outside.

"Ladies, ladies!" Clemens said, hands up before him, palms out. "I personally guarantee the safety of our young adventurers. I understand that they may have acted... rashly in the past, under their own recognizance," here, he looked to the twins, who both cast their eyes to the gray flagstone floor. "But this outing is of a wholly different kind. There will be a man along, and though I hesitated to don its carrying belt inside this fine house..." As he spoke, Mr. Clemens drew forth from the top of his pack a length of brown leather, and attached to it was a holster bearing over a foot of metal and wood in an unmistakable shape.

"You brought a pistol into my- our- the Becketts' house?" Liza exploded. Again, Clemens raised his free hand, the gun belt twisting freely. Martin stood in awe, a hand absently rising as if to reach for the weapon.

"Now, I assure you, it is safely carried and always stowed in my bags when traveling. And it will keep your young ones safe as we venture forth. There's not many creatures I know that would shrug off a slug from Mr. Remington's device, and none of them live on this continent. I do not bring this out to dismay you, but to reassure you." Liza crossed her arms and blew a hard breath out her nose. Abigail had seen this pose before. The woman was reluctant, but would ultimately agree.

Clemens beaming, gun on his hip for the first time since leaving Virginia City, the twins reluctant, they headed out, hitching a ride on the ore wagon to the Landing as it ascended for the second load of the day.

"This is ancient forest, indeed," Clemens noted. "Every tree reaches out to one, eager to tell its own story. How many Indians must they have seen, stalking prey? How many wolves and catamount, even before Man impinged on its depths?"

"Not too many Indians, I'm afraid, Mr. Clemens," Abigail pointed out. "The Paiute took these lands for haunted by ancient spirits. Having been up here, I can see why. I wouldn't want to risk running into the things we saw again as regular as they must have hunted."

"Oh come now, young lady. I'm sure it's not as bad as all that. Your young minds, frightened at being lost in the woods, added to whatever fearful thing you may have seen. A bear, no doubt, must be a terrifying beast to two unfamiliar with nature, alone, cold, hungry, exhausted. Don't blame yourselves. But still, I already get a sense of this place. It's certainly a fitting setting for the kind of stories your brother has been trying to sell me on. Terrifying tales, tall tales of a different stripe, to more than amaze and delight, but titillate and chill. Perhaps the kind of thing that sticks with you, haunting you for days after reading it. Such an impact..."

"Certainly that's true of having witnessed the events myself," Martin admitted. "It was quite a few nights before I slept soundly." Clemens nodded.

"And that kind of wilderness adventure may be exactly the kind of story city readers are yearning for. Something to bring them the frights and chills of the wild frontier, untamed, unpredictable. Beyond cowboy stories of today's dime novels, into a new era of exploration and extranormal events. Do you suppose there are any burial grounds around here? The one thing your stories seem to be missing, monstrous creatures, deep, foreboding forests, houses that come to life and try to abscond with you, is ghosts, spirits! Ha! Yes, a good ghost story told by the fire is just the thing for this kind of collection!"

"Did you see that?" Clemens pointed, practically hopping out of the wagon. "It was a frog, well, it was mostly a frog, but it had the most unusual splay of over-sized, delicate, insect wings. I know I saw long, narrow dragonfly wings that must have been as long as my hand, and a few other sets that may have been from house flies. Oh, you weren't stretching the truth much, were you, lad?"

"Oh! There it is!" Martin peered between the towering firs and oaks. Abigail turned just in time to see the copper and black and tan mottled frog swing into a patch of sunlight, glistening and gleaming. Her breath caught in her throat. It wasn't in itself frightening, but somehow majestic as it landed on gray bark and folded its wings away in a kind of tent which provided it camouflage. Like a flash of sunlight directly to the eye, the afterimage of the creature hung in her vision for a time after she looked away.

"I did pretty well with the story of jumping frogs, but I doubt anyone would take something so outlandish as a flying frog seriously. It's not even frightening except in how alien it is. It's something to keep in mind, but I want to see something truly bloodcurdling to base a story around. If this new genre is going to take off, we need something that will grip the readers and not let go," Clemens insisted as though giving a lecture.

At the Landing, the trio debarked.

"Did you kids want to check in with your parents? From what you said, they're working in one of those buildings,"

Clemens offered. "It would seem proper to introduce myself and all."

"That's a well-mannered proposition, but I doubt they would see you, or us for that matter. When they're in the office, of late, they're interested in nothing else besides the business of running and expanding the mine. We spent the day at the office recently, to see what they were about, how the project was coming, but..." Abigail trailed off.

"But everyone was acting quite oddly," Martin picked up from his sister. "I suppose they're all very focused and wearing themselves thin. I hope the project is all arranged soon and we can have our parents back, though it looks like it may take some time. They plan to run a rail all the way up to the proposed new shaft."

"A railroad up a mountain? At this inclination? It seems impossible," Clemens noted.

"There's a lot of impossible on this mountain," Abigail said. "Although it has been done, in New Hampshire, by Mister Marsh."

"Oh? How did they manage it?" Clemens asked.

"He designed a secondary cog wheel to pull the train up a track not unlike a ladder, with rungs the teeth of the cog push on rather than relying on smooth metal wheels on smooth metal rails."

"Fascinating, and you hope to reproduce that here?"

"Something like it. The challenges are somewhat different, with the hopes of carrying loads of silver ore down the mountain rather than people, but then down is easier than up."

"Ha!" Clemens laughed. "I suppose you're right at that, young lady! I suppose you're right."

They headed up the mountain, once again following the

river. The twins were wary, but restrained their fears. On their last trip, they hadn't seen anything terrifying until nightfall, and they would be home before dark this time. Before they reached the point where they had diverted the first time, they came across massive tracks in the soft ground. Pine needles and other leaves filled the irregular pits, softened the edges, but once Martin and Abigail pulled away some of the leaves, Clemens stood back, eyes wide.

"Such a creature, such size! I *must* see it!" Clemens said, taking off along a newly blazed trail. Toppled trees and trampled brush stood to either side of the path created by the monster's passing. Abigail looked at Martin. He patted a side pouch of his pack with something like confidence and followed his guest, a white ghost striding forcefully through the dark forest, seemingly unmindful of the dangers.

CHAPTER THIRTEEN

Clemens' steps slowed. A series of thumps, or crashes, shook the ground, growing by the second. The man looked around frantically while Abigail and Martin took each others' hands.

"What a sound! I could swear I can feel it reverberate in my chest! How did you do it?" Clemens asked.

"What?" Martin asked, puzzled.

"How did you make the sound? Some large sheet of metal? I've heard of theater productions simulating thunder with such. Or maybe a landslide? A tumble of loose earth sliding down the mountain into some gully?"

"We- that-" Martin stammered.

"You think we've made all this up for your entertainment?" Abigail, too was flabbergasted.

"Entertainment, flim-flam, what have you. You don't expect me to believe these sloppy prints are from a real creature, do you? It's clearly a school-child effort at frightening the willing. It certainly reinforces the idea of scaring people for fun, but really, if we're going to go in on such an enterprise, you must tell me how you do it," Clemens insisted. "That frog puppet was exquisite. Far better than these tracks."

Before either Beckett could answer, the brush to their right rustled and a black-masked face appeared. Unmindful of the humans, the creature darted out across the flattened area of the path, glistening body in an armor of fish scales bending back and forth with each step, sending up flashes of reflected sunlight. On its striped fan-tail, a second appeared, then a handful more at once, followed by a veritable river of the creatures, trundling and shining across the path into the brush on the other side.

Without communicating, Abigail and Martin grabbed Mr. Clemens' arms and hauled him back toward a few larger trees. His hat flew off and he reached for it, breaking free of Abigail's grip, but she turned and leaned a shoulder into his side, forcing him backward. Martin tripped, bringing down Clemens and then Abigail and they all lay at the side of the trail, eyes wide as the silver stream of bandit-faced salmon flopped past. Well over a hundred of the monstrosities later, though their numbers were hard to gauge, the school began to thin and Abigail and Martin regained their senses.

Mr. Clemens recovered his hat, getting within a few feet of some of the stragglers, causing them to instinctively swerve away. "Simply amazing! I'm still baffled at how you can construct such convincing puppets and fail so miserably at a proper footprint of a great beast. Still, every enterprise requires development. We will take care of it. On to the next encounter!" Clemens said, starting off down the trail with renewed energy.

"I'm a little worried about him," Abigail said. "I don't know if he's in full control of his faculties. Maybe we should head back."

"I don't think there's much chance of that right now. Look at him. He's got so much energy, and he's determined to follow these tracks, even if he thinks they're fake."

"Probably *because* he thinks they're fake. Would you follow them if you thought a real gigantic bear awaited you at the other end?" Abigail asked. Martin shrugged and shook his head, finally catching view of Mr. Clemens and hurrying after him.

Stumbling through the forest, following gargantuan tracks, the twins barely kept up with Clemens as he pursued the bear. "Its den must be ahead somewhere, correct? I love this entire thing so far. It is a bit of a walk. Perhaps those of lesser energy might avail themselves of a cart for the entire journey? Or horses? It does seem quite a ways to the den. Do you have a map of all the work you've done? Of course you have. The clever pair of you... Have you considered making this one of many different adventure paths through the forest?

"Different paths could be made for people of different ages and temperaments, ranging from a string of hapless curiosities like the bird-headed worm and raccoon fish to the mentally devastating many-headed bear you wrote about," Clemens prattled on, absorbed by the idea of this whole episode being some sort of pitch for a wilderness attraction based around strange creatures and local legends.

"What do we do?" Abigail asked Martin.

"I have no idea, you're the clever one!" Martin hissed back, nursing a pained ankle that grew more tender the farther they walked. The ground was anything but even and stable. The edges of the bear's footprints often gave way, forcing one to slide a few inches before regaining control of one's path. "I'm just trying not to break my neck!"

"Amazing! You must have worked for months on this!" Clemens exclaimed, having pulled ahead of them again. He stopped now, at the edge of a clearing before a cliff face. Abigail and Martin caught up before he spoke again. "There are thousands of bones here, some natural, it seems, others, look at that! That could be a goat of some sort, but look at all the horns..." Indeed, the dozen yards between the trio of explorers and a low, arcing cave entrance was completely covered in gleaming white, sun-bleached bones. Many were cracked and jagged at the ends. "Is there more inside? I mean, this is really spectacular work so far. If you haven't created a cavern experience, I completely understand, and yet, I sense..." Clemens began to pick his way through the bone field.

"Mr. Clemens, we- we should definitely go. What if the creature returns while we're looking around? Or it has... cubs it hasn't... absorbed?" Martin tried to persuade his guest.

A sound issued from the cave, but nothing like those present could have expected. It sounded like nothing other than a forlorn flute calling them to dance. Notes spun and reeled in the air in a driving rhythm. The notes, high and piping, stretched over their heads. Clemens strode forward, swaying and clapping as he went, over the lip of the cave and down, his white hat bobbing as he descended.

“Where’s he going now?” Martin asked. “This can’t be good.”

“Don’t you hear it? The music?”

Abigail struggled, but the music sang to her. She felt it deep within her being, even saw shifting collections of lines like loose bundles of sticks, *The lines on the bird in my dream... in my hand, my spine, Mother...Father...Daniel...*

But these were limned in iridescent greens and blues and reds, beautiful, ominous, irresistible. Martin stumbled behind her, boots sliding on bone. The osseous ground cover clacked against itself in a poor approximation of rhythm.

“What is going on? Music?” Martin called from behind her.

No! Abigail pushed back against the music. *I've read too many faerie stories to think following music into a cave is wise! We may never see our parents again! Come on, Martin!*

Resist! Push back as we do everything else, together! Something squirmed in Abigail's brain and the sheen of color faded from the clusters of black lines swimming through the air around her. The music shifted to wheezing and shrieking.

Easily six feet across, the great bear's proper head was even more grotesque than the twins recalled from their first encounter. The dark had spared them the details of a smattering of teeth growing from the left side of the face, just below the eye. Sores, red and weeping, stood open along the edges of its round ears, along its jaw, down its neck and across its shoulder. Its mouth stood open. They could see teeth, sharp, jagged, crammed into the palate like the Devil's hairbrush. Even the lolling tongue sported ivory triangles like shark's teeth along the edge and in a line down the middle.

Abigail shook as she recognized the black clusters of lines, like cramped, irregular tally marks, infesting the whole being. She could see them, black against the deep brown, sliding behind the angry red of the open wounds, shadowed in the teeth. She knew somehow that they were not normal markings like stripes on a skunk or the band of a mallard's neck. They were *inside* the creature, showing through because... Because they were inside her, too.

The dream with the bird, the boat, the fell reflections of the forest in the water... The creature that had landed on her hand... The Western Maplewing, Martin had dubbed it... It had left behind something... infectious, that something that twisted when she resisted the whistling snores of the bear, thinking them faerie music.

But if the black lines cause that delusion... why is Mr. Clemens affected?

As if in response, Martin stumbled on a bone hooking his foot in a rib arcing out of the general mass. He pitched over and slid down the slope, causing a grim avalanche of clicking and clacking remains. The bear lifted its front leg, revealing a red-eyed cub head, as pitiful, as terrible, as it had been that night. Abigail shuddered as the flesh beneath it writhed, trying to move independently of its mother. Its jaws worked noiselessly for long seconds before a small roar issued forth.

Clemens, for his part, stood, transfixed, one foot on the edge of a massive hip bone. Abigail couldn't tell whether he was simply under the creature's spell or if he was stupefied by proof that this was not in any way a hoax. Picking her way down to Martin, she saw that his leg was impaled by the narrow jaw of some poor animal. She pulled the bone free, revealing square teeth framed in crimson blood and charcoal colored fibers from Martin's trousers. She waved a hand before his eyes and watched them focus, then dart around, taking in the scene.

"Mfhwahfr!" he tried to cry out, but she muted him. Abigail pulled her hand away from his mouth.

"We need to get out of here, quietly." The cub's roar cut across her words, louder this time, as if it was coming around, more able to assert itself as it awoke.

"Quietly? Much more of that and it won't matter if we bring a brass band through," Martin said, prodding at his leg and wincing. "Not going to be moving anywhere too quickly like this. I was already practically hobbled."

"At least it's fitting you're taking on most of the injuries. It's your fault we're in this mess... again."

"You can't let anything go, can you? Keep the... small head quiet. I'll get Mr. Clemens out," Martin said. Abigail nodded, uncertain of how she would do her part. She turned back to the bear. She had ridden an elephant once at a circus in the city. This beast dwarfed that. Its deep brown fur, she could now that she was closer, was sparser than it appeared at a distance. The black crisscrossing lines made up for some of the difference. Many scars, some long, thin trails, others blotches and short sweeps, told tales of many battles.

The smallest head leaned toward her, accompanied by small tearing sounds, wet, sickening. Without really thinking about it, she began to sing, softly, "Hush little baby, don't say a word, Mama's going buy you a mockingbird..."

The head settled back against its mother, rocking gently as she sang. After a couple of verses, she realized that she was surrounded by a great furry arm, strong musk making the air heavy. She stroked the cub between its closed eyes. When she realized what she was doing, she tried to back away and immediately tripped over a deer antler, which entangled her left ankle while keeping her from regaining her feet.

The small bear's eyes opened dreamily and it began to lean forward again. She could see the fur separate, red, raw flesh revealed beneath. Unable to get her feet under her, she pushed back with the heels of her hands and crab walked a few more feet before the larger head stirred.

"If-" she sang a sour note, "If that diamond ring don't shine..." She sang again, keeping the melody flowing as she slowly backed up the hill. Bones cascaded around her. Something grabbed her under her shoulders, causing her to squeal.

"It's us, keep singing!" Martin whispered harshly in her ear. She continued as best she could, but her mouth was dry, her throat constricted in fear. She barely made it through the verse before she found herself mute. She kicked at the antler, finally freeing it, but levering of the boot at the same time.

The bones tumbled down to flop against the massive bear.

This time the greater head rose, looking straight at her with what her panicked mind was certain was recognition. Turning now, she and Martin and Clemens sped from the cave as best they could, crossing the gleaming boneyard and entering the dim confines of the forest once again.

The crunch of bones forced them to turn and look at the head the size of a street hawker's cart, deformed and encrusted with gore and misplaced teeth. The mouth opened. Desperately, Abigail pressed her hands over her ears, which were just beginning to truly mend after the last encounter.

The roar washed over them like a fetid low tide, filling the air with not only a rumble and shake of the force of great lungs, but the foul air of decay and disease. Clemens took off, whooping and waving his hat in one hand, while Martin and Abigail trailed after him, little chance of outrunning the beast.

CHAPTER FOURTEEN

When there was no sound of falling trees after a few minutes, Abigail and Martins' pace slowed. They tried to call to Mr. Clemens, but he was either too frightened to respond, or too far ahead to hear them. Abigail tracked his white suit for some time, moving between the trees as the path arced west toward town.

"Do you really think it's stuck in that cave during the day?"

"I think it's very ill and while its roar is quite impressive, it may not be in any condition to chase anyone down," Abigail said.

"You sound like you feel sorry for it."

"Every beast under the sky deserves sympathy. Just because we think of it as a monster doesn't make it so. It's a predator like any other bear or wolf or snake."

"You were as scared as I was that night. What happened?"

"I sang to the cub. I saw it react. I found myself... Patting it."

"You *touched* that thing? Are you mad? What if it *is* diseased? What if passed you a plague?"

"I..." Abigail looked around conspiratorially as though there might be a passerby to hear. "I already have it." She pulled at her glove, revealing the dense mesh of striations. It had grown to the size of a half dollar on the surface, though she knew the infection reached all through her body now.

"What do you mean? Why are you showing me your hand?" Martin squinted at the skin. "There's the tiniest of scars, where you scratched at it, no doubt."

"You don't see the spot. Hmm, only the infected can see it, recognizing the mark..."

"'Spot?' 'mark?' Sister, you're beginning to frighten me."

"You think you're frightened? I'm the one with this... whatever it is inside me. It's in the bear, and the raccoon-salmon, and... it looks like everything in these woods. Except you, apparently."

"It's a long walk back. Why don't you start at the beginning?" Martin said.

"It started... I *think* it started, with the Maplewing landing on my hand."

"Hey! You used my name. I didn't think you liked it. Sorry, continue."

In the distance, she could feel the bear, like a bit of noise at the edge of her perception. It swirled like a storm on the horizon. As it dwindled, she noticed other spots all around, resting high in the trees, or down amid the roots, flying a ways off to the side as she recounted her dreams, the spots she'd noticed on Mother and Father... On Daniel and how the flower he'd brought that day moved.

They worked their way back along the bear's path, keeping keen eyes out for the position of the sun in the sky and Mr. Clemens' white suit.

"You should have said something earlier. I know I couldn't probably do anything to help, but I could have been there. I wonder, if all of these people in our lives, in the town, are affected... infected..."

"Why aren't you? I don't know. Perhaps some people are immune, or resistant. Perhaps you eat something or have contact with something that protects you."

"Master Beckett! Miss Beckett!" A yell from a ways off alerted them to Sam Clemens' position. They found him in the low branches of a convoluted tree. A pack of what at first appeared to be wolves padded around the base of the tree as though a way up would suddenly appear, or their prey might drop down, sacrificing itself.

Abigail sensed a connection to the creatures before they were close enough to see their deformities, the hooves at the end of their legs, the swept-back, ridged horns like mountain goats'. Their long, shaggy jaws were still just as full of pointed teeth for snagging flesh, though.

She felt out the connection in her head, tried to reach out to them with a low howl. They glanced at her, but nothing more, snapping at her and Martin when they neared.

"Do something!" Clemens insisted.

"They're not listening to me," Abigail protested, "What happened to your pistol?" They hadn't heard any shots, so he hadn't fired. Martin was already rifling through his pack. He stood and threw something which struck a tree only a few feet from Mr. Clemens' scuffed shoes and the wolves' noses. A cloud of brown dust exploded forth, engulfing the heads of half the group. They began shaking their heads violently, sneezing and stumbling away from the noxious cloud. The creatures began to run in earnest as their strides came surer.

"I've never been so glad for you to have a stink bomb on hand!" Abigail sagged, the immediate danger seeming passed.

"I thought it might come in handy. I know many beasts' sense of smell is far stronger than ours. I reasoned that would make the stink bombs more effective."

"Luckily, you were right," Abigail said. Mr. Clemens stood on his perch for a few more moments, letting the cloud disperse and the wolves get farther away.

"Good show, young man! Quite the adventurer, indeed. The creatures are impressive, but one needs a main character, a hero, if you will, to really drive a story. You would have to get into danger on a regular basis, at least once per story, and then find some clever way out. Or... perhaps not. If the goal is to truly terrify, what if... the hero *doesn't* survive, and tells his story from beyond the grave? Or the story is told from the point of view of a trusted companion? Hmm... much to think about. Ah, there you are!" The man bent down and plucked his Remington from the leaf litter. He gave it a cursory inspection and slid it into its holster.

"We won't tell Liza if you don't," Abigail offered. Clemens bowed.

"Indeed, Mr. Clemens, interesting takes on the tale, but I think the first order of business is getting back. We know where the bear sleeps now. I think we have an obligation to... deal with it in some way." Martin grew a hard look on his face.

"What are you saying, brother?" Abigail asked.

"I think we need to bring a group of men back up here and slay the beast, before it slays others."

"We don't know it's hurt anyone, not really," Abigail said.

"Did you see the expanse of bones outside, and inside, its cave? It has killed *thousands* of animals. Something like that must have an immense appetite. How long before it comes to town? Or takes out an entire wagon full of miners? Especially now that we're venturing farther up the mountain into its territory?"

"I know, I know, but it's..."

"Oh lord, you don't think it's your pet, now, do you? Because you were able to charm it with a little song?" Martin asked, aghast.

"No, nothing like that," Abigail said, though within, she wondered if that was true. She felt a connection with the creature. She glanced at the glove covering her right hand, where the black tally marks still clung from her encounter with the leaf-winged caterpillar. "It just seems like there must be a different way."

Peter Smalls paced behind his desk, the only space open in his office, with Abigail, Martin, and Samuel Clemens taking up the side where the door stood closed, along with some filing cabinets and a single chair. After some discussion, Abigail had taken the chair. She wasn't happy about the blatant sexism, but tried not to let it distract her from their goal.

"I don't see another way," Smalls said, dropping a fist into his open hand. "It's hard to believe such a thing as my men described during their storytelling really exists. At first, it was, you know, darkness, shifting shadows, fatigue, a little spirits on the way back to town, these can all affect one's perceptions, recollections. It could have been a harmless cub looking for its mother for all I knew. That bat thing was disturbing, but small, easily dealt with. This is..." Smalls turned to Clemens. "A giant? Mad with sickness? There's only one thing I can see. Bullets have a hard enough time taking down a regular bear. I think we have to, yes, we have to blow the cave entrance, trap it under tons of rock, keep it from getting out. If we get lucky, maybe kill it straight out between the impact and the falling rocks."

Again, Abigail cringed at the idea of killing the creature she'd begun to connect with, but she couldn't ignore the vast field of bones they had crossed, the hypnotic tune the whistling produced.

They had held that part back from Smalls, knowing the more fantastic elements of their encounter would not be believed.

How many of the miners were infected? That was another important question she didn't know ow to broach. She decided to stick with the facts. They reiterated their report of the creature, the injuries they had sustained from that night, how it had knocked down solid, large trees with seemingly little effort.

As they had told their tale, the sun had sunk, until it peered just over the mountains on the opposite side of the valley, casting orange light through Smalls' window.

"It's too late today, Sir," Martin said. "I think it's afraid of the daylight, or perhaps injured by it, somehow, sensitive eyes. All I know is when we saw it the first time, it was full on night, and this last time, it didn't chase us past the entrance of its cave."

"It would take some organizating, at any rate," Smalls said. "We need to gather men and women willing to brave the danger, and enough dynamite to do the job. I wager we can be ready by morning. Let's go!" Smalls waved his arms at his visitors, indicating they should leave the office. He followed Abigail out. "I'll address the miners. They should be heading for the mess hall by now. Which one of you remembers the way well enough to lead us on the trip back up?"

"I'll go," Martin said, not sounding excited about the dangerous trip, but resolved that he was doing the right thing.

"Well, you're not going without *me*," Abigail countered.

"I don't like it. Your parents will be furious with me, but I've seen enough up there myself, and your descriptions of events are dead on... If this *is* some kind of joke, now is the time to tell me. It will be a dangerous task, hauling crates of dynamite up the mountain to some off-the-path location. People could die, monster bears aside."

"We're absolutely telling you the truth, Mr. Smalls," Abigail said as steadily as she could.

"We are," Martin agreed, sticking his hand out to the foreman as though striking some kind of deal. Smalls looked to Mr. Clemens as the adult of the group.

"I- I just don't know." Mr. Clemens seemed disoriented now, lost. "I thought it was all a game, an entertainment..." he said, looking Martin in the eye. "Your letters spoke of terrifying tales, a new approach to really getting readers' attention. I... a flying frog? A giant bear with three deformed heads... The bones!" Clemens collapsed onto a bench at the side of the hallway. "I was a carriage-length away from..." His eyes were distant, unfocused.

"I'll take that as a 'no,'" Smalls said.

"He's just now accepting what he saw was real. It's an awful lot to take in. I remember," Martin said. A bell sounded in the distance. At first, Martin thought it was the dinner bell, but it was louder, and kept ringing. Smalls ran for the nearest window.

"Fire! There's fire at the gate! Monsters in the woods will have to wait!" he cried, running for the door.

"Should we go help?" Abigail asked.

"I'm not sure how much good I'd be right now. I'm dead tired from that chase through the woods, and you need a shoe, at any rate. Let's get Mr. Clemens back to the house and then figure out what to do."

The palisade was ablaze. Abigail could see it as they pulled Mr. Clemens onto the front porch of the bunkhouse. Smoke didn't just spiral into the sky as from the bonfire. This was no thread of gray reaching up like a mythic beanstalk. This was a storm front of thick, black, smoke lit from beneath by raging orange flames.

Being the last ones out of the building, the miners who had arrived to dinner first running out before them, they stood dazed, staring at the distant conflagration. It captivated them, enchanted them as had the bear's whistling snores.

As though bidden by Abigail's recollection of the beast, a great roar washed over them. Trees just beyond the fortified wall fell, snapping branches off their neighbors, sudden, sharp retorts like rifle fire. Then she saw it, unmistakable, glow of the fire upon its hide, picking out the scars as the dark hill of flesh moved back into the forest.

The twins said not a word as they guided their guest back to the estate, passing through wrought iron gates standing open, greeted by Liza and Jacob and Elle rushing out of the door before they reached the stoop. Hands and tongues fluttered like busy birds, checking the youths over, cooing and reassuring, inquiring into their health and safety. Abigail was sure they looked a fright, but the true terror was so close...

The trio were swept into the mansion by the servants and looked over for injury more systematically. Their clothing was whisked away. Wet cloths swabbed wounds and swept away dirt, even as Abigail's anxiety over the proximity of the bear grew. The bells continued through the night until after she passed out in her bed. They haunted her dreams.

When the front doorbell rang, she sat bolt upright, chest heaving, a dream she couldn't quite recall hovering over her. She looked down at her hand and in the dim, pre-dawn light.

The mass of black tally marks seemed to dance beneath her skin.

She dressed quickly and dug through her closet for an appropriate shoe to replace her lost boot. After seconds of internal debate, she chose her riding boots, purchased a year previously when there had been talk of getting a horse. The plans had fallen through, and she had had little call to wear the knee-highs. They seemed the best choice over a cluster of flower-toed, higher-heeled shoes which wouldn't aid her in traversing the darkling wood.

She was halfway through lacing up the second boot when a knock came at her door. "We've got to go!" Martin stage-whispered through the wood panels.

"I know!" She said back in a similar low tone. "These boots don't lace themselves!"

"Do you need help?"

"I've got them, thank you!" And a few seconds later, she had. She picked up her pack and they headed down to the kitchen, where once again they raided the pantries for fruit, crackers, and other foods. After two trips into the woods that took strange turns, they were going prepared. "Do you have more of those stink bombs?" Abigail asked as they joined Smalls in the foyer.

"Of course. I only brought the one the first time, but I'm loaded for bear now... If you'll excuse the expression."

"I don't think I will. That thing still gives me the shivers," Abigail shot back. It was true, but not entirely in the way Martin would interpret the phrase. She looked down at her gloved hand, wondering what the mark was, how it connected her to the bear, the insect that had given it to her.

Was it some kind of faerie mark? A demon's calling card? The thought made her stomach sink. What if this was all a devilish infestation? A possession as the priest railed against on Sundays? Why now? Why her? Why the others? Her parents? Possibly the others at the Landing offices? Thoroughly unsettled and unfocused, Abigail followed Martin and Peter Smalls down the path to Silver Hill proper where a wagon waited to bring them once again into the dreadful forest.

CHAPTER FIFTEEN

"Giant Powder Company" the side of the box read. "High Explosives" and "Dangerous" also stood out in block letters. It didn't settle Abigail's nerves in the least to have to ride in the same wagon, bumping and jouncing up the rutted road. The miners, though, seemed perfectly at home sitting right atop the wood crates

"Come on, girlie, if yer comin'!" One of the old miners she recognized from the fireside tales extended a hand. Tentatively, she took it and was lifted from her feet with a force she hadn't expected. "There we go! Let that look slip off yer face! It'll be fine," the older woman insisted.

"Do you... do you know what we're doing this morning?"

"Sure do, saw the beast m'self last night. Don' tell any of the guys, but it were me who tipped the barrels, smashed 'em right good, and lit 'em, too."

"So *you* drove the bear off? Saved Silver Hill?"

"When ye go down into the depths of the earth, ye have to learn to swallow yer fear. Ye walk out of the light into the places where no light's ever shone, ye have to accept that any day a knocker or a goblin of some kind is gonner run off with yer lunch or yer pick. Ye gotta know how t' deal with the fey. Once they know yer not afraid, they're not general so trickish. 'Less o' course, ye make 'em angry, eh Stan?" The woman nudged the man next to her. He turned, showing the far side of his face. It lay a ravaged field of parallel scars, from his damaged ear down to his chin, the scars interfering with the growth of his black beard. Abigail gasped.

"What ye want, Janny?" The man asked.

"Just tellin' the little one about dealin' with the faeries of the earth."

"Blasted little demons, they are. I'll tell ya," the man growled, fingers tracing the lines on the side of his face. "Keep yer hands on yer tools and always bring an extra bite of food. The last bite of yer sandwich won't do."

"Maybe they don't like yer spit on their food. Can't blame 'em," the woman said. The man grimaced and turned back to the conversation he'd been having. "Ye got sommat good for the faeries today?" Janny asked, looking at Abigail's pack.

"I've got some apples and such," Abigail admitted. The conversation was strange, especially sitting on boxes of dynamite.

"Ah, yeah, they like the apples. I think you'll do all right."

"Have you ever worked with dynamite before?" Abigail asked.

"Nah, not me. They mostly take care o' the blastin' before we groundhoggers come snufflin' along. I've helped put up supports for new shafts before, but never the blowin' things up. They say it's good for to learn new things, though."

"They do say that, yes..." Abigail agreed. Janny got absorbed into Stan's conversation, leaving Abigail to her thoughts. At first, she was grateful. She felt unprepared for interaction with the woman, who seemed to her to be the epitome of Silver Hill folk.

She and Martin had never had much contact after they left school for private tutoring, beyond a few shop keepers, the postmaster, and Daniel... Her mind dwelt on him, the strange flower he had brought, and his saving her and her brother from ruffians.

When they came to the point where the bear's trail veered away from the path of the river, there came a collective gasp. Abigail noticed even Janny swallowed hard looking down the lane of destruction. What before had been a game trail past massive sequoias and other ancient growth was now a lane as wide as Main Street, with drunken trunks leaning outward against their fellows.

The going was slow, but at least the damage the bear had wreaked left a corridor for daylight to show their way instead of relying on light playing through the dense foliage in slim swords, doing little to press back the tide of shadow.

They trudged along, dragging toboggans laden with two crates of dynamite each along the uneven path, dodging between splintered trunks of trees felled by pure brute force.

Abigail and Martin took the lead, Mr. Smalls just behind them. Martin periodically gasped as his ankle bent the wrong way at the edge of a massive footprint.

"You going t' make it, young Mister Beckett?" Smalls asked more than once. The silence was oppressive, and Abigail thought he was just trying to keep some human noise in the air above grunting of the folk dragging the dynamite.

"I'll get there and back again," Martin would always say, imitating a character from one of his adventure books. Abigail cracked a small smile, wary of letting anyone else see, as they wouldn't understand even the tiny blossom of joy in the nightmare they traversed.

"I chose the people with us because they're hardy, they won't run if the going gets tough, but we're armed, too. Half a dozen shotguns and rifles. If this bear surprises us before we get the charges set, there'll be gun play. If you hear a metal click, I'm going to need you and your sister to drop to the ground, cover your heads with your arms, and stay there until someone comes to get you."

"Yes, sir," Abigail said. Martin hesitated a moment, then

repeated the words.

"We're not going to have any trouble from you, are we, young Mister Beckett? Coming back up here, that's hero enough. Your parents might have my hide just for that. If you get yourself shot, or mauled, I might not see another sunrise." Smalls knew what he was talking about with regards to heroes. It was an open secret, something everyone knew and no one spoke on, that he had been in the war between the states, fought hard, seen a lot of death.

"No sir, hit the deck when we hear guns readied, aye," Martin said, taking words from his pirate adventure books, but giving them with a steady, serious tone. He might not have seen war, but the forest was a battleground between nature and... something. Abigail and he knew it well enough.

They made the final approach to the cave in as close to silence as they could muster. The sleds ground against soil and whispered through grass. Tiring miners grunted and blew hard breaths. When they saw the bone field, a few swore, but after a short burst of oaths, the quiet was palpable. No whistling tune came to them. The bear was either out, or awake. Looking at one another briefly, both Beckett twins edged forward, stepping as nimbly as they could along the edge of the bones, trying to see into the cavern.

Finally, Martin let out a breath. "It's all clear!" He called out in a stage whisper. Peter Smalls nodded and waved the dynamiters forward, wrenching the crates open with crowbars and removing a stick at a time to carry just past the mouth of the cave.

"Careful," Abigail said, "The bones aren't well set. They'll shift and slide." Janny and the others nodded, picking their way slowly across the field, then unrolling long coils of detonation wire. Progress was steady and quiet. Everyone seemed to know exactly what they were doing, requiring little direction or communication.

And then someone fell. The middle-aged Mexican man stepped on a length of bone that broke like a shot beneath his heel, causing him to step back, arms windmilling, searching for balance. He went over, hat flying in the air as he rolled back, an avalanche of bones clacking around him, taking out a younger man, then Janny. Abigail reached out as though there was something she could do, then put her hand to her mouth, silently praying for them all to be all right, for them to find their footing and escape the cave.

Somewhere within the cave, one of the charges went off. The ground shook. More bones cascaded toward the cave mouth. Just as many were thrown back out on a blast of air thick with dust and debris. She thought she heard Mr. Smalls yell to get down, but the concussive wave struck her across the chest and she was airborne, choking and struggling against a force she had no hope to affect.

Abigail slammed to the ground in the deeper shade of the forest proper, away from the break in the canopy around the cliff where the cave stood. For long moments, she lay, pain wracking her torso and back, limbs unresponsive. She coughed again, the fit pulling her from her stupor. She tried to sit up amid the clumps of moss and stands of ferns, but success took ages.

When she finally had a better view, she could see the white expanse of bones, a cloud of dust settling, but still thick across the area. Men and women cradled limbs or lay limp, having clearly been thrown against trees. She silently prayed that Martin was all right and gave thanks that she had missed the deadly obstacles.

She was just testing her balance when another sound echoed through the forest. Wherever the bear spent its days, it had heard the blast.

Abigail stumbled toward the cave, searching each face she came across to find her brother. Heads hung at unnatural angles. Glazed eyes stared blankly at dirt or sky. The weight of these peoples' deaths dragged at her, pulling her toward the ground, trying to steal her hope that Martin had survived.

But we're twins. We're supposed to have a great bond. Wouldn't I know if you were gone, brother? Wouldn't some mysterious connection be broken? Or at least change? She struggled with the need to know, to feel something beyond what she could see and hear to find him.

Once again, she felt presences all around, in the cave past the collapsed wall, in the trees above. A huge mass some distance hence closed in quickly from the northeast. A dense cluster of tally marks rose and fell with an exaggerated gait.

The reality of the bear coming outstripped the quandary over whether Martin lived or she could sense him. She could feel the bear approaching, and if they didn't find a way to deal with it, it would deal with them.

"It's coming!" She cried out, as loudly as she could, knowing that it didn't matter if something heard her because the most dangerous beast was already on its way. "It will be here soon. What do we do?" She hollered, hoping to draw in Smalls or Martin, or someone who knew how to set the charges. There was one box left, nearly full, and the plunger boxes still stood in their neat row at the edge of the bone field.

The man with the mangled face, scars running from scalp to chin, who Janny had tried to draw into conversation on the wagon rose up from behind a fallen tree. Bits of moss clung to his clothes and the stubble on the side of his face. Blood beaded up in a few places across his cheek, but he stood able, pointing to the dynamite and the rubble at the base of the cliff where the cavern had been. He wanted her to place the sticks.

"I have no idea what I'm doing. Where do I put them?" She asked.

"An'where along the solid face. Avoid the loose rock," the man advised. She tried to comply, fully aware now of the bear charging toward them. The bones began to dance slow waltz to the beat of tremendous footsteps. The closer it got, the more they moved with each impact with the ground. She placed one stick, then another beside it. She took two more and tiptoed as quickly as she could across the bones to target another place.

"No time for more! The bones are dancin'! Get the wires in!" The old timer ordered, and she sped her pace, running back to the spools of wire and then to the explosives. Her heart raced. Her face was hot with exertion and fear. Would she place the wires fast enough? Would the bear show up before she was done, forcing the old miner to blow them up while she stood too close? Would she be buried with the monstrosity, Janny, and the others for all time?

A roar echoed across the forest, shaking flying things from tree branches and loosening a small slide of rock from above the cave. Stone clicked and rattled down through the bones. A curtain of dust fell. Someone coughed, stumbling out of the cloud, swatting at the gray grit. *Janny!*

CHAPTER SIXTEEN

Abigail stabbed the wire into the end of one blasting cap, then the other, then started across the base of the pile of rubble to the second location, wire catching on bones as she moved. "Come on!" She told it, waving her arm.

A hulking head, raw chin easily six feet off the ground, dagger-laden tongue sipping the air as nostrils flared, washed Abigail with noxious breath. Great eyes, that seemed the size of her entire head, bore down on her. Clusters of black lines twisted and rolled through the brown irises. Holding her breath, she tore her eyes away and glanced down at the second set of dynamite sticks. They lay between her and the bear.

So much like birthday candles... Abigail thought, the happy birthday song running through her head. Slowly, she crept forward. The tune crept up her throat and she found herself humming quietly as she fumbled the ends of the wires into the sticks. Once, twice, putrid breath caused her hair to flutter, her eyes to narrow against the stench.

Eyes closed, all was not darkness. The lines danced like stars forming a constellation of the bear behind her, a deeper dark against the shadow of her eyelids. She could see her hand, as well, small grouping of black marks moving as she groped for the ends of the dynamite sticks. Finding them in the dark, she plunged the cords home and turned away from the bear, knowing it could snap her up and she would be gone in a single bite.

The bear reared up onto its hind legs. The fused cubs Abigail had noted before were very clear now, clusters of black in the red gray. She ran forward, then turned left, veering away from the cliff. Then she was flying again, this time struck much harder and from behind.

Before Abigail stretched a void. At first, there was nothing, though she sensed something, perhaps just out of reach, the ground? But then lights appeared ahead of her, in the direction she was traveling. They were glowing clouds collapsing into fireflies, pin pricks, stars, she realized through a haze that gripped her mind. They seemed like new things, things that had not existed before, though she also knew them to be ancient. She saw her reflection by their light, a reflection whose feet vaguely shimmered in the wake of her passing.

In the surface, perhaps below it, shone tiny crisscrosses of black lines, like the mark on her hand, in the bear, and on the bird she had dreamed once... Above, the stars burst and reformed into new spots, which exploded like fireworks, coalescing back into discreet points. The points began to form recognizable shapes. She had seen sailing charts rife with constellations for the horoscope signs, Greek heroes, animals of all kinds, including greater and lesser bears...

In the void beneath her, the black spots and streaks performed a similar dance, coming together, erupting outward, evolving into shadows of the creatures above, twisted by the ripples across the water, stretched. A mockery of the bear of light charged at her across the water, hovering there, encompassing her reflection. The black striations fought at the edge of her image, entangling her outline. Her hand tingled and thrummed with energy that tried to push its way up her arm.

She watched her hand, unbidden, reach out for the water. Remembering the bird, how it was so quickly overcome, she

The Silver°

Vol XIX - No. 46 • SILVER HILL, NEVADA

GARGANTUAN BEAR

SILVER HILL- The terrifying tales told around campfires since time immemorial in these parts have just come into crystal clear view with last night's sighting. The last wagon of miners and ore coming down from the number nine shaft arrived at breakneck speed, pursued by an impossibly large bear! Said bear took a score of lives before turned away by brilliant insight or tragic accident!

J. Brain & Co.

Maufacturers and Dealers in

HARNESS, SADDLES,

BRIDLES, WHIPS,

COLLARS, SADDLERY WARE, Etc

ALSO

Best Quality of Silk-Sewed Assorted Buckskin Gloves always on Hand

Oil barrels, stored just outside the gates in their own enclosure for the safety of the citizenry, caught fire, spilling across the breadth of the road down from the mountains and igniting, threatening our great wall, but also repelling the invading monstrosity!

Peter Smalls is quoted as having said, "This is something you might call a 'lucky tragedy.' It will take some time to repair the damaged wall, but who knows what kind of havoc the creature could have recked upon Silver Hill if allowed to pass?"

* * *

R. JORDAN

DRUGGIST

Apothecary,

Dealer in

Drugs, Medicines and Chemicals, Soaps, Sponges, Brushes, Fancy and Toilet articles, Perfumery, Patent Medicines, Pure Wines for Medicinal Purposes.

Voice
f Hill

Weather

Slim winds means the smoke from the recent fires will persist. Those with weak constitutions might do well to remain indoors.

SUNDAY, NOVEMBER 1, 1874 • 1 cent

STARTS PALISADE FIRE

And again, this reporter calls upon the Becketts to do something! Hire guards for the town! Arm them! Buy cannons if you must, but surely burning down the palisade is not the best option every time one of these monstrosities comes calling.

SILVER HILL- In other blood-chilling news, the werewolf, yes, you read that right, WEREWOLF which had been harassing miners, shephards, and pedestrians of an evening, has finally been laid low by one Mariah Marquez.

Mrs. Marquez, one of our miners, had been taking pot shots at the beast for at least a week, to no avail, until she finally thought to cast her ammunition with silver from our mine. Once the connection had been made and a true shot fired, the creature was felled.

It was too dark, and the creature too disfigured, to identify who it might have been before its supernatural malady.

Eyewitnesses report standing guard over the misshapen creature until the sun rose, at which point it ignited itself, reducing with unbelievable speed to smoke and ash.

Take care, citizens! And perhaps invest in the old protections and remedies. Their need may be back.

resisted, pulling back at the shoulder, her upper arm, bringing her other hand around to help. It was in vain. The hand, buzzing with dark energy now, fingers wide, shaking, grew closer and closer to the surface. Desperate, not wanting to succumb to the dark, she spun her body away.

Whispering. Voices Abigail almost recognized. Her name. Concern. These impressions wove through her emerging consciousness as she fought to pull herself out of the cocoon of cloying shadows holding her mind between her terrifying dream and waking.

"Did she make a sound?" one voice asked. They were the first words that cut through the black wool bundled around her.

"She's been doing that. It's been days. I'm really getting worried. How long can she last without sustenance?" The other voice... As it went on, she could feel the concern, but more than that, the pitch, the timbre cut away strands. She struggled harder. "We should never have gone back up there. What were we thinking? The bear's path was a straight enough shot. Smalls and his crew couldn't have missed it." *Martin!* The first clear word in her own mind connected itself to the voice, like a hand outstretched. She grasped it tightly, hauling herself upward. Thousands of shadow strands burst in a running trill of pops and snaps.

"Ugh!" She erupted into consciousness, opening her eyes to see her brother and someone their parents' age standing by the door. Aunt Helen? Her vision was clouded.

"Abigail!" Martin cried, hobbling over to her bedside and kneeling with a grunt of his own. "You're awake!"

"Martin!" Abigail finally got her tongue to respond. "I

didn't see you after the first explosion. And then the second... If we made it... the bear?"

"Buried under half a mountain. Workers are rebuilding the palisade and the gate. We haven't seen any more creatures. Do you think it's over?" Martin asked. Abigail looked down at her hand. The black lines, about the size of a large coin before, covered the back of her hand. The narrow tendril leading up past her wrist, a formidable vine.

"I don't-"

"Oh! You're awake, thank the Saints!" Liza squealed from the doorway. She pushed past Mr. Clemens and came to stand beside the bed. "I heard talking and thought I was going to have to tell these two to leave. I've been trying to keep them from bothering you, but Master Martin insists on being here. Your parents have sent a note. Apparently, they expected you to come back up to the office to have a training day or some such? At any rate, I sent back that you were under the weather and would join them when you were feeling yourself. Don't you worry about rushing back to the Landing. I don't understand how they can spend so much time up there, especially with that bear..."

"We did take care of the bear," Martin put in.

"Yes, of course, that Mr. Smalls is quite something, isn't he? Braving the forest with his crew to face off against a giant bear. Did you get to see it after he slew it?" Liza asked.

"He didn't slay the beast. If anyone deserves credit, it's Abigail. She risked her life to wire up the dynamite."

"Oh, come now, Martin, you and your stories... No one would believe a young lady like your sister would go anywhere near something as dangerous as dynamite," Liza brushed off Martin's claim.

Abigail was thrown back to the moment, the bear looming

over her, massive, imposing, filled with the black stars and tally marks. She remembered the feel of the dynamite, cool, yielding as she pressed home the wires. The whole time, the bear breathed down her neck, but it didn't act to stop her, didn't try to eat her. She wondered if her marks had something to do with that. Did they mean the two of them had something in common? A connection? Now that it was crushed under tons of rubble, it seemed unlikely she would ever know.

CHAPTER SEVENTEEN

"Sir who?" Martin asked, latest note from their parents hanging in his hand.

"Sir William Thomson," Abigail said. "You should really know who he is, or be able to pretend to. He's a famous engineer and scientist. He helped, risked his life, really, laying the transatlantic cable, a major feat of human ingenuity."

"It sounds like you're already in love. Perhaps you should meet his train on your own and you two can have a date," Martin snapped. "You can use some of those 'wiles' Helen's been teaching you."

"*We* need to go retrieve him as representatives of the town and Beckett Mining Company."

"What about Mother and Father?"

"They appear to be too busy with the project to be able to tear themselves away from the office for nearly a whole day to come down the mountain, go to the station, greet him, bring him back here-"

"He's coming here? To stay in the other guest room? Have we ever actually used all three guest rooms at once?" Martin asked.

"Not that I recall. I suppose you could ask Mother or Father."

"I really can't."

"You'll get your chance, soon. Not only will Sir Thomson need to get up to the Landing, Mother and Father want us to come up for an orientation day. Remember the other note Liza got? She told them I was ill, but I've recovered now, more or less. Their post script note here reminds us again to come up."

"Orientation? But we already did that."

"Maybe there's a new phase of the project starting. Last I heard, teams had begun clearing trees. Or maybe they just want to see us. They *have* only been back twice in the last month," Abigail said.

"I should should be most gratified to meet Sir Thomson, myself. I don't believe I've ever met a knight before. I expect he has quite a number of harrowing tales of crossing the ocean, as well," Martin said, warming up to the idea of a full house with such interesting guests.

"I'm sure he does. It was quite a dangerous mission. A number of sailors were badly injured," Abigail said. "At any rate, we would love to have you accompany us, Mr. Clemens." The older man nodded, swallowing his latest bite of egg before speaking.

"I'd be delighted. I'd love to see more of the town and this Thomson sounds like an interesting fellow, good instincts there, Martin."

They met the eleven o'clock train, where a middle aged man with an impressive beard and a fine brown suit awkwardly navigated the stairs, then limped toward the middle of the platform carrying a brown leather valise.

"Sir Professor Thomson, sir!" Abigail waved and strode up to him with purposeful steps.

"Professor will do, young lady," the man protested with a soft Scottish burr.

"Professor Thomson, I'm Abigail Beckett. This is my brother, Martin. And our chaperons are Liza and our new friend, Samuel Clemens. You may know of him as Mark Twain. He's a writer of some note here in America."

"I'm afraid," Thomson said, "I don't have much time to read for pleasure anymore. The wonders of the natural world keep me quite engaged. To whit, I'll need my equipment seen to. There are three trunks on the train." He turned, nodding and pointing. "Yes, they're being removed now. Careful! That's irreplaceable scientific equipment! Quite unique!" He hollered at the porters, who seemed not to hear.

"Yes, the Becketts have everything taken care of, Professor Thomson," Liza said. "They left explicit instructions for the care and transport of your equipment up to the offices and for me to conduct you to the estate if you need rest."

"It has been quite a long journey," Thomson agreed. "Perhaps getting the lay of the land, so to speak, and beginning fresh in the morning would be wise."

"Professor Thomson!" A man's full voice yelled across the platform. The party whirled as one to see Mr. Beckett charging across the boards, hand out at a downward angle before him as though to shake hands in greeting. He closed the thirty feet in seconds and pumped the stunned professor's hand with incredible vigor. "We're *so* glad you could make it! So glad!" Mr. Beckett said, barely lowering his voice from the greeting. "You've met the children. Aren't they just great? They're supposed to come up to the office to see what it is Mother and Father do all day. Tomorrow is as good a day as any, right Martin? Abigail?" Father looked toward them, eyes wide, but unfocused, as he addressed them. "Let's get going, shall we? Your equipment is being handled!"

"Y-yes, your nanny was just telling me."

"Oh! Great! Liza's just a peach, isn't she?" Without waiting for an answer, Mr. Beckett spun on his heel, legs pumping like he was leading a parade down Main Street. He stopped beside a large carriage and stood at attention, one hand up to his forehead in a salute. He remained stock still as everyone else caught up, as though he'd been turned to stone.

"Your father is quite... enthusiastic," Professor Thomson noted.

"He does seem especially energetic today. I think he must really look forward to your visit," Abigail agreed.

"Or perhaps they've had a good break on the cog railway project," Martin said.

"A cog railway? What's this then?" Thomson asked. Abigail explained as they neared the carriage and got situated. Only when they were all seated did Mr. Beckett break from his stiff stance. He slammed the door shut and leapt up into the driver's bench of the carriage, causing the driver to make a small noise of surprise.

"Don't mind if I drive, do you, Alexander?" The man asked and then they were off with a jolt.

Daniel and his Pa sat beside the campfire in Beckett Mining Company's disused number two shaft the gang had taken over after Pa had lost his position with the Becketts. Nobody who wasn't part of the gang came up here, since it was a distance from the active shafts, so motion at the entrance caused Pa to stand and draw. The newcomer stepped forward into the light coming from the hole in the ceiling above where the smoke from the fire slithered away like a snake into the sky.

"It's just me, Señor Swindon, Miguel," the man said, his outfit of all worn cloth except the boots and belt, which were marred leather. The whole figure presented something that had been dragged through the dust for an extended period. Only the pistol on his hip gleamed in the narrow patch of sunlight.

"Miguel, you're supposed to be keeping an eye on the train station with Jerome," Mr. Swindon said, lowering his weapon and sitting again. He hadn't holstered his gun, though, and the hand bearing the weapon rested on his knee. He accepted the other's presence, but wasn't about to trust an unusual appearance. "You weren't followed, were you?"

"No, Señor, I have news. It's just the kind of thing you sent us to find out."

"Do tell," Pa said, scratching at his jaw with his empty hand.

"Mr. Be-" Pa's gun clicked and rose a few degrees. "That is to say, the owner of the mine," the gun drifted back down. "Summoned a scientist. I don't know what they're up to with their new project, but they have engineers in the offices all day long, and all night, it seems."

"You're losing my interest, Miguel," Pa said.

"The scientist has equipment, three trunks that were sent up to the Landing. He said it was real special stuff, non-replaceable. To me, that means it must be worth quite a lot, don't you think, jefe?"

"I do. I do. Well done, Miguel, bueno to you. This equipment is on its way up the mountain now?" Pa asked.

"Si, señor. I rode as hard as I could over the rough land. They must still be on their way.

"Get the boys together. We're about to get us some non-replaceable scientific-type equipment! He'll pay through the nose to get it back!" Miguel nodded and backed out of the cave. Pa ranted on. "He thought he could just fire me, that I'm just a nobody miner. I'll show him! We'll make enough money to get out of this backwater, set up real fancy in California!" Pa holstered his pistol and pulled a glass bottle of amber liquid from under the stool where he sat. "Things are looking up, son. Things are finally looking up!"

"Yes, Pa," Daniel said, not at all certain that stealing something they knew nothing about would bring the results Pa wanted.

In minutes, they were on the trail, six men who had gathered around Pa because of the fire with which he spoke about pushing back against the Becketts' power in Silver Hill, because he talked a good game about his plans for the future, for making them all rich, or because they had nowhere else to go.

The sun was high in the sky, the light as good as it ever was in the mountain forest, and they reached a place scouted long ago on the path between the train station and the Landing. They checked the trail on foot and saw that a carriage had been through, with its narrower wheels, and a cargo wagon had followed. Neither, as far as Bolin could see, had returned.

Bolin was born in China, had come to work in America, and found only mines and railroads, both more dangerous professions than the farming he had done back home. Still, he had a keen eye for tracks, having also hunted for food from a very young age. He had a bow, but it looked very different from the ones the Paiute and other Indians carried. Rather than a simple elongate "C" shape, Bolin's weapon bent more drastically at the ends like a massive, thin, mustache.

They heard the ring and jangle of the wagon's harnesses and hid. Daniel's heart felt like he had just sprinted up all the way up Main Street. He remembered when he did that more often, when he had played around at school and raced boys his own age instead of hanging around in a mine with his father, waiting for an opportunity to rob wagons. What would Abigail think? The notion struck him and he sat heavily on the ground, causing a bush to shake.

One of the wagon's horses, spooked by the sudden sound, whinnied and shook its head, rattling the metal loops on its harness again.

"What is it, girl? You smell somethin'?" The teamster asked the disturbed animal. Pa glared down at Daniel, but waved for the other men to make their moves. Two men stood behind the wagon, rifles raised. Three stood in front, with two pistols each, training all six barrels on the teamster.

"Drop the reins!" Pa called from behind a tree.

"I don't think so, Swindon! Oh yes, I know the sound of your damnable voice! I worked beside you for thirteen years. I thought you were a good man, raising your son on your own after Annie died, but then you had to ruin it. Instead of turning yourself around you what? Become a highwayman? Do you even know what I'm carrying here?"

"Some very valuable scientific equipment. Some fancy scientist that your boss hired," Pa answered. While he spoke, he waved to Daniel to get up, to go over to the wagon and take the reins. Daniel looked over at the man, recognizing him vaguely. He thought he recalled him being kind when Daniel had been a small child. Yes, he was the one who gave him honey candy on so many summer evenings. Daniel hesitated.

"A European. There's lots of mines in Europe, no, jefe?" Miguel put in.

"Indeed there are. I don't much care what your boss is up to, but I know he keeps so much of what comes out of this ground for himself. I think it's time he shared a little more of it, with me. And he will, if he wants whatever this scientist fella will do for him." Daniel finally rose to his feet and edged close enough to the wagon he could almost touch it.

"Aww, Daniel, I had hoped your father wouldn't drag you into this life. He used to be a good man..." the teamster said. Something in the man's tone, implying that his father wasn't a good man, lit a fire in Daniel's chest. He grabbed onto the wagon's frame and launched himself up, throwing his other hand, balled into a fist, at the other's face.

"Constance sends her deepest apologies about not attending your arrival, Professor, but we're up to our eyeballs in this newest project. It's our most ambitious yet! We're clearing a path through the dense forest to run a rail up to the newest shaft site. We've had a number of very promising test digs right along the ridge, and hope to sink a number of shafts over the coming years. Perhaps in a few years, when the initial sections have played out, we'll build a hotel up there. The view is amazing. We can call it The Overlook, or The Perspective. It's always wise to keep a good perspective!"

"Indeed, Mr. Beckett," Thomson agreed politely. "Such energy you have, and ingenuity. I was initially surprised at your letter offering for me to use your mine for my experiment, but I came to understand that your son was an avid scientist himself, and as a professor, how could I pass up the opportunity to make history *and* instruct? It was quite a journey, but as pleasant as one could expect for the thousands of miles traversed."

"Good! You see, a good perspective, right kids?"

"Yes Father," they responded in unison.

"Is anyone else hungry? I really can't recall when last I ate,"

Mr. Beckett said with an unsettling sudden tilt of the head. The twins looked at each other knowingly. *Had* he eaten up at the Landing? He must have. It had been weeks.

Abigail peered at Father. There was definitely *something* off about him. The black spots she had seen on previous occasions seemed to have gone... No... She realized as she inspected him. The black wasn't gone. It was diffused, spread out through his body. Unlike her own marks which collected on her nerves, plainly visible to her, at any rate, she could barely see Father's, but he was definitely still infected.

During their day of visiting, which seemed to have slipped Father's mind, they had been concerned that none of the engineers and project planners seemed ever to take a break, drink coffee, eat lunch. They all seemed unnaturally focused. Abigail was all the more grateful for Professor Thomson's arrival if it meant Father would actually eat something. She resolved to bring Mother her favorite apple pastries the next day.

"We'll help," Abigail offered. Liza nodded.

"Master Beckett can get acquainted with our house guests while we throw together a luncheon feast," the maid said. At the kitchen door, she pulled the cord to a series of brass bells set throughout the house and grounds to summon the servants. Father, Mr. Clemens, and Professor Thomson strode off to Father's study. Father immediately launched into an animated story before he had even slid the pocket doors shut on the opulent, silver and dark wood-filled room.

Once lunch was ready and Professor Thomson had been ensconced in the east guest room, the Becketts and guests descended upon the dining room, which had not been properly used in weeks. Now, the curtains stood wide, a fire roared in the fireplace, and platter upon platter of food lay in formation down the center of the grand table.

"It's a shame Constance couldn't be here for this. I'll need to head back up early tomorrow and give her the chance to come down and have some leftovers. If there are any!" Father laughed at his own joke and began piling sliced ham and roast beef, and four kinds of potatoes, carrots, radishes, broccoli on his plate. He followed it up with brown gravy and a cheese gravy he had sampled in his travels while looking for investors for the mine and brought back the recipe for. Abigail paled at the thought of eating all that food and wondered again about the last time he had eaten.

"You certainly have an appetite to match your energy, my good man," Professor Thomson noted, taking barely a quarter of what the master of the house accumulated. Mr. Clemens was likewise conservative in his portioning, while Abigail and Martin, who had other things on their minds, picked and placed little on their plates.

"I understand you've had some unexpected excitement on the mountain. Strange sightings?" Professor Thomson said.

"Sensationalism," Father scoffed. "Codswallop and poppycock. Some miners down from the city saw a bear and panicked, did more damage than any bear ever could, spilling hundreds of gallons of oil and kerosene and lighting the palisade on fire. Now we're exposed to the real threat of Paiute coming down from their hidden places."

"Father exaggerates," Martin jumped in at Abigail's urgent stare. "The damage wasn't that bad, and they'll have it fixed up in a few days. The Paiute barely even live around here anymore. They don't like the mountain any more than anyone else. They say it's cursed."

"Oh?" Thomson asked, bemused. "How so?"

"They have many tales of strange creatures, outsized animals, and even people, twenty foot tall men with flame red hair," Martin said.

"Sounds like faerie tales we have back home in Scotland about giants. Regale me." Martin shot a glance over at his father, but the man was fully involved in devouring his food.

CHAPTER EIGHTEEN

Martin's relaying of local legends evolved into his, Abigail's and Mr. Clemens' experiences, including a number of descriptions of strange creatures and finally, the bear which pursued them to the river.

"You are quite the storyteller, young man, verifying Mr. Clemens' account. I gather that's why he's here, to discuss some form of collaboration. He told me you had quite an impressive imagination, and I can see he was correct. While the study of science rarely leaves one a surfeit of time for other activities, if one is serious about one's work, that is, you could certainly sell a few stories to the more flamboyant periodicals."

"I know what I said, and it's all true as can be, but so, I shudder to say, are his stories of the creatures," Mr. Clemens said.

"Oh?" Thomson raised an eyebrow. "An ordered mind hardly succumbs to folklore and superstition."

"Yet one often finds a kernel of truth in every story," Clemens countered.

"I far prefer the hard numbers and rigors of the scientific method to hearsay and the fumbling attempts of the ignorant to explain things far beyond their understanding."

"Science relies upon observation, does it not?" Clemens challenged.

"Observation and measurement." Thomson nodded, taking a bite of a cracker. "Have you seen these creatures?"

"A few, such as the raccoon-salmon, and most damnably, the bear. It has... No, I shall not endeavor to build upon the frightening details young master Beckett as given. Neither do I wish to dwell upon them for nightmares I still endure on their behalf, nor I do not wish to disrupt anyone's appetite or ruin this fine meal. Suffice to say it exists and is if anything more terror-inducing than Martin has let on."

"It's all well and good to encourage creativity my good man, but this pushes the bounds to accept such tales as reality," Thomson said.

"I understand your reticence, sir, and assure you I felt the same way. I thought for certain these youths were having fun at my expense, or trying to convince me to invest money into some kind of tourist attraction to compete with the other natural wonders of the west, such as the Yellowstone National Park which houses geysers and other spectacles. But then I experienced the horror myself, and I tell you, I do not relish risking my life on a second trip up into those woods."

Thomson stared, eyes narrow, appraising Clemens. Was the man pulling his leg? Or merely duped by some local trickery? He looked to Martin, to Abigail. She wilted under his stare, unable to support her brother in the face of such a worldly, widely regarded man of science. He had been knighted for his contributions! How could she sit at a table with him and tell him he was wrong?

"I have never heard of the creatures of which you speak, but I am far more rabid a student of the physical world and its mysteries than of the biological world. I deal not in creatures strange or mundane, but in materials, energies and forces. It is these I'm here to study in the depths of one of the Becketts' disused mines. It provides the perfect setting for my experiment, and I am eager to unpack and place my equipment tomorrow. I am weary from my journey and this fine food. Unless there's something else urgent, I intend to excuse myself and retire. I may join you for dinner, but do not come wake me if I am not about. Travel does take its toll."

"Of course, Sir Thomson, er, Professor," Abigail said. "Don't hesitate to summon my brother, myself, Liza or one of the other servants if you need anything at all," Abigail gushed.

"You are most kind, young lady, and this house most hospitable. I had expected a much coarser reception, given tales of the 'wild west' which filter back across the pond. I must say I'm pleasantly surprised and look forward to discussing my experiments with you, Martin, but that can wait." Martin stiffened at the mention of his name and the implied demand of his engaging of his alleged knowledge gained from the correspondence courses. He tried to smile and nod to Thomson, pretending to have a full mouth, then stared at Abigail as soon as the professor turned away.

"What is the subject of your experiments, Professor Thomson?" Abigail asked as the man reached the door.

"Dark bodies, and dark motivators, something far enough outside the scope of the average education, that without meaning any slight, I'm sure you would be lost at even the most rudimentary attempt at an explanation."

"My sister is very intelligent!" Martin blurted out.

"As I said, 'no offense was meant.' You do know something of what I speak, though, I hope. It could be your studies are not quite so advanced." Martin was about take the easy way out and admit his studies had not included such things, but Abigail jumped in.

"We would be glad to listen to the hypotheses behind your experiments. Perhaps I could learn something," she said. Thomson gave a smile that couldn't help but being half smirk and nodded, leaving.

"What did you do that for?" Martin asked.

"I really want to hear what he has to say about dark bodies. You would too, if you kept up with your studies," Abigail said in a low voice.

"Oh, did Professor Thomson go?" Father asked, crestfallen. "I'd hoped we could have discussed the details of his experiment and what he needs from us." His face reset, from disappointed to excited. "Dessert!" He called out exuberantly.

Daniel wasn't particularly bulky, but he caught the teamster by surprise. The force of his full one hundred and fifty pounds found its way through his fist and into the older man's nose. Reins fell from the other's hands and blood poured over his mustache. Daniel landed with one foot on the toe board beside the teamster's feet and his knee on the seat. Still seeing red, he shoved the man with all he had and the other rolled away over the side. Someone on the ground reached up and grabbed the man's arm, half-catching him, half-pulling.

"Well done, son. I knew ye had it in ye!" Pa yelled from the mossy boulder. "There's a turn around just ahead. We'll get pointed in the right direction and get the loot back to the hideout, then we'll figure out what it's worth."

"Yes, Pa." In position, Daniel picked up the reins and gave them a gentle flip to get the horses moving again. The path curved around to the left, past another boulder and a trio of massive redwoods. Past the ancient trees, he could see the clearing his Pa meant. There would be plenty of room to turn the wagon around.

Daniel took it slow, talking to the horses and pulling the

reins as he had learned years before. Then he heard it. At first, he was reminded of the dried gourds the men and women would shake at the bonfire beside the miners' bunkhouse of a night. He missed those get-togethers, the stories, the popcorn from time to time, and especially seeing his best friends, his only friends close to his age, the Beckett twins.

The immediacy of the sound cut through his reminiscing, though, and as it grew tremendously loud, he realized the sound was coming from all around him. A boulder shifted in the tall grasses, then rose inexplicably. No, not a boulder, a massive, scaled head with vertically slit eyes stood on a tree trunk of a neck. A long, forked tongue flashing out from the crevasse of a mouth. Within seconds, another and another head rose up. The smell of stone dust rolled over Daniel, along with the urge to sneeze. He held out, with narrowed, watering eyes, and he tried to get the horses to back away.

The wagon rolled a few feet and then stopped dead. Daniel was at a loss. He considered turning to the right and left, but the right was a mass of writhing, scaled, bodies, swaying heads threatening foot long fangs and excruciating death. He'd seen a rattler bite before, the swelling, the discoloration... They'd had to put the dog down. It was better than suffering.

He wondered if he should just run across the space. He'd either make the trees or get snapped up, maybe eaten, swallowed whole. Suffocating wasn't a great death, he'd heard, but it had to be better than the fire of venom flowing through his body. The way old Ginger had whimpered before Pa did what he'd had to... Daniel had one hand on the vertical bar he'd used to board the wagon, ready to launch himself as far as he could before the giant snakes could react.

"Son! Where in tarnation are you? It shouldn't take that long to- Lord a'mighty!" Pa cried out. "Ok, you just stay where you are. We'll take care of this!" Pa gave orders to the crew to move to around the edge of the clearing, to aim for certain snakes. For long seconds, Daniels' heart pulsed hard in his throat, his stomach was a ball of iron. His hand sweat on the bar.

"Fire!" Pa yelled, and guns went off all around. Bullets careened, only two striking their targets. The horses shrieked and tried to run in opposite directions, straining the leather and wood of the harnesses. One bullet struck thick, stony scale and winged off into the trees, the other struck one of the monstrosities in the eye, sending a stream of clear fluid arcing into the air. That head recoiled, flopping back and forth, striking the ground, spooking the horses even more.

A snake the width of a wagon wheel launched itself at the wagon, knocking one of the large trunks off into the grass with a crash and clang. A second struck, laying fangs into the left horse's shoulder. The falling tongue, a length of wood from the front of the wagon to the yoke which attached to the harnesses, snapped. The horse fell. The other horse reared up, trying to kick out at the snake, but the weight of the harness and the fallen horse skewed its aim and it tumbled over backward. More wood broke, leather tore. The wagon settled to stillness for the first time since the first serpent head appeared.

Daniel took his chance, and leapt from the driver's seat, tumbling in the grass even as another head rose up, smaller, but still large enough to eat a retriever whole, still terrifying. Daniel traced its body back to where it intersected one of the larger serpents and saw that it was fused. His eyes widened as he realized the whole shebang was pulling itself this way and that as individual heads launched themselves. They were all melted together like a pile of candles left in the summer sun.

A gunshot punched through the air right by him. He felt the thump in his chest as he watched the scaled head, bigger than his own, explode in a burst of red. He felt wetness on his forehead, across his cheeks.

"You all right son? These are huge sons of guns, ain't they?"

"Uh, yeah, Pa, real big."

"You ok?"

"I will be, I think. Just got blood in my eye. Thanks for shootin' it."

"Of course, son. Don't mention it. Well, you can mention it every once in a while..." Pa said with a chuckle. Daniel smiled despite the sting of giant web-snake blood bringing tears to his eyes.

Abigail and Martin were still clearing their heads of dreams when sharp raps came at first her door, then his.

"Come along, children, no dawdling! We're needed at the Landing!" Father, in his new energetic mood, called through their doors.

"I'm getting dressed now, Father!" Martin called back.

"As am I!" Abigail said as loudly and clearly as she could with her blouse half over her head. She shrugged into it fully and added, "We'll be down to breakfast in just a few moments."

"Breakfast?" Father asked as though it was a foreign word he had never heard before. After a pause, he said, "Oh yes, of course, we should probably eat, shouldn't we?"

"As eager as I am to get to work, I do think it would be

wise. Will we need to also pack a lunch for a full day's work?" Professor Thomson asked. Abigail blanched at the thought that the man was standing just outside her room while she was dressing. And she had just admitted as much, thinking only her father was on the other side of the door!

"Very well, it seems prudent. Let us adjourn to the kitchen while the children ready themselves," Father said. Abigail listened to the footsteps on the landing grow quieter. She let out a breath and finished dressing and stole a minute to throw some essentials into her exploring pack. Even though they weren't expecting anything terrifying and strange, one never knew on this mountain.

Breakfast was eaten at the kitchen island again, and consisted of toasted bread, porridge, apples and pears, and some leftover meats that had been stashed in the ice box after dinner. "Bless Liza, this is still amazing the next morning!" Father exclaimed, devouring a few more slices of ham and roast beef. They packed up some chicken legs and meat wrapped in layers of brown paper and packed the bread, cheese, crackers, and a bottle of wine for the day's revitalizations. Abigail and Martin each sneaked an extra sandwich and some fruit into their own packs with knowing nods to one another as they worked.

“And this must be the damaged palisade,” Thomson noted as they passed. “You said it burned? That seems a logistical problem more than a mishap.” Martin and Abigail were caught between keeping themselves warm and being awed by the charred poles and scorched earth.

No one spoke. It seemed too soon to say anything not suitably somber enough, and nothing came to mind before the moment passed. Abigail wanted to tell the professor about Janny, how she had confessed to turning the barrels over and lighting them to scare the giant bear away, but it didn't feel like the right moment. She couldn't help but think Mr. Clemens would have had the words if he had not stayed behind in Silver Hill to gather stories from the townsfolk.

The sun crept up over the mountaintop, tentatively poking through the trees in some places as they ascended to the Landing on the wagons they used to move ore.

"I do hope my equipment made it to the Landing all right. Some of it is quite sensitive, even fragile."

"I'm sure it's fine, my friend!" Father boomed to the chagrin of everyone else present. It was simply too early for that much enthusiasm. The nascent morning was full of ghostly breaths blooming in the darkness, occasionally catching the slanted rays creeping through the forest and flaring to roiling life before fading away. Abigail and Martin leaned into one another while Thomson rubbed his hands together and blew into them repeatedly.

At the Landing, it was a tie between Thomson and Father as to who leapt out of the wagon first. Once they had their feet, Father hooked his arm through Thomson's and dragged him toward the closest building, already speaking loudly about the ingenuity of his project and Thomson's experience with such innovations.

The twins, thankful for the freedom to take their own pace rather than keeping up with their manic father, slowly crawled out of the wagon, the last to debark. Abigail wished she knew what was going on with Father, if it had to do with the marks. She was certain it did, but that didn't lend her any insights as to setting him to rights. He seemed little harmed, in the end.

As they gathered their packs and started toward the offices, fearful over what they might find, they heard Professor Thomson's scream through the office walls.

"The wagon with my equipment *what?*"

CHAPTER NINETEEN

Thomson stormed back out of the office and glared around the open yard. "You!" He targeted a random woman headed toward one of the three open shafts in the face of the mountain beside the building. "Do you know what rock this Rudolph Swindon hides under? It seems he has something of mine!" The woman shook her head, not knowing this stranger demanding information about someone everyone knew was dangerous and uncouth.

"Do you know? You?" Thomson interrogated miner after miner until Mr. Smalls appeared from the mouth of one of the shafts and strode over to him.

"Sir," he tried, failing to get the Scotsman's attention. "Sir!" He said more forcefully, the other wheeling on him. "Allow me." Smalls drew a silver whistle on a loop of twine from the pocket at the front of his overalls and blew a shrill, warbling note. Every face on the Landing turned toward him. "Listen here! Our esteemed visitor, a personal friend of Mr. Beckett's," Smalls began, absorbing the attention of all present, "requires a posse to reclaim his goods. I will offer the first five men and women to step forward an extra half day's pay. Weapons and ammunition will be provided by the company. You leave now to find Rudy Swindon and recover Mr...?"

"Professor Thomson," Thomson informed him in a quiet tone.

"Professor Thomson's affects." The party filled quickly, and rifles and shotguns dispensed from one of the smaller buildings.

"I thank you, Mr.?"

"Smalls, Peter Smalls, foreman of these yahoos. They'll get

you where you need to go. I would accompany you myself, but I have to keep the rest of them in line. The recent attacks have them rattled. I'm sure you saw the damage to the wall on the way up here. We took care of the bear, but who knows what else skulks in the trees..."

"You're the one who led the raid on that beast? You are a braver man than most, sir," Thomson said.

"I got through the war between the states, fields so obscured by gun smoke you wouldn't see Death riding up to tap you on the shoulder. And he rode hard near to daily. This one creature, no matter the size, had to be dealt with," Smalls said.

"War forges iron resolves, that's a surety. These folk are safer for it," Thomson said, extending a hand. Smalls shook it.

"Good hunting to you. He'll likely have armed men, too. He'll try to extort you for the return of your equipment, but if you get the drop on him, he'll be reasonable." Smalls nodded and turned, rejoining the workers headed back into the mine.

"All right, ladies and gentlemen," Thomson began, eliciting a round of snickering. He was used to dealing with two groups of people, those who had devoted their lives to education and science, and those youths who came to them for knowledge. The faces before him were anything but clean and bright eyed, though they had raised their hands to hunt down Swindon quickly enough.

"Who among you knows the whereabouts of this scoundrel Swindon?" Two of the five raised their hands. He chose the steadier looking one. "Good, you, lead on. The rest of you feel free to fill me on what kinds of things we'll expect. I don't suppose booby traps are a danger?"

"Uh, no sir, it's unlikely. I been workin' fer the Becketts for nigh on forty year an' I watched Rudy Swindon walk through that office door the first time afore his son was born, sixteen year ago, and watched him walk out it the last two year ago. In my whole career minin', I never saw a lazier, unforthright, snake of a man lift up a pick. About the only thing you can't fault him for is how much he loves his son."

"Well, that's a ray of light, at any rate, but how does that apply to my question?"

"'Less'n he got someone else to dig the pits and tie the ropes or what have you for a humanperson-sized snare, I guarantee you he never would lay one," the man responded.

"Aye," one of the women said, "He's big on plannin', tell ya all day long what he hopes to do, what he's gonna do, but when it comes t' doin'... Forget about it."

Pa guided Daniel back to the number two shaft. As they stumbled along, Daniel could feel the strange serpent's blood under his eyelids. It was a vaguely scratchy, burning sensation. It set off fireworks in his closed eyes like being struck or sometimes just as he was falling asleep, he would see shifting lights. Or more specifically now, he saw flashes of deeper darkness, little tangles of twigs, clusters of long pine needles.

Finally, they stopped. Pa set a bucket down in front of Daniel, had him kneel. The man splashed a handful of water up into his face. The water was frigid. He shook his head and sputtered, but he could still feel the dull fire of the cursed blood there, doing *things*, he imagined. Daniel reached down and splashed himself.

With the approach of winter, the cavernous mine shaft was tough to keep warm. Soon he would have to go around every morning and break the ice that formed across the tops of the horses' trough and the buckets of water they retrieved from the nearby spring. The spring itself, at least, never froze. That was a small mercy, but one he couldn't focus on at the moment.

When he couldn't take the cold water on his face, in his eyes, any longer, he sat back and went to his bedroll, where he wrapped up in his blanket. Pa brought him another. And still he shivered. "Just lay back, son. I'll get the fire to roarin' and you'll warm up right quick." Daniel lay back, face feeling like frost would form any moment, hair wet, shivering so much he had to grip the blankets tight to keep them from sliding off him. He vaguely heard his father messing with the fire pit, but then drifted off.

The next thing of which Daniel was aware was a softness against his cheek. He opened his eyes and saw it was dark, but he was outside, somewhere. The horizon was a line of faint light, like an hour or so before dawn, with stars filling the sky to his left and his right a dark mound, fuzzy with growth of some kind. He ran his hand over the barely discernible mat and found thousands of tiny stands of moss, like he was a giant lying atop the mountain, looking out over the forested slope, over the plains beyond, East toward Oklahoma and on, to the lovely coast, the sea, broad, dark, unfathomable.

He peered up, and before each star, a tangle of black lines. He thought of them as cages, now, something capturing the stars, grasping them, deciding their destinies. What must it be like, to control the lives of so many? He could hardly conceive of gaining control over his own. His mother gone, his father out of work, turned to banditry, him unable to go to school, to learn as Abigail and Martin did. He would never be able to climb out of this pit where he found himself.

Motion closer to the ground attracted his attention. An unblinking face rose from the moss, which seemed deeper now. It swayed slowly, surveying him. Another head appeared, smaller, but still with staring, golden, vertically slit eyes. Another face, eyes peeking through the dark moss, flashing as though reflecting a lantern. The tangled creature rose as one, showing flicking tails making no noise, fangs curving in the almost-light, threatening... What? What was there to lose now? Pa, he supposed.

The black cages at the junctures of snake bodies winked. Bodies slipped apart. Daniel reached out, and the black cages gathered in his hand. He saw them trailing through the massive creatures' bodies, clustered around where they joined, he called them to him, piling them in his hand. As the serpents fell away, wriggled off into the foliage, freed from the will that brought them to face him, he sat up.

With his other hand, Daniel reached for the sky. The black lines around the stars shook, pulling toward him, but ultimately remained. The sun crested the distant horizon, sending golden spears across the land, striking the remaining members of the serpent web. They recoiled as when they had been shot in the clearing, thrashing, and the whole mass curled up in a ball that rolled away down the dark side of the mountain.

He held up the mound of vibrating black lines in his palm, trying to get a good look at them in the sunlight, but as soon as the beams struck them, they exploded in a burst of impenetrable black.

"What catastrophe has passed here?" Thomson asked rhetorically as he surveyed the clearing, turned up dirt, torn away grass, and an abused wagon. Its tongue had been shattered, its yoke missing, one sideboard splintered on the ground beside the listing vehicle. "I can't imagine men did this work, lest they be truly savages."

"There's beasts in these woods. Like Smalls said, giants, terrors. They usually stay to themselves during the day, but at night..."

"Nobody comes up here at night, or stays into the night if they have a choice. Most who do..."

"Don't come back," three of the miners said, passing the thought around.

"Giant beasts? The children tried to tell me the same tales, but this is Nevada. People have been mining here, ranching here for decades. It's not deepest Africa," Thomson protested. A couple of the miners jumped down from the wagon, approaching the derelict with rifles to their shoulders, fingers beside triggers.

One of the two exclaimed wordlessly. The other swung around, ready to blast whatever had surprised the first. The Irishman bent down and worked at something for a moment. He came back up with a long, curved, white bone in his hand.

"What is it? Part of one of the horses?" A miner from the wagon asked.

"It's... I think it's a snake tooth!" the Irishman said, holding it up. "It'll make a fine trophy, assumin' we don't come across the thing that lost it!" He joked. He turned back to the group on the wagon and his comrade fired, causing him to jump, dropping both the tooth and his shotgun. "What in the name of Gabriel was that all about, Hiram?" He protested. Hiram merely pointed at the headless serpentine body slowly falling into the grass, blood continuing to spurt across the ground.

"That was a large one, but not large enough to bear that fang. Both of you get back up here. We still need to find my equipment. Hopefully that blast hasn't alerted Swindon and his men to our presence."

They followed the drag marks along the road for a bit, then off into the woods along a disused path, far more overgrown than the one down from the Landing.

"That's the way to shafts two and three. Ain't used them in years. I suppose it's as good a place as any to have your gang hole up. Nobody's gonna just stumble across ye," one of the miners informed Thomson.

"Shaft number three? That's where the equipment was bound, anyway. Could be, that aside from the missing teamsters, horses and destroyed wagon, they did us a favor moving my things closer to their goal."

They followed the drag marks and soon came to all three large trunks sitting alongside the trail as though delivered. One looked damaged, possibly having been dropped at some point, which immediately set Thomson to worrying over its contents, but there were more direct concerns at the moment. He reminded himself of this and gestured silently for the miners to spread out and approach the number two shaft opening, framed in heavy timbers.

A sign propped sideways beside the entrance warned the shaft was closed and dangerous. *Indeed.* Thomson thought, lifting his borrowed rifle. He wasn't overly accustomed to firearms, but the concept was straightforward. The weapon at his shoulder, pointed at the ground some twenty feet before him, trying to mimic the others, he advanced.

CHAPTER TWENTY

Thomson met two of his appointed crew at the entrance while the remainder moved around to the side, perhaps seeking another ingress. Thomson trusted the miners to do their best and use their knowledge of the mines without running everything by him. Stopping for a planning session now would negatively impact the element of surprise, if they still held it, and so they moved on.

At first, Thomson's eyes needed to adjust from the growing light outside back to the gloom of the mine shaft. The low ceiling of the entrance gave him a sense of being buried alive. His chest tightened and breathing became more laborious until they reached the broader area that the gang had turned into a living space.

Burlap cloth hung on wires and wooden frames to create semiprivate spaces, a central fire flared with heat Thomson could feel as soon as he could see it. A number of bedrolls lay about, one occupied by a youth. Thomson's heart fell that such a boy as might be in one of his classes back in Scotland would find himself entangled in a gang of highwaymen.

A standing figure drew his attention. Metal glinted in his hand.

"Beckett send you?" The man growled.

"He did not. Those trunks out by the path belong to *me*. They have no value to you, and will not serve you in any ongoing quarrel with the Becketts," Thomson explained.

"Lies! I know you came to Silver Hill to see Beckett. You workin' for him? On his new big secret project?"

"I am not. I have very little knowledge of mining or cog railways, as I'm told it entails. I am a scientist, a professor from Scotland. I have come thousands of miles to conduct experiments in natural philosophy within the depths of the earth."

"What kind of experiments?" The man demanded, suspicion thick in his tone. He edged over to stand between the interlopers and the youth. *A protective stance?* Thomson wondered. *This is surely the man himself, and the other, his son.*

"I don't mean to patronize, but it would likely take the course of a year to explain all the relevant aspects of the world to you."

"Use small words." A metallic click rang off the stone walls between wooden buttresses.

"Very well, Mr. Swindon," Thomson said, noting the other's weapon dip slightly when he revealed that he knew his identity. "Ah yes, I have you at a disadvantage. My name is William Thomson, Sir William if you like, or Professor Thomson."

"Just get on with it, unless you just want me to shoot ye. I'm fair sure I can take down your lackies afore they get me. They're just miners, after all, and I'm the big bad leader of a *gang*, isn't that right?"

"As far as I know, that's correct, Mr. Swindon," Thomson admitted. "However there are currently more of us than there are of you. Even if you slay one, or two of us, if we kill you, what happens to your boy? He doesn't look well. I can see the sweat on his brow from here, his restlessness."

"Don't you look at him! Don't talk about him!" Swindon growled even louder, elbows edging out to make himself look larger, like a cat raising its fur.

"Nobody *has* to die at all," Thomson said. "I just need my equipment. I see there's damage to one of the trunks, but it seems accidental. I came in here so there wouldn't be any surprises while we loaded my trunks onto the wagon. I came for an agreement that what's mine is mine."

"Didn't see where they had your name on 'em," Swindon spat.

"I assure, every trunk has a full name and address inside the lid, and many of the pieces have my name on them. Scientists can be almost as light-fingered as highwaymen... A pursuit of knowledge, like working against the law, guarantees no honor amongst compatriots. We can make sure your son sees a doctor." Swindon's expression flickered. He *was* more interested in protecting his son than imagined profit on unseen scientific equipment. Good.

"No doctors 'round here except in town, and we can't go there," a new voice cut in, followed by a series of metallic clicks. "We'll be keeping what we found, and taking whatever you have on you. Drop the rifle and empty your pockets," the newcomer drawled.

Thomson was not a military man. He was no hero. The end of his rifle drooped as he saw the burlap walls shoved aside and the miners from outside the mine shuffle into the open space, hands in the air.

"I'm sure we can come to a reasonable agreement," Thomson said. As the tip of his rifle touched stone, the whole room shook mightily. Wood screamed. Stone fell. Burlap curtains, free of anchor points, drifted to the floor, providing avenues for the fire's escape from its pit at the center of the space.

Lost, blind, Daniel hugged the earth. As if in reaction, the ground beneath him shook violently. He could feel it split against his chest, under his hand. His feet dangled over a void, the soil crumbling beneath his shins. The shaking stopped. He took a deep breath, feeling around with one hand, then the other, trying to find the edges of his new world. The threat of falling into an unknown abyss taunted him.

Abyss, a voice whispered from far below, echoing as it traveled up the cracks, or perhaps coming from more than one source. *Abyss, yes... So close, I can feel you. Reach out to me...*

Daniel opened his eyes, immediately slamming them shut again as dust hanging in the air and heat from the fire assaulted him. The fire was so close. He wriggled out of the blankets and pushed himself up to hands and knees, opening his eyes again as he backed away from the heat he could feel baking into his face. He continued to crawl backward, looking around for his father. His foot slipped over the edge of a crevice and he noticed the cracks ran across the floor. Huge rocks from the ceiling, broad wooden joists, blocked his view. Was there even a way out of the mine anymore?

He spotted a man with a rifle, then a woman with a shotgun. Neither were part of the gang. He heard a moan nearby, saw a bloody hand reach from under a pile of rubble. *What's going on here? How is this happening?* He thought, crawling toward the outstretched hand.

"It's all right, we'll get you out!" He called, choking on smoke that was no longer drifting up through the hole in the ceiling, but collecting in roiling clouds. He touched the fingers.

In a flash, blackness appeared in his vision again, but now it was like thick smears of ink, a smudge coming up from far below, traveling up the walls of another crevice. No, not just the stone, up a river of blood seeping out from the trapped man.

The black spread as he watched, filling in the form as though pouring ink into a human-shaped bucket. It spread across the torso, out the limbs in each direction, up the next until it engulfed the head. As it neared the other's fingers, they twitched and spasmed, grabbing hard on his own. Daniel struggled to pull away, finally releasing himself and falling back just before the shadow reached his own skin.

The whole experience was strange enough, but he was sure, very certain, that in the last second as he pulled away, the shadow had reached beyond the unfortunate miner's skin, forming a trail of tiny black cages in the air, backed by the dying curtain of flaming burlap.

"Daniel! You're all right!" Pa yelled through the crackle and roar of fire catching the aged timbers of the mine. Pa ran up to him, grabbing him by the shoulders, his pistol pressing into Daniel's arm. "Oh, thank the Lord! We've gotta get out of here!" Turning, Pa pulled Daniel along behind him. "You better let us pass, mister!" He raised his pistol at a gentleman in a fine suit who swung his rifle clumsily, then lowered it, nodding.

"Come ahead. I never- Great Caesar's Ghost!" The man said, struggling to bring the rifle up quickly and aiming it to Pa's right. Daniel and Pa turned to see who he was aiming at. Woolsy, one of Pa's gang, stood unsteadily, shoving aside a joist as wide as his hips. Rubble fell behind him. Some struck his back, shoving him forward. It took Daniel a moment to see what frightened the interloper so much.

Woolsy's head had smashed against a rock when the joist struck him, splattering half his brain across the wall. Gray chunks simmered there now as Woolsy jerked and lurched forward. The invader fired, barely winging the man near the shoulder. The arm jumped back, but then reached forward. And it reached. And it reached. The arm blackened, stretched like taffy. The fingers splayed, reaching individually, lengthening into terrifying claws.

"Shoot, Pa!" Daniel encouraged, and he did. The interloper and his crew fired as well, knocking the body back while the claws neared the main interloper. Daniel looked around and saw the axe they used for chopping wood for the fire. He picked it up and swung at the arm, knocking it down to the floor, but doing no visible damage. With a grunt, he struck again while the arm rose up, inches from the interloper's rifle. He heard bone snap, then grind as the break acted as a new joint. The forearm bent toward him, claws clutching at him.

He swung crossways, launching the hand back toward the fire, where it burned and smoked, withering away into glowing embers in seconds. He swung at the second arm, but Pa pulled him away and the interlopers fired their shotgun and rifles, knocking Woolsy's body back in a jerky jig into one of the burning bedrolls. The thing hissed as air within expanded. The outside crust flaked away and fluttered into the smoky void like evil snow.

"We gotta go!" Daniel yelled over the fire, which seemed to catch on the fallen beams with extraordinary speed. Even the wood over their heads danced with flame as he hooked an arm around Pa and guided him toward the exit. The interlopers dropped back, weapons up to fire on any other attackers. The smoked roiled, growing thicker, blacker by the second. Pa stumbled, but Daniel helped him up and they all staggered to the mine entrance together.

Plumes of noxious smoke pouring out over their heads, Daniel and Pa fell into the cold, damp, fall grass, relieved to gasp the sharp, clean air.

"By rights, I should run you into town to talk with the sheriff, or at the least leave you here to fend for yourselves, but if you'll come, I'll bring you up to the Landing. You'll at least have shelter," the leader of the interlopers offered.

"We don't need your charity," Pa said, coughing through the last and laying back in the grass in defeat.

"That would be mighty kind of you, mister. I know we haven't done anything to earn your mercy."

"I'm not a vengeful man, and you've just lost your home. I know that these are no ordinary woods, that the tales Abigail and Martin told were likely true, as bizarre as that acceptance is. It doesn't fit rightly into the shape of the world, but neither does... whatever creature I just saw in there."

"You know Abigail and Martin? Beckett?" Daniel asked, trying to sound nonchalant after he heard excitement in his voice.

"None other, do you know them?"

"We were friends. I don't know what we are now."

"The world is a confusing enough place for young people without," the stranger gestured to the mine, with angry orange fire illuminating a churning wall of smoke. "Professor Thomson." The man held out a hand to Daniel, who exerted himself to rise to his feet. As they clasped hands, Pa began to shiver and shake. "Some kind of fit? He may need real medical attention, though you seem to have recovered from whatever gripped you. Perhaps we *should* go back down to the town."

CHAPTER TWENTY-ONE

Abigail spent half an hour being poked and pinched and peered at by Dr. Le Guin as he constantly adjusted his glasses under a helmet of straight gray hair. The office was plastered with advertisements for medicines and hung with various equipment for listening to and looking at various body parts.

"You're coming along fine. The ears are looking better, your eyes are clear and focused, breathing is easy and clear. With some rest and good, hearty food, you'll be fighting fit in no time. Red meat is a must. I'll write you a prescription to help you sleep. You can pick up at the apothecary down the way."

"I don't think I've been having trouble sleeping," Abigail said.

"It's my experience that when one is stuck asleep for a time, when they awake, further sleep, which is necessary for good health, can be elusive for a while."

"Ah, I understand. Thank you, Dr. Le Guin."

"Yes, thank you, Dr. I'll take the prescription and have it filled immediately," Liza said from the doorway. "Then straight home. You need your rest, as the doctor says."

"Really, Liza, I don't require such coddling. I feel fine." Liza was already back through the office door, one hand swept dramatically down Wendig Street.

Martin strode along Main Street, crossing Wendig. He wore his best plum suit and top hat. The shoes still squeaked as he wore the ensemble so rarely they were practically new.

"Where are you going all dressed up?" Abigail called to him. He turned mid-stride, joining them.

"Arden Miles' funeral, not the first this week, or the last. The families of the miners killed at the cave collapse where the bear was killed and another incident at the number two shaft involving Professor Thomson, Daniel, and his father. They're all right, though a number of Swindon's gang didn't make it, and some of our people didn't either, including Mr. Miles and Mrs. Jacobs."

"That's sad. I wish all of this wasn't happening. Why couldn't we just live our lives without monsters and explosions?" Abigail asked. The doctor bobbed his head as he replaced equipment and scribbled a note for the apothecary.

"That is a question I'm sure everyone asks during such times. I know I did just a few years ago when I was a medic for the Union Army. So many bayon- never you mind. Suffice to say, it was a difficult time for the nation, and this is our small version of that turmoil. I pray that we'll see an end to it sooner than later. You rest well, now, and don't let such disturbing thoughts fill your head. It won't do your recovery any good to worry." The doctor finished writing and handed off the slip of paper with his prescription to Liza before sneaking past Martin and away.

"How much time do we have?" Abigail asked, resolute.

"What do you think you're doing, young lady?" Liza demanded.

"I'm going to the funeral. The doctor was right. I don't much feel like sleeping just now. I think a little walk would do me good, and the fresh air. I'm getting dressed and I'm going to represent the Becketts alongside my brother to recognize the loss of one of our community, and our company."

"Your brother is representative enough," Liza said, but Martin leveled his best pleading stare at her. Abigail joined in a moment later. Liza held out for a few seconds, then threw up her hands. "All right, let me help you dress if you must go."

The Voice of Silver Hill
ISSUED EVERY SUNDAY
by
C. Valente and S. McGuire

Terms of Subscription:
One copy, one year......45 cents
One copy, six months......25 cents
Single copies......1 cent
Contact purveyors for advertising rates.

The Silver°

Vol XIX - No. 46 • SILVER HILL, NEVADA

FAMOUS SCIENTIST INV

SILVER HILL- Professor Wm. Thomson has come to town at the behest of the Becketts to hunt down and aid in the extermination of the plague of monsters which has befallen our small mining town. Word has it, he arrived with a wagon-load of specialized equipment, and may even have recruited famous author Mark Twain for his mission, as the latter man has been seen around town, asking curious questions about recent events.

Will this team be able to rid us of the giant bears, serpent vines, fanged frogs and other monstrosities set upon us by the eldritch forest? Will there be others arriving? What kind of weapons do they bring to the fight beyond wit and muscle? We look forward to updating you, good reader, on these points and more in coming days. I think we can all agree it's about time that something was done and we look forward to speedy results.

ELKO- On Copper Bars- We were yesterday shown a 20 pound of almost pure copper reduced from Railroad copper ore by Mr. A. J. Roulstone. Mr. Roulstone informs us that the process by which it was reduce is very siilar to that pursued in the reduction of galena and no more expensive. Arrangements are being made to thoroughly test the new process on a larger scale, with propositions to test the new reduction process on silver and other ores around the State to the benefit of all who rely upon the production and reduction of metals.

Voice
f Hill

Weather

Increasing clouds, liklihood of rain. Finish knitting those sweaters, ladies!

SUNDAY, NOVEMBER 8, 1874 • 1 cent

ESTIGATES MONSTERS!

SILVER HILL- Two explosions were witnessed by miners at the numbers nine and ten shafts today. Shock waves were felt as far away as the work ongoing at the East Gate. They appeared to issue from the same locale, but smoke was also seen in the direction of the number two and three shafts, which we all know have been abandoned for some time.

Could it be that a scheduled blast created a bigger boom than expected?

Perhaps connecting the two mines through some natural cave system? As always, anyone with further information about the incident is asked to come forward while our reporters dig for more dirt.

* * *

Cleaning and Oiling Harness.

Many a harness is spoiled for the want of a little care at the proper time. The Chicago *Journal* gives the following directions for cleaning and oiling harness:

Our advice to those intending to clean harness, is first to unbuckle all the straps, and remove all the metalic portions possible without ripping the stitching; then, if a thick coating has formed on any part where the harness came in contact with the horse, remove it by scraping it with a wooden scraper; then place the straps in...

Aunt Helen, Mr. Clemens, and Professor Thomson accompanied the twins, the five of them dressed in the finest clothing they had, a chocolate brown dress, the most subdued thing Helen had packed, a white linen suit, a charcoal suit, a plum suit, and a pale yellow dress. They walked two by two, with Professor Thomson bringing up the rear, up to the front pew of the church. It was the biggest indoor space the twins had seen, even more spacious than the miners' bunkhouse. Dozens of families sat, heads bowed, waiting for the priest to begin the ceremony of remembrance.

Abigail and Martin broke off from the adults, who took seats near the outside end of the pew. The twins crossed the narrow aisle, hands waving in distracted reverence before their bodies, and knelt before Keiko Miles.

"We are so sorry for your loss. This is a trying time for all of us, and Arden was a brave soul trying to right a wrong. All any of us can truly ask in our last moments is that, to face our creator with hearts full of bravery and honor. If you need anything in the coming days, please do not hesitate to come to us. We are here for you," Abigail said. Keiko, one arm around her daughter's shoulders, reached out with her other hand and squeezed Abigail's for a moment.

"Thank you for your kind words. I appreciate you and your brother being here today, at least." Abigail winced at the rightful implication that her parents should be in attendance.

"I'm certain that if they could, my parents would be here as well. They have always valued the people who worked with them and for them."

"It's all right, Miss Beckett. You don't need to make excuses for them. We all know where their priorities lie, and that you and your brother don't see them often enough, either."

"The shadows ate their brains," Keiko's son, sitting on her other side, said, seemingly out of nowhere.

"Kirayoshi! You'll have to forgive him. He's been having the strangest dreams lately, and he keeps forgetting that's all they are- dreams," Keiko said, looking back at her son as if to drive the point home.

"Of course," Abigail bowed her head briefly and stood, squeezing Keiko's hand again before letting it go and moving back to find a seat beside Mr. Clemens. Father Gerrold walked up the aisle to stand before the casket.

"We are here today to remember a man of great heart and great merit. He served his community all his life, from his beginnings in Boston, Massachusetts to his journey west to meet his lovely wife and finally settle here in Silver Hill. He was a man of joviality and wisdom, always ready with a story to lighten the heart or deepen our understanding. He was truly the salt of the- Lord Almighty!" The priest pulled up short from his rehearsed speech. His hand shook as he raised it, forefinger extended toward the doors at the back of the church. Every person in attendance turned to see who had the audacity to interrupt a funeral for such a pillar of the community.

"Them's some mighty fine words, Father. Who are we celebratin' today?" The voice was a little rusty, but very recognizable from the bonfire where the twins listened to so many spooky and silly stories from miners.

"A-arden Miles!" Father Gerrold managed, and then passed out, falling backward and knocking the empty coffin from its pedestal.

Mr. Clemens was one of the first to break the tableau, but instead of running to the priest's aid or to the miner, who he did not know, he drew forth a small notebook and began to scribble with a pencil, making some kind of notes about the goings on at the church. Abigail wondered if this scene would end up in one of his stories one day. How unexpected, for one to attend one's own funeral.

Keiko stood next, running down the aisle toward her husband returned from the earth after he had been reported dead, buried irretrievably in the collapsed mine. She wept and laughed as she ran until a pair of men about halfway down the aisle stood from their seats, boxing her in.

"Don't rush into anything, dear. You don't know it's him. It could be a spirit, or a revenant. We don't know why he's back, or if he's even himself!" Others took this logic as sound, stepping between Arden, whose clothes were torn, scorched in places, and who was caked with dirt and blood from many scratches across his whole person, and his tear-streaked widow.

Keiko reached and screamed to be allowed to touch her husband, to embrace him, but the wall of Silver Hillians grew thicker. Arden stood, confused, but unmoving.

"Keiko? What's happening? Why are all these people here? It's not Sunday... is it? I remember being in the old number two shaft, going in the side to corner Swindon and his gang, get the professor's stuff back and all... There was a big bang, the ground shook, the ceiling... Smoke everywhere, fire, beams burning, splitting, falling... Darkness. It's not Sunday, is it?" Arden asked again, confusion and worry in his voice.

"Let's just have the good doctor look you over, son," one older man suggested.

"That's a good idea, and maybe Father Gerrold... once he

wakes up," said a younger woman. Others began yelling suggestions until the scene of solemn remembrance was churned into a sea of voices and waving arms, with Keiko collapsed on the floor, face in her hands, weeping.

"All right!" Sheriff Hornsby raised his voice, hands in the air. Abigail and a handful of others heard and quieted, but the riot continued through the rest of the congregation. "ALL RIGHT!" The man boomed at the top of his lungs, this time reaching a larger crowd which turned to him, eyes glazed with surprise. "We'll get this all sorted in short order. The doc and I will take Arden down to the doc's office and get him looked over. If you want to send Father Gerrold along after he wakes, that's where we'll be." The man set a stern expression and walked steadily forward. At first, people were too stunned to move from his way, but then the frieze shattered and people shuffled back along the pews, allowing him to pass. "How ya feelin' there, Arden?" The sheriff asked with something approaching nonchalance.

"Tired, I guess... are all these people really here for me?"

"Seems like. Come on, now. Let's figure out what happened to you and have the doc check you out," Hornsby said, putting an arm over the miner's shoulder and turning him back toward the door.

Having a somewhat different thought, Dr. Le Guin extricated himself from the crowd and went to the fallen priest, patting his face and calling to him to waken. When the other came to his senses, he said, "I don't know what came over me. I had the oddest feeling and then... While I was out, I dreamed that," Father Gerrold dropped to a whisper so that Keiko and the children would not hear, but Abigail stood close enough for every word. "I dreamed that Arden Miles walked through those doors." Gerrold pointed again with a trembling hand toward the rectangle of daylight.

"Just take it easy and breathe, Father. Sit as long as you need to," Le Guin told him, patting his shoulder.

"But that's not possible, is it? I need someone tell me that's not possible. Nobody's been brought back from the dead since Jesus' time..."

"This is a modern age, Father," Le Guin skirted the subject. "Who knows what miracles these mountains might give forth? You, come on over here and help the good Father to his chambers. I need to check on... a patient..." Le Guin caught himself while waving a pair of young men over. They hoisted the priest up and half-dragged him toward a door past the altar, each waving their hands before them as the twins had, and nearly dropping the older man. "Careful, now," Le Guin admonished. He watched the youths for a moment before making haste in the other direction.

"Demons!" Abigail heard Gerrold mumble before the nearer door closed behind him and his caretakers.

CHAPTER TWENTY-TWO

Demons? Abigail thought. *Is that true? Does that mean I'm... possessed?* Her left hand grasped the back of her right, though the marks were hidden by yellow gloves matching her dress. Her hand slid up her other arm to the elbow, covering her hand and forearm. She was certain someone would see the growing vine of black crisscross marks.

And what then? Would that be so bad if everyone knew? If Mr. Miles can come back from the dead, what can you *do?* She didn't think the voice in her head sounded quite like her own, which made it all the more terrifying. She pushed through the chaos of bodies until she was able to run down the front steps with a heavy clop clop of shoes not designed for actual walking.

The sheriff and Mr. Miles hadn't made it very far, but it looked like the miner was having trouble coordinating his movements. His right leg never bent, and each step took a swing of the body. His right arm looked like it was bending between the shoulder and elbow. Even from here, Abigail could see the tally marks sliding up and down his limbs, swirling around his chest. Dr. Le Guin caught up with him and the sheriff, getting a nod from the lawman, but no response from the miner that Abigail could see from her vantage.

She hustled across the dirt street and up to the boardwalk as quickly as she could in heels and dress. As soon as she set foot on the boards, though, her shoe striking like a dropped book, Arden spun around. Le Guin fell back a step, while the sheriff reached for his pistol.

From the front, Mr. Miles was even more disturbing than from behind. Abigail could see the black clusters of lines leaking from his eyes, his mouth, a slash across the base of his neck above his clavicle. They burst into nothing in the light, but in the shadows, they gathered like ants around a dropped candy.

The broken arm jerked, hand flipping up at the wrist, then turning, elbow pulling up sharply, then the upper arm folded turning most of the arm to point at her. The shoulder joint popped audibly and the hand reached toward her through the shadows cast by the Cobbler's storefront. When it reached the break between that block of stores and the next, it stopped as though striking a wall, sliding off to the side, then creeping up like a vine on the side of a brick building, weaving around, looking for a way in, or up.

As the arm stretched and wove, Abigail stood, confounded, mesmerized by the motion, by the wrongness of the display. Arms weren't meant to move like that, to twist and reach so far... Mr. Miles himself stumbled closer, until his whole body pressed against the imagined wall. A few of the swarming black lines edged too far out and exploded in tiny wisps in the sunlight.

Abigail wasn't certain, but the pattern of fizzing, whizzing sounds created by the evaporating lines almost formed a word or words, but she couldn't quite make it out. It sounded mostly like a snake hissing or a soda pop effervescing. The thing that definitely wasn't Arden Miles anymore spread out to the sides, a split forming right down the middle, one leaking eye drifting away from the other, mandible splitting and spilling even more black lines in a rush.

"Abyss," the word came more clearly and Abigail shuddered. She felt her hand raise toward the spreading mass of twisted flesh and crisscrossed black lines. Black antennae sprouted from the eyes, branching, splitting again.

A film formed between the segmented lines, forming approximations of insect wings. They fluttered for a moment, then crumpled, turning into reaching, writhing worms. From one wrist, a long, arcing, pincer emerged, scraping against the wood shingles of the shop's wall. "Abyss..." She heard the word again, growing louder toward the end.

In one convulsive wave, the thing rolled out into the light Abigail felt as though the eyeless monstrosity was watching her, seeking her reaction, approval, perhaps. The exposed black clusters ignited first, burning like fuses rapidly back to the bifurcated shell. Abigail gasped as the distorted form exploded outward, fragments spinning through the morning sun, burning up and hissing so loudly it seemed more like a roar. The back of the body slumped to the shadowed boardwalk, a loose pile of skin and tattered cloth. She pulled her drifting hand back, covering her mouth. Her eyes wide, she stared for long moments. Her entire arm buzzed. Her stomach turned.

"Are you all right, Miss Beckett?" Sheriff Hornsby asked, sounding as though he himself was at a loss. "That sure was... something..."

"I- I'm shaken up, but I don't think I'm injured. I had wanted to talk to Mr. Miles, to ask him something, but I... suppose I've missed my chance."

"I guess so. I don't know how I'm going to explain this to those people back up at the church, especially Mrs. Miles."

"I don't envy you that task, Sheriff," Abigail said.

"Nor do I, Hornsby, and I can hardly explain it from a medical point of view. I'm going to need some kind of sack to scoop up the pile of flesh he left behind." The doctor nudged it with the toe of his shoe, but got no response beyond a smudge of blood on the leather.

"Mehhhhhhhh," Pa tried to speak again, but only produced one drawn out sound that didn't seem to mean anything. Daniel sat in a wooden chair beside his father's cot in the doctor's offices, hoping Le Guin would return soon from Arden Miles' funeral. Professor Thomson had gone, too, in support of the Beckett twins, so it was just the two Swindon men alone again. To be with his father inside a real building was strange after the last few years in the mine, as were the thick books on the shelves and racks of intimidating medical tools.

"Just rest, Pa. The doc'll be back soon and run some more tests or listen to your breathin', or somethin', hopefully he can snap you out of this." Daniel prayed silently that whatever had happened to Woolsy wouldn't happen to his Pa, that he wouldn't turn into the monster the townsfolk already mostly thought he was.

Pa's eyes opened wide as if in great pain or surprise, then closed again. His mouth opened in a similar manner, then he made a sound deep in his throat that started out very low and rose and rose in pitch like he was singing, but he didn't give the tune words. Eventually the voice cracked and his mouth shut with a snap. His head turned toward Daniel, then away, eyes still closed. His shoulders rolled and his arms jerked, hands grasped at air and blanket, but released a moment later.

Pa breathed in deeply, sharply, then exhaled, lips pursing as though he was blowing smoke rings.

"Melllllllo," he said, nonsensically, and his hips shook from side to side, then his right leg lifted a few inches off the thin mattress. Daniel spotted a black, swollen spot at the back of his ankle just before the leg dropped. A few seconds later, the other leg lifted, knee bent, toes pointed down, then up, foot turned one way then the other.

"Mellloooooddddddyyyy," Pa said mournfully. The sound dragged out for seconds and seconds.

"Melody?" Daniel said, stricken. "No, Pa, Ma's not here. She... left ages ago. It's just us, just Rudolph and Daniel."

"Daaaannnananananannnnnnnniieeeellllll," Pa repeated in his drawn out way. "Rudolph, Rudy, Swindon," the words came quicker now, with almost no hesitation or elongation.

"That's right! What else do you remember?" Daniel encouraged the man.

"Darkness, stillness, expanse, collapse, the endless void, trapped in stone."

"The mines? Are you talking about working in the mines? You don't do that anymore. You don't have to go down in the darkness."

"Explosion, cracks, escape, light, so much light..." Pa rambled.

"Yeah, Pa, you escaped the darkness and came out into the light. No more mines." The door opened, Dr. Le Guin framed by a brilliant blue sky. A cold wind whipped through the room and Pa moaned. The doctor stepped inside quickly and closed the door behind him.

"What are you doing he-" The doctor stopped himself, seeing Rudy laying out on the examination table. "How is he doing, son?"

"After the mine collapsed, he had some coughin', but then he seemed fine. He slept late, calm as stone down at the boarding house. Now he's... lost, ravin' and movin' strange. Is that better than lyin' there like a log? At least he was peaceful like before."

"Does he have fever?" The doctor asked, then stepped up

to the table and lay his hand upon Swindon's forehead. "Hmm, it's hard for me to tell with my own hands so cold. He doesn't feel hot to me, though. I'll give my hands a few minutes to warm up and see what the thermometer tells us."

"'Thermometer?' Is that some crazy gizmo from Europe?" Daniel asked.

"Yes and no. It was invented in England a few years ago, but it doesn't spin or whistle or anything. It's just a glass tube with some material that... well, when it's hot it goes up, when it's cold it goes down. You can see it's got little marks and numbers to tell exactly how hot something is. It will take a few minutes to get a proper reading. It's far more accurate and helpful than the thermoscope I've been using since I began practicing, but I've just got this new device in a few months ago. There. Now we wait. Would you like some tea?" Le Guin asked.

"No, no tea, thanks, doc. Pa's been ramblin' talkin' about dark and light and Ma..."

"It's not uncommon for patients to see lights or tell of moving from the dark into the light or vice versa during an illness. Fevers especially can make you see some troubling things."

"I just can't do it anymore. I know you want to go back up there to see if things have really changed, but I..." Abigail, sitting on her bed, turned away from her brother. She felt tears welling up in her eyes, but fought them, focusing on a small shelf of figurines by her window.

"What happened? You were fine this morning. You were cheeky and smiling and now you look like you've seen a gh- well, okay, Mr. Miles was kind of a ghost, but really, whatever happened to him came out of the number two shaft, and that's sealed now. The bear is buried. I had hoped it was over before, but now it really seems to be. No more weirdness. At the very least, though, we need to go back to the Landing," Martin said.

"No," Abigail shivered again, wrapping her arms around herself. "I was foolish to indulge you in the first place. My scientific curiosity got the better of me. *You* got the better of me."

"So now this is all my fault? Is it my doing that Arden Miles is dead... again? That a giant bear with three heads tried to crash the gates and they got burned down? Does it have thing one to do with me that Mother and Father are acting so strangely and we haven't seen Mother for over a month except one very strange dinner?"

"It's your fault we got involved. We're not sheriffs, we're not in the army. We're still children, Martin! We might be old enough for adult things on paper, but we've been... cradled here for too long. We knew it was dangerous, and we went up there anyway. We were attacked by that same bear, and a creepy Paiute house, and blown up by dynamite. Any of that could have killed us, *should* have killed us! And now, hours after I watched a man turn into... something and explode in the sunlight... I just can't. Go on your own if you must, but I'll see Mother and Father when the project is on schedule and they return to living in the house." Martin, stunned by this revelation, stood and stared for a long moment before turning around, his pack already on his back.

"I would be crushed if you didn't come back," Abigail whispered.

"Then come with me. We've always been better together."

"Mother and Father would be doubly crushed... more... if

we both got ourselves killed. They're really too old to start over with babies, and I'd like to think, at least, that they love *us* specifically."

"Of course they do. You're saying some very strange things, Abigail."

"What's out there... We're not equipped. Maybe no one is. It's beyond a rogue bear or running across an angry swarm of bees. There's something... deeply wrong, terrifying."

"Don't turn into a baby now," Martin said. Abigail's eyes squeezed shut, forcing the building tears to race down her cheeks, but turned away again so her brother couldn't see.

"If that's how you need to think of me, don't forget, we're the same age. This baby is staying here. I'll do some reading, resting as Dr. Le Guin ordered. I'll hope to see you at dinner." Martin said nothing this time, but a few seconds later, Abigail's bedroom door closed quietly.

CHAPTER TWENTY-THREE

"Daniel," Pa said, his voice wheezy, weak.

"I'm here, Pa." Daniel reached to take his father's hand, but the other pulled away.

"I'm afraid."

"You don't have to be. The doc told me nobody's tryin' to put you in jail. The professor said he wasn't gonna to hold any grudges or anything. You're safe here. Once you feel a little stronger, we'll find a place to stay in town and I'll get a job, maybe runnin' papers or even up at the mine. Word is there's workin' on a big project, need all kinds of help."

"Somethin's not right. I feel..." Tiny black cages rolled out of the corner of Pa's mouth, spilling onto the pillowcase and soaking into the fabric. Daniel looked from the pillow up to Pa's eyes, and saw the tiny swirls and crisscrosses of black lines rolling along the edges of his eyelids. The eyes opened wider than they were meant to, pulling away from the eyes, laying bare white and iris alike. Minuscule trails of black lines pulsated along blood vessels and folds of pale brown around the widening pupil.

With a wet sound of tearing, the eyelids stretched past their limit, flapping like eight triangular flags, splattering tiny droplets of blood across Pa's forehead, cheeks, and eyeballs. Daniel reached as though to help his Pa, but recoiled as blood painted his fingers. He cringed and turned away.

"Doc! Doc! Come quick! Somethin's happenin'!" Dr. Le Guin stood from his desk, the chair creaking as he rose, and came to the bedside with sleepy, heavy-lidded eyes. He smacked his lips as though trying to wet his mouth as he turned to see his patient. His eyes flew wide. He reached for a box of gauze pads and a roll of bandages.

"His eyes, what's wrong with his eyes?" Daniel asked, torn between embracing his father to comfort him and running from the room.

"Did he claw at them? How were they damaged like that?" The doctor asked, pressing the gauze against the man's eyes and beginning to wrap them in place, winding the bandages around his head. A conical point burst from Pa's chest through the light sleeping shirt he wore, through the thin blue blanket. To Daniel it looked like a goat's horn, with ridges across it.

"Look out!" He yelled, grabbing the doctor's shoulder to pull him back, but the horn shot forth, curling into a broad spiral that caught the doctor in the upper chest, tearing through, separating bone as it came drilling through the doctor's back in a spray of blood which splashed across Daniel's face and chest. He fell back, tripping over the chair, and lay, stunned, tangled, as the horn arced around, piercing the doctor's lower back, causing him to arch backward like a dancer.

It didn't stop, but continued through, forcing ribs apart in the upper chest, and continuing to grow through the man's belly before appearing again and diving back into Pa in an ever growing spiral. The whole scene was too much. Daniel felt his gorge rise and tried to turn away, but his legs were up over the fallen chair. As his breakfast reappeared in surges, Daniel struggled for breath, struggled to disentangle himself, struggled to move away from the ongoing crunch and splatter of the scene before him.

When he managed to get his legs out of the chair and lay over onto his side, his stomach calmed and silence fell over the doctor's office. Slowly, shakily, he stood with the help of the doctor's desk. He looked at the entwined bodies of his father and the doctor, wondering what force in the world would cause such horror, or even allow it. In the back of his mind hissed the word again, *Abyss*.

"Silly girls..." Martin muttered to himself, dropping one foot after another down the stairs, not quite stomping, but by no means walking quietly. "She knows she wanted to go up there just as much as I did. And now she hates me, and I have to go up there alone if I want to get the rest of the story. She probably won't ever go up to the Landing with me now. I'll have to go stand around with all those manic people working and working, like bees in their hive. But what's the honey, really? More silver dug up out of the ground? It hardly seems worth it, with all this trouble..."

"Master Martin?" Liza called from the kitchen. "That you learning a new dance number on the stairs?"

"Ha... Ha, Liza. Have I mentioned what a light you are in my world?"

"Save the lip for your street rat friends, young man. Your parents have left me with complete authority over you for the time being. I could restrict you from going out, or swat you if you need it."

"Going out, that's a great idea. Don't mind if I do!" Martin said, leaping down the last few stairs to the carpet running from the front entrance to the stairs. Detailed leaves in at least three greens and roses of red and peach and yellow wove patterns at angles across and back. When he was at the door, Liza poked her head out past the kitchen door.

"Where do you think you're going? Why do you have a knapsack?" That wasn't the last question the housekeeper asked, but Martin was already through the door and it was closing behind him. He was halfway down the hill by the time he heard Liza again, still demanding answers from the front gate, and yelling threats he could barely hear and paid even less credence.

At the intersection of Main Street and Silver Road, the new road that led up the mountain, Martin turned and stopped, watching the men finishing off repairs, and from what Martin could see, improvements to the East Gate.

The palisade itself was reinforced from within by long, angled beams, and atop, a new tower a dozen feet to the side of the gate, adding another ten or fifteen feet of height for guards to watch from. He didn't really want to go up the mountain, not alone, not without Abigail. He looked one way, then the other down Main Street, searching for a sign of what to do. He spotted the newspaper office and decided he needed a copy. He headed toward the general store.

Paper in hand, Martin stepped out onto the boardwalk, wondering where the best place in town to read would be, without going home to sit on one of the garden benches. While he considered, a flash of white caught his attention. He focused on it and immediately a new avenue occurred to him.

"Mr. Clemens!" He called out, waving the paper over his head. "Mr. Clemens!" The older man turned and waved at Martin, remaining still while the boy ran along the boards and crossed the rutted street to meet him. "Thanks for waiting for me," Martin said between labored breaths.

"Of course my young explorer. I see you're packed for another expedition."

"I was, but then Abigail blamed me for all the danger we've gotten into, all the times we could have died."

"Certainly a valid concern, but I doubt it was entirely your fault," Mr. Clemens said.

"Thank you! We had no idea what was really up there the first time, and the subsequent trips were for you to see what was going on, and to deal with the bear... No one listens to a bare-faced boy or any woman but Mother. Even you didn't believe until you saw it for yourself. Abigail's right about one thing, though. It is dangerous, and it's all just right there. What can we do about it?"

"Well, the bear's buried, so I would call that a big step forward. I'm afraid I can't tell you what to do about miners showing up to their own funerals. In all my travels, I've never seen a thing like it. But I do know that family needs to stick together, and you and your sister are the closest I've seen. Don't let a disagreement about fault get in your way, especially when that," Mr. Clemens gestured toward the forest visible above the rooftops. "Isn't anyone's fault. It *is* a problem, and I have no idea how to solve it short of leaving the whole place to be taken back by the forest and lighting out for more civilized lands. Perhaps not every acre of God's green earth is meant for us. Maybe there need to be spaces for the old things, the dark things."

"You're saying we should just leave it be and it will leave us be?"

"That does largely seem to be the way of nature," Mr. Clemens agreed.

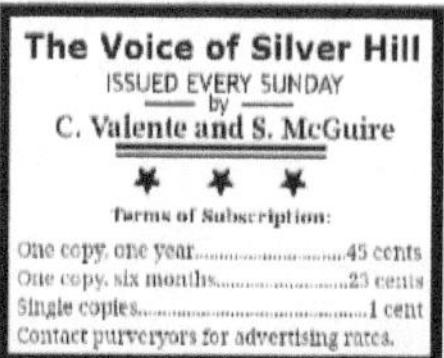
The Voice of Silver Hill
ISSUED EVERY SUNDAY
by
C. Valente and S. McGuire

Terms of Subscription:
One copy, one year........................45 cents
One copy, six months....................25 cents
Single copies.....................................1 cent
Contact purveyors for advertising rates.

The Silver°

Vol XIX - No. 47 SILVER HILL, NEVADA

LOCAL MINER ATT

SILVER HILL- After joining a posse to bring Rudolph Swindon to justice, local, admired miner, Arden Miles was crushed when the number two shaft collapsed. Despite a number of witnesses attesting to his demise, the man himself, covered in dirt as though having clawed his way from his grave, walked through the doors of the Eternal Mercy Church to gasps of surprise.

After his brief appearance, Miles was led away by Sheriff Hornsby and Dr. Le Guin to be checked over and to get his official testimony as to what happened at the mine. No report has been filed as yet, and no answer was forthcoming at the doctor's office. Professor Wm. Thomson and Mr. Samuel Clemens were both present for the event, though neither has provided an interview as yet. Is this strange occurrence part and parcel of the matter of their investigation? Will Mr. Miles be able to give account of what lies beyond the veil? Will he have messages from the land of the dead?

Voice f Hill

Weather

Clear, sunny, but still cold. Old Man Winter is right around the corner, sharpening his icicles!

SUNDAY, NOVEMBER 15, 1874 • 1 cent

ENDS OWN FUNERAL

AURORA- A new illness has appeared that has local doctors flummoxed. It appears to have two separate sets of symptoms, but the doctors feel certain there is only one disease, changing its course based on unknown factors within each patient.

Over the last month, many Aurorans have complained of listlessness, a lack of energy, and poor sleep. This impacts their concentration while working in the mines and felling trees, resulting in a far higher rate of injury. The other group seems to have more energy, but no appetite, developing small black sores, especially on the neck and underarms. Both groups report hearing voices and hallucinations of dark figures and creatures.

This a worrisome development in our sister town and we wish them all the best while suggesting a voluntary quarantine, urging Silver Hillians not to visit or elicit letters from friends and relatives in Aurora, and to halt moving of goods between the towns, as the doctors still do not know the cause or means of transmission of this mystery illness.

A JURY was brought into court in order that one of their number might be instructed upon the following point of law: "If I believe that the evidence was one way, and the other eleven believe different, does that justify any other juryman in knocking me down with a chair?" The Judge answered in general terms.

SILVER HILL- In addition to monstrous sightings, spiritual manifestations have begun plaguing our fair town. Water barrels have been tipped over; pictures have waltzed off their hooks and skipped around the room; windows have been cracked without cause. I call for an investigatory committee to be appointed by Sheriff Hornsby and Farther Gerrold at once.

CHAPTER TWENTY-FOUR

"Why does he do it? What can be so important about going up into the woods? Putting himself, *us,* in danger?" Abigail asked Liza, who had come up to inquire after her brother after he'd walked out the front door against her instructions.

"He's a willful young man, and you're a willful young lady. You're not really children anymore, and you both have to acknowledge that and take more responsibility for yourselves." Liza straightened a pencil on Abigail's desk absently. "How angry can you be at him if you're still helping him study?"

"Those are *my* notes."

"What? You understand all these squiggling lines and piles of numbers?" Liza asked disbelief filling her voice. "I knew you were often together while he studied, but I didn't know he was tutoring you."

"Ha! Martin tutoring *me*? In engineering? He couldn't tell you the difference between friction and a fraction! He doesn't care a thing for maths or science, or building things. All he wants to do is grow into one of those old men who sits around the campfire or the potbelly stove at the general store telling stories of his daring adventures fighting off wild beasts and exploring untamed wilderness. "*I'm* the scientist! I'm the engineer!"

"You're what?" Another voice joined Liza in asking. Behind her in the open doorway stood Professor Thomson.

"Did you say that *you* are the one who has sent all those papers and made such brilliant leaps?" Thomson asked, letting his valise slip from his fingers to rest against the door jamb.

"What?" Abigail said, turning to stare at the Scotsman.

"Oh yes, I've seen many of the papers from 'M. Beckett.' I do teach at the university. Though I'm not generally involved with the correspondence courses, which are mostly in things such as business and law. My colleagues have called upon me to evaluate some of your more ambitious work. Come to think on it, I did find Martin rather vague on many points whenever I attempted to begin a discussion with him on the subjects of his schooling."

"Perhaps *that's* why he was so upset with me. He knew we couldn't keep up the ruse forever. I told him to avoid speaking with you when I wasn't around."

"Planning to coach him around to the right answers? You're a good sister to help him, but you're not really doing him any favors, pretending to walk one path while yearning for another. Neither of you would end up happy."

"Our parents, Mother, especially, she's very keen on us advancing ourselves, and having the best of lives. Of course, for me, that means finding a wealthy or otherwise desirable husband."

"That is a common expectation, though not universal back home. There are successful women whose power does not derive from the men to whom they shackle themselves," Thomson said. Liza looked stricken that he should use such imagery, or make such suggestions.

"I don't think this is the best direction for this conversation. Were you planning on taking your leave, Professor?" Liza asked.

"I had intended to, yes. My equipment was severely damaged when it was carelessly handled by Swindon's gang. I'm afraid I don't have a means of making more metallic foil thin enough to be useful, or wire, or-"

"Metallic foil? We could make that up at the Landing. I know you didn't get a chance to explore it, but there's a twenty stamp mill for crushing ore, a smelting refinery, and a set up for casting ingots. I'm sure that we would use silver and modify a stamp or find some other tools to mash a few ounces of silver into foil... if you think silver would suit," Abigail said.

"Silver... I've been using tin, as it's more readily available, but silver is quite conductive, and may in fact work better. I'd have to assess the machinery the Landing offers, but that may just solve my problems. It might require a little calculus to come up with all the adjustments to the overall devices, but I think we can work that out together, if you'll help me." Abigail almost accepted without thinking, but then she realized the equipment she'd offered was all up on the mountain. The Landing had seemed to be a safe enough place, but it was hard to say how long that might be true. Martin could have been right when he suggested it might all be over, and she prayed he was right, but what if he wasn't and he was walking right into danger?

"I... the Landing..."

"Yes, your parents are up there still, aren't they? Do you want to bring them some more food? It's been days and I still haven't met your mother."

"Oh yes, of course." The professor was right. She was worrying about herself when her parents could be in danger they didn't even know existed.

Knowing he couldn't move his father's and the doctor's bodies during the day, with people wandering about the streets, Daniel sneaked away from the office, looking for a cart or something he could steal in order to do the job in the night. As he stalked the lesser streets of Silver Hill, a familiar face flagged him down.

"I hear your Pa's mighty sick," Cutlass said. Daniel had no idea what the man's real name was, only that he carried a short, curved blade on his hip across from his pistol. The sword often got more of a reaction than the gun, and saved on ammunition when it was called into real action. Aside from the weapons, the straw-haired man, ten years older than Daniel and getting round about the middle, wasn't very intimidating.

"I'm afraid it's worse than that." Daniel looked down at his hands. Tiny specks of blood had dried across his fingertips.

"Oh?" The other man raised an eyebrow.

"He's gone. I just came from the doctor's office."

"You have my condolences," the other said sincerely. Then he drew his namesake weapon.

"What's that for?" Daniel asked, falling back a step. The blade leapt forward, nicking his arm. Blood flowed freely. "OW! What's gotten into you?"

"Yer Da's out of the way. You're the only thing between me 'n' leadin' the whole gang. I don't take no pleasure in it. Jus' the way it is." The blade jabbed forward again, sweeping across Daniel's belly, but this time, the blade stopped before it touched flesh, only cutting a tiny nick in the shirt he had stolen off a clothes line minutes before to replace the one he'd sullied with his breakfast.

Both men surprised, looked down. The blood leaking from Daniel's arm had risen up and wrapped itself around the metal. Cutlass pulled back, but couldn't wrest his weapon from the blood's grasp. He thrust forward and made no headway. Daniel only felt a mild pressure in his arm where the blood was anchored, though his stomach turned. Cutlass lunged again with all his weight, leaning forward, heels off the ground.

His arm swung up away from his body, the blood and sword following in an arc. Cutlass stumbled forward and Daniel stuck out his foot to trip the other man. Distracted by the spectacle of prehensile blood, the attacker failed to regain his balance. The sword slipped from his fingers as he went down. Competition for the weapon gone, the blood slid down to the handle and held it vertical for a moment before plunging it down into the bandit's upper back.

Daniel stood stricken as the blood fell away as though returning to normal, but as it flowed down the steel blade, he spotted the tiny black cages zipping around as though in search of something. When the blood touched the fallen man's wound, it vanished. Having seen quite enough, Daniel began to sprint. He pumped his arms and legs as hard as he could for nearly a minute before running out of breath. Stabbing pain in his ribs, he took a side alley, then returned to his search for a cart.

Something Cutlass had said to Daniel returned to him as he regained his breath and cursed the lack of carts in Silver Hill. He was in charge of the gang. He hadn't thought of it himself. He had never had any aspirations toward leadership, didn't really know what it meant besides telling people what to do. Pa had seemed to like it well enough...

Abandoning his initial goal, he turned toward the mills on the east side of town. The river afforded them power to grind grain, work bellows for smelting, and other jobs, but they also required a lot of space for storing the material going in and out. The warehouses held that stock, as well as giving the Swindon gang a place to meet in town. Since the mine shaft had been closed down in a rather permanent manner, Daniel expected those remaining to gather here.

They didn't use the warehouses very often since settling into the mine, so the first door Daniel tried opened onto dim quietude, with only a few stray beams of sunlight sneaking between boards to illuminate drifting motes. In the dim light, he could only make out stacks of crates and bags of grain.

"Hello?" He asked, uncertainty tightening his neck. The handkerchief tied around his arm brushed the rough wood wall, making him jump, but then he blew out a deep breath. At worst, it was someplace no one would find him for a little while. He could certainly use some rest as much as he needed to face the remaining members of the gang and tell them that both Pa and Cutlass were dead. How would he get through those explanations? Maybe if they thought he killed them they'd be afraid of him and do as he said. He supposed he had killed Cutlass, at least.. hadn't he? *We did.* A voice said inside his head.

Contemplating this possibility, Daniel climbed up on a low stack of crates and pulled a few sacks of oats over to make a bed of sorts. As he settled in, starting to relax and feel sleep take him, he heard a low scraping sound. "Just rats," he whispered to himself. He yawned. "Rats."

Abigail and Professor Thomson talked as they walked, he throwing out questions to test her knowledge and she answering and going beyond, asking counter questions about the materials and forces involved in the hypothetical scenario he had spun. It was liberating. Though Abigail knew the proverbial cat was out of the bag, that Liza would no doubt tell her parents and there would be a lot of screaming later, she shoved away those thoughts to enjoy the mental exercise the professor offered.

They visited the general store in search of large tin cans and came away with a trove. They visited the telegraph office and convinced Mr. Herbert to part with a spare coil of wire. At the blacksmith, Professor Thomson picked up a small hammer, chisel, and nails, which replaced such tools as had been looted by Swindon's gang as immediately useful and taken into the cave.

Throughout, they continued their conversation and Thomson outlined his hypothesis to Abigail.

"Interesting," she said, "You suspect, that given the apparent mass of the universe as a whole, there must somehow be matter we cannot easily see or interact with."

"Indeed, for the celestial bodies, the planets and comets and such, to keep in their orbits, there must needs be more to the seemingly empty spaces than we can yet detect. I have been calling them 'dark bodies' in my notes."

"And they add to the mass, but can move through mass as we know it. It brings to mind stories of ghosts."

"It's not impossible that what we interpret as ghosts are somehow echoes of these other bodies, visions caught at just the right angle. A rainbow, as you know, is the aggregate splitting of many beams of light by many raindrops acting as prisms. We can not generally see the passing of light, until it impacts something. Likewise, we have to give the dark bodies something to interact with which will give us some reading, and hopefully, like a camera trapping light..."

"Forming an image? That would be amazing! To not only prove the existence of dark bodies, but to photograph them... And because they pass through most mass, the photographic paper, if you will, which might be developed by other forms of energy, from visible light to other waves like the ones James Clerk Maxwell discusses, maybe?" Thomson nodded. "If everything else is blocked out, only the dark bodies would show up, which is why you need a deep cave or mine to do the experiment."

"Exactly. You have quite a mind. Your instinct about saving yourself from a life of darning socks and starching shorts is a good one. That would be a terrible waste. I know you're worried about your parents finding out about the courses, but I'll put in a good word for you, and if needs be, see if I can arrange admission to the Royal Belfast Academical Institution. You would learn far more quickly than by post, with access to real equipment and like minds with which to collaborate."

You have like minds right here. A voice said within her mind. She endeavored to ignore it.

"That's so far away..."

"We often have to extend ourselves, reach beyond what even we think we can do in order to make the impossible happen. Do you know how long it took to lay the transatlantic cable? How many pounds were sunk into its success? How many injuries and lost materials? The greater the reward, the greater the risk we must endure to achieve it."

"Speaking of which, let's see if we can borrow a wheelbarrow from someone around here. My arms are getting tired of carrying all these cans, and you're already carrying the wire and tools. We can run them up to the house and find a way to pack them up for tomorrow."

"Another fine idea, though I don't think we need to bother anyone about a wheelbarrow. Let's just head back. Who knows how much energy we could end up needlessly expending in search of something to help us conserve energy?" The absurdity made Abigail smile. Thomson smiled. Abigail laughed, and he followed suit in that as well. It was great to have someone to talk to who understood all the things in Martin's books. Taking a few years in Scotland didn't sound terrible at all.

CHAPTER TWENTY-FIVE

Daniel stood beneath a caged sun, a mad tangle of black lines blotting out most of its light. Still, he stood atop a hill and could see for miles. The upper plains rolled before him like a lumpy blanket. Grass swayed in every direction, swishing back and forth as the wind caught it, pulling until the spear-like stalks snapped back into place.

The wind whispered something, but again, it was just outside of his understanding. He leaned down, ear out, and saw that each leaf of grass was alive with terribly thin rows of tiny cages. When the wind came again, he heard the word, "Abyss." A cold wind flew into his ear, drilling deep into his brain, settling in.

He stood up, and as he did, hundreds of forms rose from the tall grass. Amongst them were some of the strange creatures Martin had told him about, with mismatched body parts of various animals. Others were clumps of bone, not arranged in skeletons, but as though someone had taken a number of bones at random and thrown them down and affixed them together as they fell, laying across and atop one another. Near to hand stood a number of gray-skinned people who looked otherwise normal.

"Pa?" Daniel said involuntarily when he recognized one one of the figures. "Am I dreaming? Am I dead?" He was torn between running away from his father and toward him, no matter the man's state or his own.

A dream is just a different perspective. The voice came again. *As is death.*

"Who are you? Are you giving me this dream?"

It is amongst many gifts I lay before you.

The gray image of his father turned. Daniel gasped. Pa was

still attached to the doctor with spirals of goat horn. Black streams of shifting tangles of lines poured from his eyes, framing a similar stream from his slack mouth. The three streams fell between Pa and the doctor, vanishing from sight. What did they have to do with all of this?

A few feet farther away, Cutlass turned around, momentarily showing his signature weapon still sticking from his upper back. Instinctively, Daniel turned away, but he was surrounded creatures rose up from collapsed positions in every direction, down the hill at his feet and off into the distance.

Daniel closed his eyes. Still before him in the darkness, a deeper, shifting black filled each form, delineated misshaped arms, legs, antlers, pincers, chaotic figures the nature of which he couldn't even discern. They swayed and shuffled toward him slowly.

"Stop!" He screamed, turning again, seeking a way out of this nightmare.

The forms paused in their motion, becoming entirely still as though he stood in a field of statues. He opened his eyes again and saw the same. Clusters of bones stood like strange trees. Men and women, killing wounds evident, features gray, gawked, but did not draw closer.

In the great distance, a shadow swept toward him like a wave on a pond, but much farther away. He had seen dust devils across the desert move in a similar way, sliding one direction, then another, but always nearing. Daniel noticed that in the wake of the movement, the figures and conglomerations lay on the ground. With each passing moment, the shadow grew deeper, darker, closer.

A wind kicked up, blowing the fallen creatures away like so much smoke rising from a campfire. The shadow began to show details of form, a whirlwind with arms reaching out and receding, taking something from those along its path with long-taloned fingers. Eventually, it towered before him, taller than any building in Silver Hill, or even Carson City. It was a mountain made of starless, deepest night. Where it blocked out the sky behind it, he could see tiny pinpricks of that sky.

"Abyss," the thing said, the word sounding as though it was formed by a thousands blades of dry grass sliding over one another.

"I-I heard," Daniel said, quaking. "Are you going to kill me, too?" He asked, thinking of the meandering path of destruction behind the creature.

"Kill?" The word thrust at Daniel. He turned slightly, as though to take a blow on his shoulder. "Abyss doesn't kill, only consume. Just as you do."

"I? I don't consume anybody. That's horrible."

"You consume to survive. Abyss has persisted for so long surviving on the infinitesimal."

"I don't know what that is."

"So much potential, so much more, but the vessel is empty. The orchestra stuck playing a single note struck by a triangle in the back," Abyss said.

"What? Orchestra? You want me to play music?"

"We could, if that's what you want. You are a grander vessel than any I have seen. You exceed the centipede, the bat, the butterfly, even the bear and the deer. You have... capacities..."

"Vessel? Are you... of course you are, you're a demon looking for someone to possess. You just want my soul in return for what? Three wishes? To live as a king?"

"Every mind I touch grants me the knowledge, the skill,

the understanding of the world it carries. For endless ages, I have advanced by grains of sand, by the breadth of hairs. But you can carry me forward and I can learn so much about this world I've been trapped within for so long, so very long."

"Yeah, I get that. I know what *you* want. But what do *I* get?" Daniel asked.

"What do you want?" Abyss asked.

Paper in hand, Martin headed back toward the estate to talk with Abigail. Of course she didn't want to go back to the forest. Who in their right mind would? They'd both been injured in their previous excursions, every time. Her hearing was mostly back, but were the burst eardrums, bruises, scratches, and broken bones worth it? Not for her, and he had to accept that.

She was the book learner, he the hands-on adventurer. They would both contribute. That they were twins didn't mean they had to do everything together or in the same way. They would have to have their own lives at some point. The thought saddened, but emboldened, him. How much time did have left with his sister by his side? He would apologize for insisting she do what she wasn't prepared to do.

"Martin!" The familiar voice came to him as if in response to his thoughts. But how could his sister make herself heard all the way into town? Then he realized the call came from behind him and turned.

"Abigail! Professor!" Martin said, striding toward the pair, who were laden with arm loads of seemingly random goods. "I'm so sorry for the way I acted back home. You're right, of course. I should never have tried to pressure you into going back up there. I'm probably mad for going myself."

"Apology accepted," Abigail said without a trace of disagreeability, pushing a number of large tin cans into his hands.

"What? That's it? 'I forgive you, carry this?'"

"Don't press the issue, son," Professor Thomson said. "We've got a plan for how to repair or rebuild my equipment."

"You- the pair of you- came up with..."

"Wipe that stricken look off your face, boy. I know that your sister has been doing all of your schoolwork. I'll do what I can to smooth things over with your parents and the school. She's quite intelligent, you know. Solved a number of problems that the original designs suffered from and grasped the rather advanced concepts of my hypothesis without missing a beat."

"That's our Abigail," Martin said, turning to follow along. "Sharp as a tack."

"Stop," Abigail said, feeling her cheeks begin to color.

"Quick as a whip. Bright as a-"

"Sto-op!" Abigail started to walk faster. Martin saw her face redden and knew he had to keep up the barrage. There were so many comparisons, but most of them centered on 'quick' and 'sharp.' *Ah!* He thought of another one.

"Wise as an owl!" Martin called after her. Weighed down as he was by the cans and other things she'd unloaded on him, she was getting away. "Sly as a fox!" Abigail broke into a run. Thomson, unable to keep up, let out a sigh and fell back to walk with Martin.

"You certainly know now to get under each others' skin."

"She knows I'm just playing. I think we've made up. At least she didn't turn around and hit me with one of these. Why do we have cans of beets, anyway?" Seeing as they had a walk ahead of them, and Abigail didn't seem to be stopping,

Thomson started explaining the plan, trying to stay away from the scientific terminology Abigail had a good handle on but Martin didn't.

Daniel spotted Abigail running along the boardwalk on Main Street and started running to catch up. He had awoken from his very strange dream surrounded by some members of the Swindon gang and others who had gone missing from town in recent months. At first, their presence frightened him, but then he realized this was what being the head of the gang, and Abyss' host, meant. They weren't there to attack him, but to serve him.

Abigail turned to see him and let out a squeak. "Daniel! You startled me. How is your father doing? Professor Thomson said he helped get him to Doctor Le Guin, but then some odd things happened at Mr. Miles' funeral and I didn't get a chance to talk to the doctor."

"Pa's... Still at the doc's office." Daniel felt like he was lying to Abigail, but she couldn't know the truth. He could barely stand to think of the monstrosity on the examination table, let alone frightening her with the tale.

"I'm sure Dr. Le Guin is keeping a close eye on him," Abigail said.

"You don't know the half of it," Daniel said, mostly to himself.

"Hmm?"

"No-nothing. So are you headed home?"

"Yes, Professor Thomson, Martin, and I are going to work on some science experiments. Well, first we have to build some things."

"We can help you. I'm in charge now. My people will do

anything for me. Watch," Daniel said, waving a few of the returned members of his father's gang forward. "Stand on your heads."

"You don't have to do that, Daniel, and neither do they," Abigail raised her voice to speak directly to the men and woman who had come forward and were now bending over in the street, trying to put their feet in the air.

"You're right, that's silly. I should have them do something useful. I see Martin's carrying some cans. Do you have enough? I could send them to get more. Wouldn't even have to worry about money. Never have to worry about anything again. I can get whatever you want." He knelt, taking her hand. She gently, but firmly, took it back. He could feel his cheeks reddening. *How can I really impress her?*

"That's all right... I think we have what we need for now. I'm... uh... glad you're taking these changes in stride... You always felt restricted by what your father wanted. I guess we all feel that, sometimes. If you could make your own way, you could choose to do what *you* think is right."

"Right? For who? You're starting to sound like Father Gerrold." Daniel stood.

"That's not so bad. He's a wise man. He helps a lot of people get past their problems. It wouldn't be a bad idea for you to go see him. Having your father injured can't be easy. I don't know what I would do if my father was ill."

"Gerrold's a Goody Two-shoes, trying to control the uncontrollable. People are animals."

"You don't believe in a divine spark that separates us from the dogs and lizards?" Abigail asked.

"I don'-"

"Hey, Daniel!" Martin said as he and the professor drew up to join the group. "What was that with your friends trying to do acrobatics in the road?"

"I was just trying to demonstrate to your sister that I'm in charge now. They'll do whatever I ask of them."

"Ah..." Martin said.

Maybe I'll have to talk to you later about your sister. You might know what will make her like me... Daniel thought.

"Don't worry about it. We've got to go now, but I'll catch up with you later," he said aloud.

"All right, Daniel. Take care," Abigail said. Daniel noticed a flash of black as she waved. *Ah!*

"See you later," Martin said.

"Good day," Thomson said.

"Come on." Daniel turned away, walking back toward the warehouses. *Did you see that? Are you with Abigail?*

I am with many of Silver Hill, soon, I will be with all. You will help me to understand this place. Her mind is more complex than yours, though. I moved through many bodies to be able to ride along with you and not... instigate errors.

Errors? Like the goat horn? Daniel asked.

Among others. Man is a far more complex beast than those I have tested before. So much possibility.

I heard about the bear. Three heads?

It was not obvious where one creature ended and the next began. It is irrelevant. The bear served its purpose. So will you. So will she. Do not grow too attached to the world as you know it. As soon as I know it, it will be mine to re-form.

CHAPTER TWENTY-SIX

Abigail dreamed of a great, silver, blanket across the ground. Like the quilt on her bed, it was made up of smaller squares. Unlike the quilt, thin wires led from each square back to a wooden box. Across the top of the box ran row upon row of tiny glass capsules. An associate of Professor Thomson's, Warren de La Rue, had invented them. The idea was that the blanket would intercept the dark bodies Professor Thomson sought and any square struck would send electricity to the box, causing its tiny bulb, with a sliver of platinum inside, to glow.

Abigail understood how it worked, why it needed to be in the deep cave. Why it was unfurled across the mountaintop, she couldn't say. Testing, perhaps. Rainclouds raced across the sky, blooming darker and darker gray faces. She felt as though she should take up the blanket, but it was dozens of feet across, with hundreds of sections. She would never make it in time.

She tried to move forward, to save what she could, but her feet felt stuck in place. She looked down and saw that her feet vanished beneath the ankle into a pool of black like a pit of tar. Tiny tendrils of black crept up her ankles even as she watched.

No! She resisted, pulling at her feet, but she could see the black through the dirt, through the stone, like roots of a tree buried far below. The streaks and strata of black in the rock reminded her of ore deposits, as veins of silver or gold threaded through the rock as the land was formed untold eons before.

While she struggled, the air grew chill. Goosebumps raised on her arms. The sky darkened. Something even colder, wet, stung the back of her neck. Above, the sky was all but black with roiling clouds. Drops of something she knew wasn't rain pelted down. It pittered and pattered on the broad metal blanket. The tiny lights flashed over and over. The precipitation grew heavier until the little farm plot of bulbs glowed steadily.

One of the bulbs gave a little "pop" and the tiniest wisp of smoke curled up from the filament as superheated platinum reacted with the oxygen in the air, burning up. Another popped, then a handful, like popcorn. It was the "rain" striking the heated glass. She leaned forward, stretching, reaching, falling onto her belly.

The last light held out for seconds after its brethren. She held a shaking hand over it to protect it from the drops, but then it shattered. A stab of white hot pain seared into Abigail's palm. She pulled her hand back and looked. A curved fang of glass stood out from her flesh.

Dark fluid built up at the base before she could remove it. Pinching the glass, she pulled, but the blood, was it blood? It seemed darker, almost black. She leaned and saw the black tally marks roiling around as the clouds were doing above. She drew the glass again, but the fluid stuck like molasses, drawing out into strings. The strings moved up the glass, wrapping around it, pulling it back toward her hand.

Abigail pulled harder to counter the black material, but the glass broke. One piece remained between her fingers, the other shot back to her palm, slashing it. She cried out, shaking her hand. Before her, the flat area where the blanket had been was inundated. Only a few, dully reflective parts of panels showed above the black fluid.

The center of the puddle rose, black as pitch, but more fluid. It leaned to one side, then drifted in the other direction, trying to find its balance. The whole thing flopped with a splash over onto its side, but rather than finding it humorous, Abigail's stomach turned. As the thing had fallen, she felt the world shift beneath her and almost lost her own balance.

An appendage formed, long and featureless, tapered at the end, which curled into a simple pad which pressed against the submerged metal sheet to try to right an oblong body. Abigail watched in horror as her own arm reached out in a similar fashion, pressing against thin air of its own accord. She pulled her arm back to her side, cradling it in the other, and the creature fell back into the puddle, again splashing the inky fluid. She felt it against her ankles, but resisted looking down. She couldn't get away and she couldn't fight. *What can I do?*

Accept. A whisper of a word emerged from the patter of the clouds' discharge.

Martin read as they rode. Taking their own wagon to accommodate the materials and such equipment as Abigail and Thomson could make in one night afforded them the relaxed schedule he was used to before all this "creatures" and "come visit the office" malarkey started up. He loved his late mornings, his relaxed breakfasts, watching Abigail's face light up as she figured something out in one of his books and explained it in a rush of words that simply slipped by him like a stiff breeze or the swiftly flowing river.

The forest was somewhat less intimidating during full daylight, as well, and with their own wagon, they were fully prepared to leave in time to make it back to town before dark. These factors played heavily into Abigail agreeing to go.

"You've packed enough food for ten people here," Martin said, adjusting his position between pages of the paper. His eyes skimmed past advertisements for cobblers and glaziers and shows playing up in Carson City in search of the local stories, especially regarding strange happenings. Mr. Edwards hadn't promised anything, but he had told Martin there was a chance his story would show up soon.

"Of course. You saw how Father ate when he came home. It was like he had just made it across the desert. The rest of them will probably be the same way. In fact, I might not have brought enough..."

"We'll make sure your parents get to eat first if they like, and come back up tomorrow if we must. I know what it is to skip a meal whilst in the midst of a difficult conundrum. If they haven't licked it yet, I'll give them a hand."

"You're going to lick the problem with your hand? That doesn't seem very effective," Martin smirked. The others ignored him.

"The project as you've described it to me, Abigail, seems to be most formidable, containing factors outside even the consideration of the New Hampshire cog rail. As eager as I am to get my own experimentation underway, I look forward to seeing their designs as well," Professor Thomson said.

A bush shifted, leaves rustling. Martin dropped his paper, bringing out a knife nearly as long as his forearm. It shook before him for long seconds before a seemingly normal bird flew up and out of sight into the canopy.

"I understand you're jumpy. You've had some strange activity around here, but you all killed the bear and no other large creatures have been seen in some time," Thomson said. He waited a few seconds for his words to sink in then, "You can put it away. The thrush is gone." Martin felt the rock of the wagon, heard the clink and tap of the horses' harnesses. His focus returned to the moment. He slid the dagger back into its sheath at his side and bent to pick up the paper. It took him a few tries. Thomson handed him one set of pages.

"Thanks. I guess our experiences did affect me after all. It won't happen again."

"It's all right, son, I just don't want to be stabbed."

"Of course. I won't bring it out again unless there's really something there." The last half of the trip dragged on. Martin read a few sections of the paper again, having not found his own contribution. *There's always tomorrow.* He assured himself.

The Landing was busy with workers bringing ore up from the shaft, delivering it to the stamp mills where the chunks of rock were crushed into a sand which would be smelted and poured as ingots. The office where Mother and Father worked stood long and low, quiet as usual. Martin's chest tightened as they got closer.

Father hadn't been himself last time they visited, and they hadn't seen Mother in over a month. He couldn't recall the last time that had happened. Even when their parents needed funding for their second shaft when they couldn't quite pay, they all traveled together to the East Coast to schmooze with investors and play the perfect family, a solid bet for the others' money. And they were. The mine had thrived since. But now this new project... Everything seemed... off.

The Voice of Silver Hill
ISSUED EVERY SUNDAY
by
C. Valente and S. McGuire

✶ ✶ ✶

Terms of Subscription:

One copy, one year.................45 cents
One copy, six months...............23 cents
Single copies.......................1 cent
Contact purveyors for advertising rates.

The Silver°

Vol XIX - No. 46 SILVER HILL, NEVADA

MIRACLE MINER

SILVER HILL- Arden Miles, miner, husband, father of two, who we reported recently to have been slain in the apprehension of Rudolph Swindon then appeared at his own funeral has once again gone missing. Also seemingly missing are Dr. Le Guin and the aforementioned gang leader, Rudolph Swindon. Did the latter return and exact his revenge on the posse member? Did the doctor get in the way and meet his end?

Our fair town has certainly become more exciting, and more dangerous, in recent months.

✶ ✶ ✶

DR. M. W. PARSONS,

IS NOW IN SILVER HILL

To those delaying the services of an experienced and reliable Dentist, Dr. Parsons offers his services with the valuable experience of twenty years in the various branches of his profession.

All work done in the most perfect and satisfactory manner or no pay required.

Office-At the Post-office

SILVER HILL- A group of townsfolk was seen yesterday moving down Main Street, apparently led by Daniel Swindon, son of Rudolph Swindon, and heir apparent of the gang his father had built up in the years since he was laid off from the mine for stealing equipment. Why has Sheriff Hornsby not addressed this gang once and for all? This reporter would like some answers.

PARDONED.- Rich. Simmons, who was convicted four years ago of murder in the second degree for the killing of a man named Cartwright, at Elko, and sentenced to twelve years in the State Prison, was on Monday last granted his freedom by the Board of pardons.

Ezekiel Merriweather, who was sentenced to three years for burglary, having served out his time, was at the same time restored to citizenship.

Voice f Hill

Weather

The first snows of winter threaten to fall on us soon. Get out your woolies!

SUNDAY, NOVEMBER 22, 1874 1 cent

MISSING AGAIN

AURORA- Telegraph communication with Silver Hill's sister city has ceased. A number of attempts have been made in the last day to contact the town for personal and business reasons, none eliciting a response from their telegraph office. We continue to advise, and reinforce the earlier moratorium on visiting, trading, or accepting travelers from the south at this time.

A CARD.

The undersigned being desirous of visiting frineds and relations in California and the East, takes this method of informing his ptraons and the public that he has leased his Assay Office and fixtures, for the term of three months to A. E. van Vogt, whom I recommend to the public as one competent to do melting and assaying correctly and in a satisfactory manner.

oc-3m H. HARRIS

HAWKS- Our neighbors across the range reported feeling a pair of tremors on the day of the shaft two collapse. Not knowing the cause, a party was sent up their side of the mountains, and has not returned. If anyone sees a stranger, especially coming down from the mountain, let Sheriff Hornsby know immediately.

NOTICE.

WE, THE UNDERSIGNED, hereby give notice that the co-partnership heretofore existing under the firm name of Asimov & Silverberg, is this day dissolved by mutual consent. All bills owing to said firm to be paid to R. Silverberg and all liabilities of said firm settled to same.

Silver Hill, November 1874.

I. ASIMOV,

n15-30d R. SILVERBERG.

CHAPTER TWENTY-SEVEN

Seething, wounded, Daniel spotted a sign swinging in the mid-morning wind. The Rusty Pick had been a favorite hang out of his father's since he could remember. He sensed many of the others in his throng had spent considerable hours there themselves. Never having been allowed inside due to youth and then his father's overprotective streak, Daniel resolved to now get himself a drink.

He spread the bat wing doors before him, surveying the room. A few old hands, retired from the heavy work of breaking rocks from the earth and loading them into carts, took one corner by a potbelly stove. A few strangers sat some distance away at the middle of the room, while the barkeep leaned on his bar, waiting for someone to need something. He barely looked up at the squeak of the doors.

Daniel stepped into the room proper, his gang following on his heels like a gaggle of ducks after their mother. The doors swung only partway closed before opening again and again. Quickly, the front of the room was filled with gray-skinned, slack-jawed members of Daniel's gang, waiting for his command. He left them there and approached the counter. It held a fair shine, and a brass bar ran along the bottom just above the floor.

"Help you?" The barkeep asked, voice dripping with apathy.

"I want a drink," Daniel said plainly.

"The Devil, you say." The man sneered, but stood upright, knuckles down on the bar top. "People usually come in here looking for tomatoes." One of the regulars barked a laugh while another echoed the word.

"Tomatoes."

Another said, "Looks more like a cucumber kind of guy to me." Daniel slapped a coin down on the bar, scanning the bottles along the shelf for a word he recognized.

"Rye," he finally said.

"Rye," the barkeep repeated and turned, but then turned back without a bottle or glass. "Say, ain't you Rudy's kid? Oh, hey, yeah, there he is! Hey Rudy! Rudy?" The man said, puzzled. "What's his problem?"

"He's fine."

"Hey! Is that the doc? Whoa! What happened to them? Is that a goat horn? Like one of those mountain goats? With the big..." The man ran his hands up over his head to demonstrate large, curved horns.

"Where's that rye?" Daniel said more forcefully. He tried to focus on his father, command him to raise a hand at the barkeep.

"Ah, now he sees me. He's not lookin' too good, but I guess you don't have to take him to the doc, huh?" The barkeep joked. "Y'know, with him bein'... attached to him an' all. Doc's not lookin' great either. The lot o' you look like you could go use a twenty year nap up on the knoll."

"Are you going to give me something to drink, or am I going to smash you over the head with this stool?" Daniel asked in a growl. This seemed to snap the bartender's shock.

"I was just funnin', but them's fightin' words. You take your coin and you get the hell out." While he spoke, the man ducked behind the counter. When he came up again, he had a shotgun in both hands. He pumped with one hand while the other rested along the stock, with his finger at the trigger.

Daniel felt the shame and pain at his clash with Abigail, the death of his father, and the stumbling dance of failure his life had been well up inside him. Black lines flooded down his arm to the wood of the bar. He could feel, even as he leaned back, his eyes closed, the form of the long rectangles of wood. Under his command, they twisted, curled, knocked the weapon from the barkeeps hands and lifted the helpless creature by one arm. It howled as it dangled, pawing at the plank to try to free itself.

Around him, Daniel could see in his mind's eye the throng smashing chairs and tables, getting behind the bar and throwing bottles. The air filled with sharp scents Daniel had only smelled on his father's breath. One of the throng cried out in pain, fell to the floor. Daniel opened his eyes to flame racing across the still-flat sections of bar, pouring onto the floor, engulfing one of the former denizens of Silver Hill in a halo of yellow and orange glory. Abyss withdrew from that one, raced along the floor, dislodging boards as they curled from his presence, and rejoined Daniel.

The weight increased on him, but he turned, called to the throng, even as the old timers raced past into the midday sun. They all stumbled toward the entrance. Abyss was learning how to deal with the light, but fire... fire was another kind of life altogether. How many were there? Daniel discarded the question as irrelevant and led his people into the street, then away down the alleys to the comforting cool dark of the warehouses, amid sacks and crates.

Baskets of food in hand, Abigail, Martin, and Professor Thomson walked up to the door of the office and knocked. There came no answer. They knocked again. Abigail began to get a terrible feeling in her belly. As Thomson reached to knock again, she slipped a hand past and rapped the wood panel. She looked up at Thomson with a worried smile, then over to her brother.

"Just open it. It's not like we're going to get in trouble for barging in," Martin suggested. Abigail nodded and tried the knob. It turned, loosely, farther than it normally would. She kept turning it as far as her arm would go, then let go and turned it again. The whole knob slid outward to where she could see a square metal rod leading into the door, then pointing at the sky while the flattened metal ball of the knob rested, cold, in her hand. Thomson repressed a gasp, but Abigail heard.

"That's not a good sign," Martin said.

"Perhaps they didn't want to be disturbed by the miners," Thomson suggested.

"Or maybe it's just in poor repair. There's no reason to take it too seriously," Abigail tried to convince herself as much as anyone else. "What can you see through the window?" She asked her brother. He leaned over the railing from a couple of stairs behind her and shook his head.

"Looks like they've papered over the window, something black, tar paper for roofing? I know they keep it for repairs up here."

"Hmm," Thomson said. "Are there any other doors?"

"There's a private office off the back for if Mother or Father need to have private meetings. It has its own entrance," Abigail said.

Leaving the baskets by the front door, the trio walked around the side of the building, coming to the short side of the "L," and a door of vertical planks with only a small hook on the outside. Tentatively, Abigail pushed up against the hook with one finger. She blew out a breath of relief when the hook lifted. After a small grinding of metal, the door fell inward a few inches. The smell was nearly blinding.

Abigail fell back, stumbling into Professor Thomson. Even when she regained her balance, she stepped a few feet away and battled with her rising gorge.

"What happened in there?" Martin asked, trying to pierce the darkness. Thomson stepped up and pulled the door closed.

"Perhaps we'd better not just now. Go comfort your sister and I'll head back around front," he told the boy.

Abigail, starting to get her gag reflex under control, stood upright when Martin neared. "I'm fine, that was just... whew, that was something else. I don't think they've been out of the building. They've been using the office for a pot."

"But the outhouses are just over there, not thirty feet away," Martin said.

"There was definitely a note of human waste in that miasma of terrible odors. Rot was there, too, and who knows what else?" They heard a screech of metal and crash of something heavy, like furniture, toppling, and rushed back to the front door. Thomson stood there, the door open a foot or so, a few pieces of wood, nails like claws sticking out from the edge of it.

"Did they... nail themselves in there?" Martin asked.

"It certainly looks like it," Thomson said, trying to stand between the twins and the open door while peering past the jamb into the gloom. "No lamps I can see."

"Are they? They're not..." Abigail couldn't quite ask the unaskable question.

"No, I see movement. Someone is alive in there," Thomson said.

Or something. Abigail couldn't help but think.

The feeling of being many places at once, sharing awareness with Abyss as it controlled so many bodies, was disorienting to Daniel. His head hurt, everything hurt, in fact, as he could feel all the scrapes and burns and the sickening slow burn of some of the throng's flesh rotting on the bone.

Not rotting. Reducing, refining, like ore. Abyss reminded him. God had granted life to the world, animals, plants, the birds and the fishes, and finally, Man. Abyss brought something *like* the spark of life, but different. It was sharper, harder. It didn't need all of the bulk of life as Daniel had known it, and it afforded him control over far more than just his body.

Sitting on a chair in a stranger's house that yet felt familiar, surrounded by the family that had lived there and the throng he had arrived with, he reached up to scratch his nose and saw every other right hand rise to a face as well. He dropped his hand. Dozens of other hands fell. "That's creepy," Daniel said aloud. A number of other tongues wagged, making approximations of his words. Mostly, it sounded like choking and moaning.

So, you come out of the ground, like the silver? Daniel asked in his head, avoiding the symphony of voices.

Yes, like the silver, the gold, but older. Abyss answered.

How can you be older than the ground?

I am older than this whole world. The ground, your planet, your sun, all the suns you see in the sky. I see you have another word for them, stars. Very inefficient to have so many words for the same things.

You're older than-

Your entire universe, everything you will ever see.

How does that work?

Everything blooms, fades, and dies. Except me. I found a way to escape death. When your world was born, everything was energy, flying outward. I was pulled apart. As it cooled, gasses and dust eventually formed, collapsing into planets and stars. I am... spread all through your universe.

Like God.

Hmm?

Father Gerrold said that God is in everything, every plant and animal, every rock. The divine spark was what made people live, be able to do and think and feel.

Yes, exactly. An animator, a motivator. Even when this God has left you, I can move your bodies. This God is easy to chase away. The slightest disruption in the energies, or the form of the body and he flees. You are much more stable now, stronger. It is not unlike the crushing of the ore in the stamp mills, then the smelting with heat to bring forth the pure metal, the shining material.

I can see that. Daniel nodded, and all around him, heads bobbed. *Can we make that happen less?*

You are the director. I motivate, but you know their systems better than I, so you are in charge.

Can't they be in charge of themselves until we need them? Free will and all that?

Does your God give you free will?

Kind of, but if we use it, we get punished.

And yet he flees and leaves you, and I raise you up. There is no punishment here. Only unity.

Unity? Daniel asked, a pull in the distance drawing his attention. There were more people Abyss inhabited, up at the Landing. He turned that way to try to see what they saw, closing his own eyes in the living room of the house in Silver Hill.

Bodies moved in the dark, writing, using rulers and compasses. Others worked the mines, bringing up more ore, but not silver, not anymore. This was a new vein, a new direction the mine had taken in the last months. Abyss would be delivered to cities across the west in the coming months, then across America, over land and past oceans to the other nations of the world.

Then Daniel spotted another. She carried only a small trace of Abyss. Something within her resisted its spread. "Abigail..." The word slipped from his lips. The throng repeated the name.

CHAPTER TWENTY-EIGHT

"Mr. Beckett?" Professor Thomson called cautiously at the door. "Mrs. Beckett?" Abigail tried to see past him into the gloom, but he kept his body before the narrow opening.

"Abigail..." A dozen voices said from the shadows.

"Well, yes, she's here..." Thomson agreed. A face suddenly appeared in the doorway. It was drawn, gray, with unnatural wrinkles at odd angles across the thin face. The head held no hair, and the eyes were dark, hollow, irises charcoal gray. The eyebrows were pulled back in an expression of surprise. Thomson likewise leapt back, bumping into Abigail and stumbling down a stair before catching himself using the railing. "Uh... Hello?" The professor managed.

"Professor Thomson! We've been expecting you. Did you bring the children? They're supposed to follow some of our engineers around to see what the project is all about and get a feel for the work we're doing!" Abigail's heart fell when she immediately recognized the voice as well as the spiel. These were the same words he used before. It was like listening to a ghost stuck repeating the same path back and forth down a hallway.

"Father?"

"Abigail? Abigail! And Martin! Come along, children, professor! Don't mind the door. The miners were being... unreasonable. We had to protect ourselves until they regained their senses." Father waved a skeletal hand for them to enter. She could already smell a faint echo of the stomach churning miasma they'd encountered at the back door to the office. This suggested that there was a separation, but perhaps an incomplete one. On some level the people within understood it was bad, but couldn't be bothered to rid themselves of it entirely.

Thomson pushed the door open with a foot and stood just inside. He tentatively waved the twins forward. "It's a mess, but they seem to just be... working," he told them.

"Of course we're working! Lots to do! Complicated project! No time to stop! Come right in. Abigail, why don't you follow Wendy around? She's our only woman on the design team. You'll get on famously, though, I'm sure. Martin, come on over and meet Mr. Klin. He's working on the redesign of the cog for our purposes, greater pushing power to get more carts up to the New Landing and these new carts that will slow-slide themselves back down under minimal supervision!" Father seemed quite excited to show them the projects. Abigail shot Martin a look, but he shook his head. He was right of course. They both knew this script from the first time they came up to the office.

"Oh!" Klin exclaimed with great energy, looking up from his inclined drawing table, his gray, drawn, face suddenly animated. The twins jumped back, surprised. "You must be the Beckett twins! Here for the day to help us knock out this incline problem? Klin here, Thomas Klin. Nice to meet you both. Well look here..." The man pointed to the schematics before him, leaping right into a detailed explanation of their latest issue.

While Abigail had worried about Martin following along the first time, she was now far more worried about what the man would do if they broke his stride. His words rode an off-putting rhythm, his movements sharp, sudden.

They engineers seemed to be locked into whatever they had been doing weeks before, even though Abigail could barely see the work in the dim light.

"This is all fascinating," Thomson put in. "May I see what

you've been doing about this cog engine?" Klin looked up, breaking off mid-word. His smile froze, while his gaze drifted away. Thomson pulled a device from his pocket. Holding it in one hand, he did something Abigail couldn't see with the other. Sparks flew, followed by a low, butter-yellow light. "A small self-lighting lamp. Isn't it something? A fellow back at the Academical Institution came up with it a few years ago, and I've always carried one with me since."

There was a great shuffling of bodies as Klin, Father, and everyone else the twins could see backed away from the light, clustering in the corner. Absorbed by the moment, Thomson leaned forward, unaware of the exodus. "Hmm..." he said, looking over the expanse of paper. Now that there was proper light, Abigail could see, too.

A leaning triangle of paper stood to the right, with a few scribbles on it, notes some some kind in a tight, illegible hand. Above the hypotenuse, where Klin had made approximation of the incline of the mountain, the paper was gone. Over the weeks, he had drawn that line enough times to score it away entirely, leaving just the wood, which was also scored with the incline, and a number of closely overlapping steam engines with one vast wheel on the side and clusters of worn away wood where Abigail assumed calculations and measurements would be.

The surface of the wood was stripped of varnish, leaving a blond color she had taken for the rest of the paper in the gloom. Now the scribblings of a mad man on the walls of his cell at the asylum assaulted her mind. How many hours, how many weeks, had he sat here, happily doing the same work over and over again, grinding the table to the dust which had built up at the bottom of the incline and spilled onto the floor? Thomson pulled the light away and strode to the next desk, the next. They were all of a kind.

"How horrible..." Abigail said, hand rising involuntarily to her mouth.

"What? Are they that far off? Are we going to be stuck here figuring things out for them?" Martin asked.

"We should go," Thomson said in a low tone. Then louder, for the engineers' benefit, "It's almost lunchtime. We brought baskets of food. We'll be right back."

"Food?" One of the ghoulish engineers asked as though he had forgotten the word. Thomson ushered the twins before him to the door, pulling it closed behind him as best he could.

"But Mother? Father?" Abigail said as they hurried down the short stair to the level ground of the Landing.

"I'm no physician," Thomson began. Abigail's stomach sank. Neither was she, nor an oracle, but she was certain she knew what the man was about to say. "But those men and women are not well. They are all terribly thin, hairless, so pallid as to become gray, and their flesh hangs in strange ways. We're going to need help getting them back down the mountain to see the doctor."

"That sounds like a great idea. But how? There are a dozen of them. How will we get them into the wagon?" Martin asked.

"The picnic baskets. As Professor Thomson said, they're rail thin. Father ate well when he came down that time."

"That was weeks ago," Martin said. "I have a feeling that whatever's keeping them going isn't entirely nat-"

"Stop right there," Abigail said. "Mother and Father have just overworked themselves. They're manic, but they will recover. They *have* to recover."

"Let us not argue about future possibilities," Thomson said. "Let us use the food to get them in the wagon and return to town."

Each with a basket in hand, they approached the short stair to the office door again. Thomson led, rapping on the door and then calling into the dark, "Hello? Mr. Beckett? I have that food if you'd like to come get it. Some lovely roast beef I remember you enjoy..."

"Roast beef?" A voice said from within the office. A face appeared, hovering the dark, an expressive moon in a starless sky. Bald eyebrows raised. "Food?" Thomson reached into the basket and pulled out a sandwich wrapped in brown paper. A hand shot out, grabbing the sandwich and retreating quickly. Abigail heard the paper tear, the sounds of hungry chewing, then the word "Food!" again, distorted as from a still-full mouth. Thomson offered another sandwich. This time, three hands grabbed for it, knocking it to the floor just inside the door frame.

"No need to fight, there's plenty for everyone," Thomson said, opening the basket. The door creaked, then broke off its hinges as it was thrown open. The doorway showed a tumble of faces and limbs, all reaching for the sandwich in Thomson's hand. He took a step back and down. Hands extended until they reached the cascade of direct sunlight pouring from above. When light touched flesh, the owner of the offended limb howled, falling back.

"Did you see that? A sunburn in less than a second!" Martin said. "No wonder they blocked all the windows with paper."

"Indeed, Martin," Thomson said. "But that presents us with a new problem, not just of motivating them to come with us, but to protect their sensitive skin from the sun."

"But doesn't that mean... Are they even still human?" Abigail asked.

"There are diseases of the body that can cause one to be injured by the sun. I've heard of cases across Europe. This, of course, seems to be something else entirely, as those people lived quite happily and otherwise healthily in the dark," Thomson said. "We'll need blankets or large umbrellas, perhaps."

"Blankets..." Abigail said, the word reminding her of her dream from the night before, of the creature, the "rain," and Thomson's device. She focused on her palm, searching for any sign of the cut she had sustained in the dream. Perhaps it was a different kind of message, a metaphor her brain was sending her. Then she turned her hand over and saw that the black tally marks, while not surging and trying to break away from her, had spread across most of the area between knuckle and wrist, and the exploratory tendrils from before covered her entire forearm and halfway to her shoulder. *What do you have to do with that creature?* She asked the tendrils in her mind.

Sam scribbled notes about a mine spirit the old timer called a "knocker," sure that he could turn it into a story. Mischievous, liked pasties, loitered around work sites waiting to steal and break things... He heard a lot of folk tales about a lot of creatures, mostly mysterious ape men in the woods that always turned out to be bears or lake and river monsters which often turned out to be groups of otters, but these spirit stories spoke to him. People liked the idea there was still magic in the world, despite steam engines and transatlantic cables.

His next question faltered on his tongue. He leaned forward and peered out the window to get a better view of what he thought he saw. Smoke billowed from somewhere north, but close to the river.

"Thank you for your time, Henry," Sam said, "But it looks like there's more pressing stories for a newspaper man today. I'll try to catch up with you soon!" And in the space of those two sentences, he was off the faded old wingback chair upholstered with broad pink and white stripes, across the narrow foyer filled with old boots, umbrellas, and coats, and into the cramped back street, orienting himself on the rising pillar of smoke.

Two streets later, he realized there was a second plume coming from the middle of town. "What is happening?" He wondered aloud to himself and turned toward the nearer one.

Sam got close enough to see the flames leaping from one of a row of warehouses along the river. Men with buckets were already addressing it. Someone else stood on the opposite side of the street, staring at the spectacle. The woman noticed Sam watching her, turned away and set off at a suspicious clip. With a glance back at the fire, Sam followed his instincts, and the woman.

Most of the time, stealth was part of following someone, blending into the crowd. Everyone else on the street was gawking at the fire. The buildings here were nearly all housing of one sort or another on one side of the street, warehouses on the other. Some stood alone, but many crowded together, shoulder to shoulder like they were huddling for warmth. Sam was anything but invisible in his white linen suit and boater. The woman, though, thought she could slip out of view in a narrow alley and let him pass by. But he caught sight of her and turned to face her.

"Stop! I just want to ask you- hey, I know you. We were on the wagon together, up past the Landing. When we blew the Hell out of that cliff and buried the..." Sam leaned in slightly and lowered his voice. "Giant bear." Recognition bloomed across the woman's weathered features. A smile crept over her lips.

"The writer with the Beckett twins, yeah, I remember. It had to be done. I didn't have a choice."

"I know, I don't blame you. I don't think Abigail does, either. You had your chance to stop the beast and you did. She seems well enough now, anyway."

"The beast? Oh, the bear, yeah, that too," the woman said.

"Too?" Sam had meant to be more subtle in pulling that thread, but the question slipped out. The woman slumped, then sat on the threshold of the nearest door.

"Look Mister," the woman began.

"Samuel Clemens. Call me 'Sam,'" he said. Feeling silly looking down on her like some kind of predatory bird, he crouched beside her.

"Janny Pinsker," she responded, instinctively holding out her hand. He took it briefly. "They wasn't right. Wasn't themselves, not anymore. Somethin' got into 'em. I think it came..." she paused, as though debating whether to tell him everything. "I think it came from the mine."

"What came from the mine?" Sam asked, but Janny was on a roll, staring off into the distance and didn't acknowledge his question.

"Always been stories about the mountain, the forest. The Paiute told the first comers who started the town, the Becketts, the Mercers, the Rambos... The stories came down through the years, creatures you don't see anywhere else, rabbits with antlers, snakes with ears... Most of it didn't mean anything. Only come these last months, since they bottomed out shaft nine... Things have changed. It's like they started mining strange instead of silver."

"What does that have to do with..." A smell Sam had only half noticed resolved in his mind as Janny leaned forward. Kerosene. "Janny... did you light the fires?" She leaned against his shoulder and nodded. "Because of monsters on the mountain?" Another nod. "How did they get into town? What about the wall?" Janny sniffed as she leaned back to talk again.

"Not all monsters look like mixed up nursery rhymes. Some look just like men..."

"Were there people in those warehouses? Sam asked, standing and turning to look over his shoulder. The curve of the river and the height of buildings kept him from a direct line of sight on the plume of smoke. There was a pall spreading through the sky, but he couldn't tell if the townsfolk had put out the blaze.

CHAPTER TWENTY-NINE

The smell of kerosene roused Daniel before the crackle of flame, the wall of heat smacking him across the face or the mildly irritating smoke pouring through the stacks of goods like the tide coming in. Daniel had never seen the ocean, but three of his throng had. They held great reverence for it. The waves, the tide, the storms able to lift great ships like leaves on the wind. These memories drew him, promising more, lifetimes of experience, knowledge, at his metaphorical fingertips.

A flash of pain and searing light broke Daniel from his daydream. He stood from his resting place, and the others followed his lead, all but the one which had burned. It was quick. Quicker than he expected. He supposed the changes Abyss was wreaking in their bodies made them something he couldn't really predict. Many of them were no longer meat to roast over a flame, but would catch and be consumed like oil.

He went to the door. It rattled, but wouldn't open. It was blocked from without, he realized. He scanned around for another egress and the sensory overload of so many other sets of eyes also looking dropped him to his knees.

While he was down, one of his throng found a glass bottle, shattered, reeking of blazing kerosene atop a sack of oats. He tried to direct that body to pick up another sack of oats and throw it on top, to smother the fire, but the sack only glanced off the pile, toppling it, spreading the kerosene and spilling the bag. Oats and a cloud of oat dust displaced a cloud of smoke and immediately exploded.

The sliding barn door flew off the warehouse, while the concussion knocked many of the throng prone. A few caught fire. Many shook off the damage and shuffled for the opening to the street. Pulling himself along the wall, Daniel made it out, fell to his knees, breathing in the cool fall air. A Silver Hillian ran over to him to help him up, then fell back, face twisted in fear. The man crab-walked backward a few paces, stumbled, rolled over and got his feet under him and ran.

Instinctively, Daniel reached out a hand toward the fleeing figure. A line of tiny black cages shot forth, piercing his neck and vanishing within. The man turned and ran back to Daniel, helping him up. The fresh ones with a bit of themselves left appeared to be the most helpful. He didn't have to concentrate to direct their every movement and they didn't mimic his every act. He just told them what to do and they had enough consciousness left to comply. When the man touched him, the connection was improved and the other's memories flooded into his mind. What had been a frightening deluge the first few times was now like adding a book to a shelf.

Daniel called to those remaining inside the warehouse. Most stood, some lay inert, the connection still present, but the physical mechanisms of the body failing in the face of the heat. Those who could shambled out of the building. He commanded the new guy, Earnest, to pat those on fire down to put them out.

"We must go, but where?" Daniel asked. The throng murmured a slurred and mangled response, his own words distorted, but he answered his own question as he thought of Abigail. "Up the mountain," he said. And they marched.

Abigail looked back up at the office door and saw what her mind had refused to see before. The shapes within were not indistinct to her at all. They were not shadows in a dim room. They stood, crouched, and shambled, blazingly black silhouettes of distorted human forms. Mother, Father, Mr. Klin and the others were saturated by whatever was growing up her arm. She could not help but think, *How much longer until I'm like you? Unable to think clearly? Unable to step into the light?*

"They're all..." Abigail started, but couldn't finish her sentence.

"They're what? Did you see something?" Martin asked.

"Tell me, do *you* see anything?" Abigail said, holding out her hand, palm down.

"It's your hand," Martin said. "Wait, do you mean...?"

"Did one of them scratch you? I don't see anything, either," Thomson asked.

"Not today... but yes, Martin? I think it's the same thing from that first trip we took into the woods. We chased after monsters? So sure that the miners' tales were real."

"That turned out right," Martin said defensively. "They were real, more real than I'd ever realized. Scarier, too."

"That thing that wasn't a butterfly... I hadn't realized anything had happened at the time. I had an itch. I thought maybe it was just an irritation from a scratchy bush or tree bark. But then there was a mark, a little grouping of black lines like tally marks when you're counting something. One, two, three, four," Abigail said, drawing her finger down through the air in a series of short parallel lines. "Five." She slashed across the imaginary lines she had made.

"Perhaps you drew on yourself while you thought. I know many students who trace flowers or geometric designs while they study," Thomson said. "Sometimes they don't even realize they've done it."

"I'm sure I didn't, Professor. And anyway, they've grown. I haven't had the luxury to study very often over the last few weeks, and when I did, it was all reading, no real notes to speak of, no pens. But they've spread. You don't see anything at all? Here? Here? Reaching up here?" She traced some of the major peninsulas of the growing map of shadow on her skin.

"No, I'm sorry. I don't like to say it, but perhaps the stress of recent events..." Thomson said.

"I am *not* mad!" Abigail said, eyebrows knitting together. She felt the growing sheath of darkness wriggle on her wrist in response to her outburst. A shiver ran down her back and she resolved to maintain control. For so long, she'd had to watch herself lest she reveal her knowledge of engineering, of science, the classes Martin was meant to be studying but constantly shirked.

She'd had to pretend to be dim, ready to give up her own interests and life for some random man her parents would no doubt choose for her. One of the few blessings of living so far from the big cities was that there weren't many young men her parents approved of, and the one she did socialize with, they didn't care for.

"But I think *they* are! Run!" She sensed suddenly a throng of beings pouring forth from the mine entrance, though she was looking away from it. The radiant black ore running through the mountain had shrouded their presence from her new sense, but now they neared the surface. She grabbed Martin's wrist, forcing him to drop the basket, and pulled him toward the other end of the long office building, away from the windows and door.

"What are you talking about? Who?" Martin asked, looking around, but then Thomson was behind the twins, doing his best to catch up despite his limp, which was much more noticeable at speed.

"Go! They're armed!" The professor urged. Abigail could hear the clang of metal picks and shovels striking one another as the miners disgorged themselves from the mine. She pulled up short at the end of the wall, peering around to see what happened when they came into the sunlight, but the skeletal figures, mining clothes hanging off them, helmets askew, kept forward without pause.

"That's not good," she said. "Mr. Miles exploded in the sunlight. They're getting stronger."

"Miles did what?" Thomson asked, hobbling into the cover provided by the building.

Sam turned back to Janny, taking her by the shoulders, noting soot on her blouse, in her graying hair, smudge on her jawline just below the ear. "Were there people, Janny?"

"Not anymore. They weren't people no more. They were monsters. The monsters can't stand light, fire. They were hiding, resting, planning in there. Planning their next attack. I attacked first," Janny rambled. Sam released her shoulders and nodded. *Just seeing the giant bear with three heads might have cracked any mind apart. But being forced to set off dynamite, potentially killing the girl Abigail, facing other horrors in the days since... Arden Miles...* Sam shivered at the thought. That scene would stick with him for the rest of his life, he already knew...

A great explosion rocked the row of houses. Fire reached into the sky, confirming the conflagration was still active. There was nothing he could do now, not for the people Janny thought were possessed.

"We should go see the sheriff," he suggested, taking her hand firmly.

"They set the Pick on fire," Janny mumbled, not resisting as he walked up the street. "Where are we supposed to wet our whistles now?"

"The saloon? Is that the other smoke I saw? How did that happen?" Sam pressed.

"They came in, a whole peck of 'em, gray and saggy like old rags hanging on a rack to dry. I don't know what started it, but I was headin' in and saw... The bar... Twisting, grabbin' ol' Smitty... It... I... then there was crashin' and a lamp got smashed. All that liquor up in flames... Real shame..." Janny smacked her lips.

"I think that's the least of our problems right now. So there's a gang of ghouls in Silver Hill? All the more reason to find the sheriff," Sam said, increasing his stride.

"Gang, yes, Swindon, that's right," Janny said dreamily.

"That Rudolph fella Beckett fired for stealin'? He's at the head of this trouble?"

"He was there, as gray as the rest, but Daniel... I'm sure Daniel was the leader." Suddenly, Janny's grip on Sam's hand increased and he paused to look back at her. "Daniel's got the Devil in him! I saw it! I saw him do magic, reach out and make the bar rise up and take down poor Smitty. Lifted him right up and threw him! We should tell Sheriff Hornsby!" Back in the moment, Janny released Sam's hand and started to run.

"That's what I've been sayin'!" He hollered after her, then gave chase.

Janny pulled up short at the turn onto Main Street, backpedaling to the corner of the post office. Sam caught up, struggling for breath. He tried to peer around the bricks, but

Janny waved an arm out to the side, keeping him back.

"What is it?" Sam whispered.

"Daniel and his army."

"'Army?' Please..." Sam said, taking off his hat and edging up to look for himself. 'Army' was no exaggeration. There were easily a hundred men and women, not exactly marching, but moving in lockstep as perfectly as if a band were playing. He could practically hear Johann Strauss's music popping along with the hundreds of feet coming down in perfect unison. Such organization and discipline was disturbing. He expected a ragtag group of half-dunk miners and bandits leaning on each other to keep their feet. This group appeared much more formidable. "How did the boy do it?" he asked in awe.

"No boy no more, he's lit by the Devil, I tell ya. There's a darkness teemin' all around 'em all, like a swarm o' flies thick as fog."

"I don't see anything," he said.

"You ent been touched by it. Those who have can see, that's what the Paiute said. If you eat a tainted critter or plant, it gets in you. If one bites you, its gets in you."

"Something bit you?" Sam asked.

"Thought it was a hummin'bird, months ago now. I was on m' way up to the Landin' and it was zippin' around between flowers. It buzzed on over to me and landed on my shoulder. Next thing I know, that pointy nose went right through my shirt and its belly started fillin' up with red. Ever since, I could see it. That Abigail girl has it, like me, sleepin', not like Daniel. It's runnin' through him like a rabbit in a carrot patch."

"Abigail?" Sam said.

CHAPTER THIRTY

Abyss called to Daniel inexorably. He looked up at the mountain in the early afternoon light. He saw the ore, glaring in its stark contrast to the trees and earth, seething there beneath the ground, ready to spill forth onto the surface. *I have learned so much. These last days with you, your connection to the other humans, your world. I must see more, touch more. You will come. You will free me.*

But the sunlight. Daniel tried to protest.

I understand it better now. It is the source of the other kind of life, that which infests the surface of this planet. What your people learned over eons, to make clothing to protect yourselves, shelters against weather, I have grasped in weeks. You are proving a most useful tool. And as you help me, I can help you. Come. Walk freely in the sunlight. It will no longer harm you.

Daniel took one tentative step out of the shadow cast by the buildings of Main Street. For the first time in days he felt the sun upon his skin. It prickled, uncomfortable, too hot, but he did not feel himself dying, Abyss being burning away. His mouth drew up in a sneer and he set his shoulders toward the East Gate. Behind him, a hundred and ten Silver Hillians strode, left, right, left, right. He led his own parade, his own army into battle.

He reached out to others who had been touched by Abyss. Across the town, teapots dropped onto kitchen floors, darning needles swung at the end of their thread, chairs fell backward as townsfolk who had been meaning to see Doctor Le Guin marched out their own front doors.

Ahead, he could feel the animals, the plants Abyss had first taken, turn their attention to him. He directed them to go to the road, to join the army as it came by. They would multiply the workforce carving Abyss from the earth's grip and throw down any opposition.

The miners were not just wraiths of their former selves, manic slaves like those in the offices. They were covered, head to toe in black dust. Sludge trailed behind them on the thin grass and pounded dirt of the Landing.

"Don't hide, Abigail," a voice came from the crowd. Abigail couldn't help but peek again. She immediately regretted it. Peter Smalls, foreman of the mining operations stood, rock dust in his short helmet of hair, actual helmet hanging off his neck by a strap. He had a few slashes in his denim overalls, and his whole person effervesced with the black marks. "Abyss doesn't want to hurt you. It needs you. You and Daniel, and the professor, you have unique minds, knowledge and insight and something I don't know how to say, a kind of magic, maybe..."

"Magic?" Thomson scoffed. "Superstition and hokum have no place in the laboratory or any serious discussion."

"It may not be the best time, Professor," Martin pointed out. "We are deeply outnumbered and they are armed with metal tools meant to break rock."

"Point taken, lad," Thomson said in a lower tone.

"Abyss. Is that what you're called? You infected my body through an innocent looking animal. You come to me in my dreams, trying to infect my soul with another, which you devour and expect me to stand still for that? How dare you? You take my parents from me? Worse, prance them around like puppets..."

"You misunderstand me, my dear," Smalls' voice shifted,

became more sibilant like he was using too much air with every syllable. "When your world was very young, the light bombarding it slammed the tiny bits of myself that were near the surface, breaking me down, changing me. Much of that material was lost... died... but some survived, it rooted itself in chemicals that it could move, bond together, build on each other. In small pieces, my parts are not very aware, insightful, but as they... we... accumulate, we gain complexity, understanding, intelligence.

"When I interact with certain structures which have evolved on their own, under minimal direction, certain minds, I can see so much more. Your memories are exquisite pieces of art that I relish. I want to learn more. You can help me. I can help you in return. Oh the things we will learn, wonders we will build! My little stray sheep. You've done so well for yourselves, but it's time to return to the fold."

"What is he talking about, Abigail?" Martin asked. "Mr. Smalls?"

"It's not Peter. There's something... in the ground, in the rock. When the number nine shaft was sunk, they hit something. You could call it a vein. All those stories? Of giants and strange creatures, all of the things we saw, from the bird-headed worm to the great bear mother... They were all Abyss trying to figure out... life. With the mine, a lot more of the vein of Abyss was released all at once. It... got into everything, everyone we see here. It got into me, but for some reason, it hasn't done to me what it did to Peter, or to Mother and Father."

"So harsh. I'm not *doing* anything to anyone. I'm just guiding you home. The more that join, the more powerful we will all be."

"All that... sludge..." Martin said. "They aren't even mining silver anymore. It's just that... stuff..."

"I think it just implied that this *stuff* is the spark of life, that it's somehow responsible for all of us thinking and moving and doing... anything. The very idea is sacrilege. It's vainglorious self-regard on an order I've never witnessed, even amongst doctors and scientists," Thomson observed.

"Sacrilege. I have seen this word in many minds. It is an unexpected event, this deep understanding that *something* came before you, created you, and that such creation brooks reverence, and yet here, now, you have no reverence."

"Because you are a charlatan, a monster! You claim in effect, in every way but saying the words themselves that you are God!" Thomson's voice shook with his rising temper. "Yet you do not create! No! You only mutilate! Degrade! You cause the natural creatures of the world, this good, green earth, to become stricken, mixed and twisted in ways that turn the stomach! To raise yourself up so high is laughable! Ha! You are nothing but a thief! A second rate artist who steals parts of another's creations and sets them together and calls them new! Ha!"

As Thomson railed, Abigail's attention was pulled away by movement along the ridge above the Landing. At first, she saw shadows moving in the brush, but then bleached-white patches showed through the leaves.

"So vehement, so little understanding," Abyss said through Peter Smalls. "If you join me, you will remember such history, past the formation of this planet, this universe. The old universe, my universe, was so different from this one. You would not understand it on your own, but through my experiences, you would see how everything worked, how everything works in your world. I am the only path to such knowledge."

"Science is my life. I will learn what I can, and that will have to be enough. Selling my soul for some promised wisdom is a trick so blatant I can hardly believe ones of such will, such insight, as the Becketts, building up a whole town from a single mining plot, would fall for it," Thomson said.

"That's it..." Abigail said. "They didn't *all* build up from nothing. That was my parents. The other engineers may have had to exert greater will, or perhaps will in a different way to make it through all of their classes, earn their credentials. Abyss wants people with strong wills, but sometimes the will is too strong... Strong enough to resist. Everyone in that office is infected, like me, but they don't speak with his voice. They speak for themselves, even though they're trapped in their own minds, memories damaged, perhaps, living the same days over and over again. Are you trying to wear them down, Abyss? Have they been resisting you for all these weeks?"

"Resist? Who would resist ultimate knowledge? The greatest power ever seen in the universe? In any universe. The ability to *transcend* universes! Why would they resist?"

"Maybe they saw that you were making puppets of the miners. You tried to get into their minds. You probably even sent the miners against them. That's why they nailed the doors shut. I see you, now, Abyss. You send me visions, dreams, but Professor Thomson's right. You can't create anything new and you're not God. We can resist you, and we *will.*"

"You said it, sis!" Martin chimed in. She had the feeling he hadn't really followed everything that was going on, but she appreciated the support. She glanced up again at the white amongst the green. What was it? Albino squirrels? Some kind of walking mushrooms? She had the vague sense her mind was missing something, leaving something out of her understanding.

"You're so angry, child. It's true not every experiment I've done has succeeded, but that is the way of science, is it not? To hold an idea in one's mind, to test it, to watch how the test fails, and create a new idea? You saw some of my less successful interventions, before I knew anything about this world outside of the stone and dirt. I was groping in the dark," As Abyss spoke the miners crept closer. Shovels and picks were laid on the dirt. Peter Smalls' body was only a few feet away from Abigail. She could see the marks she thought now must be some form of script. Indecipherable as she found it, there did seem to be a kind of order, patterns.

"...finding my way by touch." On Abyss' final word, the miners lunged, trying to grab Abigail, Martin, and Thomson. Smalls' fingers grazed Abigail's arm as she swatted another Abyss-encrusted miner's hand away from touching her brother. Martin stumbled onto his backside, while Thomson ducked one hand clawing toward his face and shoved the offender back with both arms. The miner fell against two others, who, without missing a beat, caught him and tipped him back up to where he could balance himself again.

"Professor! No!" Abigail cried out, too late. She watched a splotchy web of black across his hands settle into his flesh.

"I'm all right!" The older man said. From behind the throng came crashing. Objects flew from the office door. A wastepaper basket clanged loudly against one miner's dented helmet. A chair fell at the feet of another. Taking the opportunity Abigail was sure her parents were giving them, she stepped past Martin, gabbing his outstretched hand and hauling him up. She pointed to the wagon. The other two nodded and ran as quickly as they could.

The clangor increased behind them, but Abigail focused on the wagon. If she placed a foot there, grabbed that handle, she could get up to the driving bench in seconds and begin turning the vehicle around. It might be another harrowing ride down the mountain, but she felt it unlikely the miners would be able to keep up if she pushed the horses.

A long, narrow, white, object dropped from the cliff only a few feet in front of her. Involuntarily, she looked up, where it must have come from, and saw a host of other shapes that finally clicked in her mind. Tracking the massive number of pieces back over her shoulder, she saw bones raining down on top of the office building.

CHAPTER THIRTY-ONE

The thunderous hail of ribs and pelvises upon the top of the office building and the hollow clacks of femurs and radii and ulnas colliding in air and striking one another on the ground rose quickly, forcing Abigail to cover her ears. Deformed skulls and long bones with all manner of extra protuberances crashed into one another, a veritable osseous deluge. Amid this, Mr. Smalls' revenant stood smiling vaguely, unmindful of the spinning and bouncing assault from above. None of the bones, Abigail noted, seemed to hit any of the changed miners.

She nodded her head toward the wagon for Martin and Thomson to see, but the bones piled up especially to block their escape.

"My army grows," Abyss said through Smalls as the onslaught slowed. Still, Abigail barely heard. She was looking for any opening, a thin spot in the distribution of bones. She found none and settled in to wait to see what happened next. She half expected Martin to make a break for it, and if he did, she would be with him, but he stood, his hands over his ears against the racket as well.

Distracted, Abigail didn't see the vast, singular, black mass until a second before it smashed into the far side of the offices. The roof shattered, sending pieces of tin flying. The walls exploded, filling the air closer to the ground with shards of wood and nails. She shrieked, turning away, and felt a number of impacts, some rough and blunt, nearly knocking her for her feet, others sharp, impaling her shoulder.

Martin and Thomson cried out as well. When she looked up, Thomson was on the ground beneath a section of wall that had managed to remain intact. The frame hanging with broken siding pinned him to the ground.

The other thing she noticed stole her attention, though. An immense head swung one way, then the other as though looking for something, or testing the air. The great bear they had buried looked the worse for wear, with bone showing through along the side of the deformed skull and at the shoulder blade.

The head rose and she saw with horror another head below. There was no doubt that this was the same bear. Of course, how many giant bears could one mountain support? The massive bone field before its den no doubt supplied this onslaught. Did the bear know her? The black net of symbols still flowed around its body. That much of Abyss, all those brains to work with, it must. But what did it think?

The bones on the ground shifted around, trying to do something, form something. All of the bones suffered protrusions and warping.

She backpedaled from pure instinct, and tripped over a long bone that immediately began wrapping around her ankle. She yelped and kicked it away with her other foot, but another limb of unnatural design swept around from her right, across her field of vision, lifting her into the air. She struggled, but her arms were pinned to her torso by the appendages that lifted her, seemingly a long pair of curved praying mantis arm, joined at the elbow and jointed at the end, but all in bone.

Held in place as she was, Abigail could see the tiny clusters of marks she felt more and more certain were some kind of language, streaming through and over the bones, connecting them to Abyss and allowing him to animate them. She marveled at how much concentration that kind of thing must take, to individually control and assemble into groups so many bones, while also controlling so many people, or what had once been people...

She prayed that her parents were still in their husks, somewhere. A notion, the seed of a plan, began to form, but for now, she was utterly trapped and expected to be forced to listen to more of Abyss' justification for taking control over a whole town full of people, and killing others. It all sounded like the Devil pretending to be God, to her.

"You go that way, I'll go this. Rattle all the doors you can, get all the wagons and carts and horses you can together. We've got to stop Daniel. I don't quite know what he's up to, but it can't be good. There are a lot of people up at the mine, and even without strange magic, I think he and his gang could interfere with the machinery, making it even more dangerous for everyone up there," Sam said to Janny.

"You're tellin' me. You ever see a stamp throw a pin? A winch wire snap, sending a load of carts back down to miners without enough time or space to get outta the way? Ain't pretty. You head north, I'll take south. I'll meet you back here in twenty minutes."

"Do we have that much time?" Asked Sam.

"We'd better, 'cause most of these doors are businesses already closed up for the lack of custom these last weeks. Gotta get to actual houses. Tell 'em Janny sent ya if they don't listen right away. 'Sides, they're jus' walkin', an' slow at that. We'll catch 'em up easy with horses and carts."

At the first door, Sam paused. *What am I going to tell*

these people? What will convince them that they need to drop whatever they're doing and hook up whatever cart they have to ride up the mountain and... and what? Sam's writer mind spun and he nodded to himself. He rapped confidently at the door. Waiting, eyebrows raised, smile twisting his mouth, even mostly hidden beneath his mustache. The seconds passed. He began counting in his head. After a thirty count, he knocked again. Nothing. He began to count again. *If they don't answer this time, no one's at home and I move to the next.* He told himself.

The door swung open violently, striking furniture within the house. Before Sam Clemens stood a Goliath of a woman. She stood four inches taller than him, easily, and seemed to fill the doorway with broad, well-muscled curves. She also had an unhealthy pallor about her, nearly gray around the eyes and mouth. Barely looking down at him, she advanced. Sam scrambled out of the way, then turned to observe. *What are you going to do, big Bess? I can't fight you, that's sure. If you turn toward me I'll have to run, and hope that I can outpace you, or lose you in the alleyways. But I'm sure you knew them better than I, at least before the sickness got into you. Will you remember the turns and paths?*

The woman stepped off the stoop to the road and headed toward the East Gate. Sam watched for a few seconds, knowing he would likely see her again, and moved onto the next door.

"I saw her go!" A voice volunteered through the door before he could knock. "I knew she was sick. Tried to visit her yesterday, and she was laid out on the kitchen floor, dinner from the night before scattered across her and the boards. Worse, when I went to check her, the breakfast kept scatterin'! Eggs and ham squelched their way under the stove like rats caught at the cheese."

"That's quite an encounter, friend," Sam said. "Would you mind opening the door? I've got a lot of visits to make, and if I have to yell through the door for every one, I'll be hoarse before I go back to meet the army we're building."

"Can't do it!" The woman said. Got two children in here. Can't take any chances. Their father's up at the mine. Haven't seen him in three days."

"I'm very sorry to hear that. Keep the door blocked and those kids safe," Sam said. "I'm gathering folk to head up the mountain and find out what's really going on."

"God bless you, sir! And Godspeed!" A much younger voice piped up.

"And may He keep you!" Sam said, moving to the next house.

Abigail twisted in the creature's grip, to no avail. She did notice, though, something strange when she raised her hand to pull the bony appendages away. The mark on her hand and up her forearm tingled, pulled, as though a magnet pulling a bag of nails. The sensation was strange, unsettling, but when she pulled her arm away, she noticed the flow of tallies on the bones shifted, too. She experimented, bringing her arm up, then down, and saw the streams of black lines shift.

What if? She asked herself, but tried not to verbalize her idea even within her mind. Abyss could hear her. Instead, she began to hum a tune she had heard the miners sing many a night beside the bonfire. In her head, she kept the words as she set her experiment in motion.

Woodman, spare that tree! She lifted her arm again,

pressing it right against the bone.

Touch not a single bough! The lines of symbols pulled around the bone to her arm. The black on her own skin pulled, but didn't go far. It was anchored in her flesh, or something more meaningful.

In youth it sheltered me, As Abigail watched, the black marks gathered at the bone's surface closest to her arm, pooling, no longer flowing away, but many lines converging there. The pull intensified until she wasn't sure if she could pull away if she wanted to.

And I'll protect it now.

Just as she began to struggle against the force, there was a small explosion of black. The bones fell lax around her, then tumbled to the ground, separated by inches. She took her chance and ran to Martin, freeing him, and together they worked on overturning the wall pinning Thomson.

As they heaved and shoved, Abigail noticed an excruciating smell invading her nose, making her eyes water. She looked back at the massive bear skeleton and saw it splattered with a putrid slurry of... things she couldn't even bring herself to identify or dwell upon. The mess lay across the upward facing surface of the wall they worked on, the surrounding bone creatures, even the nearby cliff face. Her stomach rolled, warning her there wasn't much time until it disabled her with its discomfort.

Instinctively, she looked over at the outhouse. It certainly wasn't a priority in the current situation. Behind her, Abyss began to speak through Peter Smalls again, but she couldn't make out the words, between her remaining hearing loss after her earlier injury, the blood rushing through her ears, and all the other distractions.

As she moved her hands to another place on the shaky

assemblage of boards to try to help the professor, she saw the back of her arm. The black area had spread dramatically, reaching to her shoulder and wrapping around to nearly encompass her entire arm. Each of the tendrils had widened, branched.

Did the tallies from the bone creature holding me... go into *me? I saw the reaction, the explosion. It would have been a good tool against Abyss, but...*

Yes, our bond is stronger now. Feel my strength in you. Abyss teased, purely in her head now, a voice instead of a murmur. *Do as I say, as I will, and your parents can go. I don't need them. They aren't as...* suitable *as you.*

What about Martin? The professor?

They have their uses, their strengths, but you are far more important to the cause. Abyss said.

"Abigail! Push!" Martin insisted, straining with his side of the broken wall. Distracted, trying to focus on the job at hand, Abigail shook her head and thrust with both hands. The flesh of her affected hand shivered, writhed, and she saw black lines spread into the individual boards. She drew her hands back, dropping the wood. Thomson groaned.

The boards themselves began to twist and curl, pulling against the others and the still inert chunks of wood. Nails screeched as they pulled through. Abigail screeched as the long, flat pieces bounded away on jagged ends. Martin cried out and stepped back.

"What was that?" He demanded.

"I- I don't..." Abigail grabbed the main framing studs and willed the black symbols outward, trying to infuse them with the same energy as the previous boards. Nothing came out. The wood lay dead as it had a moment, a day, a week, a year before. She tried again, straining to recall exactly how it felt, what she had done to send the energy out the first time.

You can't get rid of me that easily. Abyss taunted. Bone creatures, which had been standing passively, began to lurch forward, closing the circle around the Beckett twins and the professor.

CHAPTER THIRTY-TWO

Arms and legs shaking with effort, Abigail and Martin managed to shift the lightened wall, tipping it up on one corner.

"Go! Professor! Crawl out!" Abigail cried as the wall neared its apex, wobbling already with their flagging control. The older man was stunned. He wouldn't be able to get himself out. Nearly to vertical, the wall began to fall back, the bottom edge, mostly composed of thinner clapboards, chipped and cracked, shedding chunks against the hard ground by the second. The whole wall dropped four or five inches at a time, each drop a shock into Abigail and Martin's arms. The whole thing flailed like a flag in the wind, threatening to fall apart as much as fall over and strike Thomson again.

Staggering forward, Abigail gauged where one of the central studs would be and turned herself around so her back would press against that spot, allowing her to use her legs to do the work and give her arms a break. Still, her legs shook at the effort. She looked at her arm. Was there less black than before? Had motivating those boards taken some of Abyss away?

Of course not, child. I am everywhere, in everything, just as the God you worship so. We are the same, He and I, and you and I. Everything is one. Life will win. It is our nature to find a way. Even as you search for a way to save your friend, you allow me to secure a structure around you.

A jail? Is that what this comes down to? Control? Keeping me here? Such lengths, all these miners, all these dead creatures' bones. You must not be very confident in your ability to hold me by sheer force of argument or will. That's it, isn't it? My will is what you want. Then why don't you try some of this? Abigail clenched and unclenched her hand, forming a fist which she drove upward into the weathered clapboards.

The boards splintered, flying upward, scratching her arm as it passed through. She closed her eyes, focusing on the cluster of black marks on her arm, sending them outward along the wood fibers embedded in her skin, into the grain of the boards. It flowed. Boards writhed. She directed the marks to the next and next boards, the thicker studs. The whole wall shimmied and leapt away, crashing through the bone wall and hurtling away even as the bones leapt back up into place, weaving together.

"That was something, girl, but you're missing the potential of an alliance with me, with us," Peter Smalls continued to speak Abyss' words. "You are surrounded, outnumbered."

Did you switch back to speaking through Mr. Smalls because you're talking to all of us? Or because I divested enough of your darkness that you can't hear my thoughts or talk in my head anymore? Go ahead, answer if you can."

"I can hear you just fine, girl," Abyss said. "But you must choose to hear me, or I will be forced to consume you all and simply seek more amenable specimens."

"Ha! Good luck with that, boyo!" Martin said. "Or, whatever. I know you're not really Peter. You're some kind of black sludge stuff that infects our brains and makes us say strange things. Maybe you're the same stuff that mixes up the creatures in the forest..." At first, Abigail wanted to cut Martin off, but then she felt the rhythm of his speech and realized he was drawing Abyss in. She had a moment to think, formulate.

The wagon seemed hopeless now. There were so many

skeletal creatures that they could swarm the area and prevent the wagon from moving. They might already be infecting the horse. *By the time I knock another hole in the wall and get through, using whatever means, the horse might already be a skeleton controlled by Abyss, whatever it really is, as Martin pointed out. What if this is all just a mass hallucination? Exposure to some toxic chemical in the mine?*

No, if that was true, there would be no giant bear skeleton, no smashed office, no scratches down my arm. In fact, most likely, I would be back at the estate, lying in my bed, perhaps strapped to it. At least then, this would be only my nightmare to bear, and not that of so many in Silver Hill. No illnesses, no death, no resurrection and explosion...

Daniel walked up the wagon path in the warming afternoon, largely sheltered by the thick canopy of leaves above and to the west, as the trees on the slope below grew high enough to provide some comfort. His attention remained on watching the events of the Landing unfold, with the giant bear crashing down onto the office and Abyss directing the massive array of bones from the bear's cave. The animation of such simple remains, bones only, without a brain or muscles gave Daniel hope that there was a way to restore his father.

Of course I can elevate your father back to his previous level of consciousness. I can do anything! Especially with your help. The Beckett girl is proving to be most difficult, even to the point of kicking me out of her body. Not entirely, but what's left is not enough to speak with her inside her head, plant thoughts, let alone enough to overcome her will and get her to submit.

Yeah, she's not much for submitting. I think it's from getting her way too often. I love her, but she's spoiled like an apple crawling with hornets.

I hope you're free enough with your attachments that you're willing to find another, one more agreeable to our goals.

A horn blew. The sound cut through Daniel's conversation, persisting with a rousing call to charge. From lower on the mountain, Daniel saw horses and drawn wagons advancing at nearly twice the pace of the Abyss-laden Silver Hillians. Behind them, a legion of miners and townsfolk not touched by Abyss carried pitchforks and shovels. As he watched, horses with only riders neared even faster, kicking dirt and grass into the air as they approached.

The lead horse pulled up at the tail of Daniel's army. A man in a white linen suit yelled something Daniel couldn't hear for himself. He tuned into the throng closest to the rider.

"...ver Hillians deserve, as every man, to determine their fates for themselves, not to be led by illness or madness to destroy themselves and their fellows in a haunted wood!"

"What are you talking about?" Daniel called back, the wave of gray faces mimicking his words rolled down the trail like a ripple in a river, the form distorted as it bounced off obstacles. Daniel growled to himself and trotted toward the stranger. "What do you want?" he called from much closer, trying to suppress the throng copying him.

"I want you to turn around, take these people back to town. We'll send for doctors. Everyone will be seen to," the older man, around Pa's age, said with some authority.

"We have a doctor! Raise your hand, doc," Daniel commanded, and Doc Le Guin, still bound to Pa, lifted one arm like a bird flapping its wing. After a moment, the arm flopped back down.

"He's... as ill as the rest of you," the man in white said. "I think you sho-" Daniel raised his own hand before him. The throng followed suit, a sea of arms reaching toward the oncoming army. He stepped forward. Left. Right. Left. Right. Terrence Davies' gray hand touched the stranger's nervous horse on the shoulder. It whinnied, but Abyss flowed into it, spreading quickly. Davies fell to the ground, no longer animated by Abyss as the whole of what had inhabited the body moved into the horse. It bucked, resisting, and the man in white tumbled to the ground, rolling over the side of the trail and down the slope toward the river.

Daniel ordered his army forward. A few of the townsfolk swung shovels, jabbed with pitchforks, but all the throng had to do was touch their attackers. Smaller transformed insects and birds also swooped in, making contact with the townsfolk. Abyss quickly inhabited the humans, growing Daniel's influence. The horses were taken, too, sacrificing the few for new troops as the horses and riders fused, creating terrifying centaurs with horse heads emerging from human bellies and feet merging with the horses' shoulders, only boot toes left exposed.

Abigail, resolved that this was all in fact happening and not a dream, despite all logic to the contrary, signaled to her brother. *We're getting out of here. Maybe find a ventilation tunnel to hide in to regroup.* She thought as she charged the bone wall. She planted her feet firmly and pressed her hands, fingers spread, against a skull on her right and a hip bone on the left. She closed her eyes and envisioned the black symbols streaming across the wall.

Nothing happened for a long moment. She turned her affected arm and pressed it against a long bone, getting her own bit of Abyss as close to the wall as possible.

"It won't work, you know," Smalls said from very close by. She imagined she felt his breath on her ear. The web of tally marks undulated and shifted like the surface of water and she was reminded of the lake in her first dreams of Abyss. The entire wall before her turned black like a curtain falling, then she felt as though *she* was falling.

Abigail plummeted through the darkness for some time, vaguely aware of time passing, of feeling some unidentifiable sensation, but unable to see even her own hands before her face, if in fact she was really moving her hands. Or she had hands. She searched around herself for any sign of light, of heat or cold, of anything by which she could judge her speed or direction.

At first it was the tiniest of tugs, like a light breeze, but pulling instead of pushing. Over time, the pull increased. She directed her attention to where she thought she was moving, and felt the pull grow ever so slightly. Experimentally, she pulled back, trying to move away from the source of the force. The pull continued to increase, but at a somewhat slower rate. She chose another direction, and found no real resistance, but still pulled to the side.

No matter what direction she willed herself, the pull increased over time, slower or faster. She was not certain she wanted to go in the direction of the pull. What force had leashed her? Claimed her for its own? Abyss came to mind, a darkness, not unlike this one, but with a will to consume, contain, capture other life.

Not consume, but infuse, improve. Only certain formulations of matter react to me. That is a sign that it is mine, and I should have all that is mine. You, Daniel, to a lesser degree Thomson, have something even more special than the other organic collectives. "Organic" relating to an organ or instrument. Do you like music? I find it such an interesting subject. That certain sounds, certain patterns, are more enjoyable than others. I suppose that's simply the way of things. Some things are more compatible than others. Like you and I.

"We are *not* compatible," Abigail said, disgusted.

Of course we are. At the lowest level, I find organic molecules to be most easily motivated. Metals, ores, are restrictive, so stodgy.

Abigail saw in the void a dimly glowing cloud of matter, falling, swirling, into a central point, like a drain. She slipped into the clouds and felt them condensing around her.

Organics are so much more reactive. I've waited so long to move. *Oh, there were some bacteria and other tiny, primitive creatures, some stray clumps of atoms I could direct, but they were insensate, unable to really grasp what was going on around them.*

Abigail saw herself, stretched like taffy, pinned between layers of rock.

When I found ants, the world exploded for me. I could see, smell, sense vibration. They were my first miners. We dug around, doing mostly as ants do, until I found a-

"A bear den? A female bear with cubs?"

So clever, yes. I didn't understand how the bears worked, where one ended and the next began. Ants had discrete forms, hard edges I found easier to interpret. With the bears, I experienced such a leap in even their sleeping minds, such an expansion on the experience of joining with the ants, that I moved on the whole mass.

"What about the hybrids? The mixed species?" Abigail asked, finding herself involuntarily drawn into the ancient being's narrative.

I'm sure you can figure that out. After the bears, but before I saw the miners, each walking independently, I came upon pairs of things, caterpillar and leaf, worm and bird. Each time I move into a creature, I take on the shape of the vessel, like water. I can only understand as far as the creature is capable of. The smaller brains, less sophistication in so many ways, were like wrong turns in a labyrinth.

But then there was you.

The sophistication of your nervous systems, your brains, your memories *gives you a sense of time, something which I had been battling with since it began. The ability to hold the past in one metaphorical hand and the future in the other, weighing them, often incorrectly... But I can see to that, guide you, show you...*

CHAPTER THIRTY-THREE

Sam lay in the brush atop a layer of dead leaves, staring up at the afternoon sky through the mixed canopy of increasingly naked oak and maple branches and dark clouds of redwood needles. The battle on the road above was mostly the buzzing and flapping of Daniel's flying minions and the gasps and moans of those on the ground. Shovels and picks and such mostly just thumped to the earth.

"Get up," he whispered to himself. "Get up, get up, getup getup getupgetupgetup." Finally he found it in himself to roll over, muscles across his back and neck crying out, threatening to spasm. Dark specks of detritus clung to his suit, his hair. He couldn't see his hat, but that was the least of his worries.

Warily, he crawled forward, taking shelter behind a boulder to peer out onto the road. The horsemen were all literally horse-men now, fused and mingled in a way that turned Sam's stomach. A few of the townsfolk were still wrestling with Daniel's crew, but only a few out of nearly seventy men and women who had agreed to join the cause and stop whatever was going on remained.

Sam spotted Janny and almost waved, but caught himself. She held a shovel across her body. One of the gray men alternated mechanically between pushing it toward her and trying to pull it away. While they struggled, another young woman walked up beside her and caressed her face with a gray hand. A gray caste spread around her eyes and mouth, the line of her neck. Sam watched the fire drain away from her eyes. Her hands fell to rest at her sides. The shovel hung in the man's hands for a long second, then fell with a muted clang. Sam's heart sank even more for the one amongst the crowd he felt he knew best.

I'm sorry, Janny. I failed you. I shall remember you. He promised silently.

The rest of the Silver Hillians stood stock still, awaiting orders. Sam couldn't even hear them breathing, though they numbered over a hundred and a half now. No one struggled, let out a single noise or was being held by the other side. No one even seemed injured in the traditional sense. They all wore gray masks of Abyss, a blank look in their eyes and slack expressions.

Daniel turned back uphill and began walking. Everyone around him walked in the same fixed step with him as Sam had observed back in town. It chilled his blood to watch it. What could the boy accomplish with over a hundred unflinching, unthinking soldiers? What happened when it became a thousand? Ten thousand? Could the world stand against such a force? Growing by the battle, no resistors left...

"Wait!" Daniel called out suddenly, turning south, toward the river, the side of the road where Sam lay. "What about the one in white? The one who led the new ones to me? Where is he?" Sam slid down behind the rock to keep from drawing attention. The dry leaves rasped and hissed. He winced, stopped, his body half under a bush. He tried to dig his arms under the loose leaves.

The enthralled townsfolk stepped forward slowly as one, and again, reached into the bushes. Some were displaced by a few boulders or the thickest of bushes, but the rest charged through, slow step after inexorable slow step. A muddy boot came down right beside Sam's head. The mix of dirt and horse manure churned into the road in town pressed up into his nose, threatening to make him sneeze. His eyes watered.

One of the possessed Silver Hillians cried out, a strangled, wordless, flag of sound that wavered in the still air and died away. Sam shrunk into himself as best he could, dreading the cool touch of a gray hand.

"That's just a hat! Leave it!" Daniel yelled in disappointment. "He's gone. Let's go." The Silver Hillians retreated up the mountain with a slow, steady, synchronized gait. Sam listened to them leave, waited until he couldn't hear their steps or moans anymore, then waited a few minutes more.

Finally, he sneezed, over and over. He leaned against one of the boulders, handkerchief in hand, assessments of the encounter whirring around in his head. Things had gone so wrong, and it was all his fault. He didn't know all of the creatures could pass the sickness, and with the merest of caresses, no biting or injecting... They had lost so many more citizens, so many able defenders of the town. If Daniel came back down the mountain, he would face very little resistance.

Untold ages of time passing weighed down on Abigail. Abyss had been less than conscious, at least as she understood it, dormant, numb to the world until life, its own lost body, changed by this alien world, found its way home.

Home, yes. Do you see? The light tried to destroy us, and you survived. You went on and on, changing, spreading. I have one form, but you have learned a barely imaginable myriad! Many even take that damnable sunlight and eat it, using it to grow! That amazes me beyond explanation.

"I only have one form, one body. But do you even have one? You're a fluid, taking the shape of whatever you're poured into, with no true form yourself. From what you say, away from a body, a brain, you're not even intelligent. Even that is something you steal from others. You claim to be God, but you are the farthest thing from it. You are a lie."

Hoping to catch Abyss off guard, Abigail threw herself toward Peter Smalls. She wrenched at the darkness in him. She could feel it move, sway toward her, break free, finally, and pour into her. Both hands were black as though she'd plunged her arms into a bucket of ink up to the elbows, then the darkness rolled up even farther.

She stared into Peter's eyes, hoping to see the moment when the spark of awareness returned, but instead, as Abyss left him, he froze in place. His eyes turned milky. The paleness, an ashen gray, spread outward from them, across his face, down his neck, across his torso until a breeze kicked up and he blew away like a pillar of smoke, his features eroding in seconds. The whole head, then body collapsed in a cloud that settled on the packed dirt and blew into the pool of waste around the broken office walls.

It is not. Abyss said in her head.

"It is not so easy to get rid of me," one of the other miners said, the words echoing across the rest of those gathered.

"Peter..."

"There was nothing left of who he was, only what I made him. When you took that way from him, you killed him," the miner said.

"Me? You blame *me?* You killed him, probably days ago, weeks? The fact that you made his body a puppet, that he still moved and spoke the words you made his tongue form doesn't absolve you."

Abigail scowled, fighting tears for all those Abyss had taken from Silver Hill. She quickly lost, water streaming down her cheeks. "He had life. Whether what you say is true, even if life came from you, somehow, that doesn't give you the right to take that life away."

"You do it all the time. A farmer plants corn and wheat and a hundred other crops for the purpose of harvest. This is no different. In fact, I gave more of myself than the farmer, who kills continually, reaping weeds and killing animals that might consume his bounty. You *are* of my body, my children, even."

"We are not your children, or if so, you are no parent, leaving us to live, without guidance or aid for all these eons?" Abigail pushed back, wiping the tears from her face.

"In that I had no choice, and I am here now. You may rejoice as your songs say, in my return."

"We don't have any songs about you."

"You have many songs of the grace of God, the power and majesty of the being that brought Man to life, created the birds and the fishes and the beasts of the field," Abyss argued via the miner.

Abigail turned away at this. *Blasphemy!* She screamed inside her head. She crossed her arms and headed back toward Martin and Thomson. They sat, leaning against one another, exhausted, injured. Beyond them, though, the wall had refined. Shadow no longer filled crevices. There were none, just a smooth, singular surface. The bones were no longer individual, organic units, no matter how deformed.

"How? Why?" She asked, the words coming of their own accord.

"Do you like my castle? Daniel has always dreamed of a castle, high on a mountain, overlooking a kingdom he ruled beside a beautiful queen. You didn't know he had such imagination, did you? There are many unexpected things in life."

"But the bones..."

"You do not use the bones of the trees as they fall. You split them into planks, nail them together into walls and doors and chairs. Why should I not optimize the form of my building material? The wall will remain even if you steal my essence from it. It will continue to be strong."

"So you're saying we're trapped."

"Abigail," Thomson said weakly from his place on the ground. He was a disheveled as she had ever seen him, hair in disarray, coat smeared with dirt and spatter from the office exploding. "I don't know what exactly is going on, but it seems that there's some... entity that can move into living beings, yes?"

"Yes, its calls itself Abyss. It can move into dead things, too, animate them in some unnatural fashion."

"What is unnatural? If all of nature comes from me, and I interact with it, it is the ultimate in natural events," said the miner.

"Most things in this world cannot simply pass through other things. They cannot occupy the same space," Thomson pointed out.

"But Abyss can, just like..." Abigail saw where Thomson was leading her, but tried not to bring the information into focus, to the front of her mind, lest the creature see whatever plan arose from the thought.

She looked around for something into which she could push the Abyss she contained, to free her mind from being read. The dirt was hard packed, holding only pebbles and devoid of grass or other plants. The walls of the office were a possibility. The front of the structure still stood, however precariously, but she sensed her parents still within.

Inspiration struck and she shucked off a riding boot. She held it up, considering. *It's leather. It should work.* She held the brown, calf-high boot in both hands while balancing on one foot. The stocking clad toes of her other foot hovered just above the cold dirt as she focused, trying to send Abyss into the long-dead leather.

What are you up to? You want a living shoe for a pet? I find humans make better ones. Abyss tried to distract her, but she focused, urging the ink-black marks on her arms into the immobile leather. Abyss resisted. She could feel it pulling back, trying to maintain its hold on her. Whatever he was getting from her, he had no intention of relinquishing it.

Of a sudden, black poured from her hands, flowing into the shiny brown leather, filling the scuff on the toe first, then diffusing into the whole leather piece, then the next, filling the entire boot in seconds. She immediately felt all the hours of sleep she had missed in the last week, all the missed meals, and she realized why her father had eaten so ravenously when presented with food. Had he found some way to free himself? At least partially? If she could learn how he had done it, it could help her.

The boot writhed and hopped in Abigail's hand. Now that she had it, she didn't know quite what to do with it. She dropped it on the ground and saw the miner who had been speaking for Abyss wiping dirt from his face. Abigail turned to Martin. He had another clod of dirt in his hand, bouncing it to test its weight.

"Thank you for breaking his concentration, brother," Abigail said.

"At your service, sister. Now get to whatever you were

going to do." Abigail nodded.

"Get that piece of tin roof. A knight needs a shield," Abigail said.

"A knight? That's not exactly what I wanted to be, but-"

"Just do it!" Abigail said, losing patience. She wasn't sure if the tin would have the same effect as the silver, but it was worth a try.

"Come!" A reedy voice called to her. A hand waved in the gloom just inside the doorway. Abyss' army was spread around the area inside the bone wall, but irregularly, clumped. None strayed too close to the offices. Abigail wondered if they still had some sense of smell.

Taking the chance, Abigail ran along the wall of the office building, under the blacked out window, vaulting up the three steps to the door and into the dank confines. The smell struck her immediately, even though she expected it. Fighting the urge to retch, even with an empty stomach, Abigail breathed through her mouth as much as possible.

"We heard through the opening back there," Father said, pointing toward the destroyed back wall where the private office had been. "You have some kind of connection with Abyss. It's different than for us." Abigail nodded.

“How did you rid yourself of him? When you broke free and came to dinner? The train station?” She asked.

“No time for that now. You’re strong enough on your own. You also have a plan. What do you need?" Father asked.

"I need silver," she said in a low tone between gulps of fetid air.

CHAPTER THIRTY-FOUR

Even as she searched around for a gap in the bone or the shadow holding it all together, Abigail watched the walls shift. The bone crept across the sky, blotting out the sun. Abigail stood, impressed. The majority of the bone wall was in the shadow of the trees, but this new arc through the air cut right across the open space. She understood that Abyss had developed a means to shield himself within people, but in the bare bones... This was not a good sign.

Come out, all of you. Abyss beckoned. *See how I have made it safe. The sun will not burn you.*

Abigail watched the arc complete its journey, creating a pavilion of bone. The black symbols converged into a solid mass above her. One side descended, cutting her off from her brother.

"What's happening? Where are you, Abigail?" Martin began to panic.

"It's okay," Abigail said, not at all certain it was. *What's Abyss' goal now? Besides to keep me present, imprisoned? Why does it want me at all? Why does it think I'm special?*

It's not just you. It's not just him, or me, it's him and me, or him and you. It's... what was that thing you tried to tell me about that time? About how things can be more than their parts? Another voice came to her head. One she immediately recognized, but couldn't reconcile with reality.

Daniel? Are you in my head, too?

I think it's more like Abyss is a telegraph wire, and you're Europe and I'm America and he's connecting us. He's making us more than we were, and we're making him more than he was on his own, down in the ground, more than he could be with ants or worms or even the bears.

Synergy? Are you talking about Synergy?

Yes! Thank you. I've been filling in the gaps, making sense of the jumble of nonsense they tried to cram into my head in school. Abyss has really helped me. Has he helped you, too? I mean, you were always smart, but there's always more to learn, more to understand, right? I know you were studying with martin's books.

I don't know. I don't think I've seen anything I would call help. I've been infected by some kind of black tally marks. I can see them in the things it's touched, tried to control. But I don't think it's made me keener, or, well... it did *show me something I couldn't quite grasp about the formation of the Earth and gas clouds...*

That was amazing, wasn't it? How gravity pulled all that stray matter into a swirling vortex of stuff that just kept squishing in farther and farther, heating up the inside, but crashing material together to make the surface, too? All that fire and rock, and eventually the ocean?

I'm impressed, more than impressed. Those are things not spoken of by scientists, yet you spin them off like you're telling the grocery clerk your order for the week. Not just that, but I understood it, too.

You've always been smart, Abigail, more than anyone I know, more than that Mrs. Marquez... Some school teacher she was.

Don't be too hard on her. She did her best with a classroom full of rowdy mine rats.

You didn't stick around too long.

Mother always wanted more for us. She had issues with Mrs. Marquez, too. She was upset that she wouldn't push Martin and myself harder, give us extra work to do. Never mind that that would all be extra work for her as well, creating the lessons, grading them, all while keeping you all on track. She took us out to give us tutors. We've gone through a dozen or so at this point, kind of like Abyss in a way, taking what they knew and leaving them by the wayside.

Abyss would never! Daniel objected. But was it him or Abyss creating the connection? Or maybe a combination of both... How much control did Abyss gain over them? If it could direct the miners and others to do as it pleased, what was it doing to their minds? Abigail and Daniel?

The space before Abigail shifted again into what she could only assume was a throne room of some kind. The chair form continued to rise on a dais, then split, drifting to the sides into two, which sat against the far wall. Fluted pillars and Romanesque statues alternated places to create an aisle to the foot of the platform where the thrones sat.

In the right throne sat a figure of deepest black. Squinting, she recognized the form, even if she couldn't make out the facial features.

"Daniel?" Abigail asked, apprehensive. "What are you doing here?" She had been talking to him in her head, but she didn't expect to see him. It was odd how Abyss making the distance feel like nothing was less jarring than the figure suddenly before her now.

"I'm here for you, my Queen. Come. Sit," the voice was a forceful whisper, loud enough to reach her ear, but it didn't seem quite like... "Sit!" The other commanded.

"I don't know who you think you are, Daniel Swindon, but I'm not much for being ordered around, by my parents, or my friends."

"Do you not recognize your King?"

"I don't have a king, this is America."

"America? No, I'm King of the World! With you by my side, we will dig mines on every continent, free more of Abyss, build an empire and live beyond anything you ever dreamed."

"What I dreamed? What do you know of my dreams? Do you think I'm here to rule? To lord some kind of power over people? Make demands and have subjects fawn over me?"

"If you don't want that, we can just slay them all. Once we have gathered enough Abyss, we'll have the power to do anything, build anything, go anywhere. None will stand against us," Daniel said.

But was it Daniel? Abigail began to have doubts. She could see where he might desire wealth, even power, to live above the subsistence his father could provide, but he had always been kind to her. Sometimes his efforts were misguided or overzealous, but he was a good person.

"Abyss, Abyss, Abyss... You're not Daniel at all, are you?" Abigail squinted at the dark mass. It was tightly woven, but she spotted a few holes, through which she saw only the bone wall and throne.

"I have his form. I have vast knowledge, experience. Soon I will exist free of these borrowed bodies."

"Stolen. Stolen bodies, from people you've *killed*," Abigail corrected.

"Everyone has to eat, this is just the way I do so. I've never had individualism before. It's quite fascinating. Before, the world just *was* around me. I passed through a worm, coming out more condensed, all else stripped away. That was a form of transcendence, like being refined. I went from the ore of myself to the true, shining metal. But being paired with humans is a revelation in understanding, of grasp of the world around me, of senses and memory and self!"

"All right, then, live your life. You don't need to kill anyone else. Experience human existence. Realize your potential as part of our society. Why do you need more?"

"Because I have no idea what I could be. Neither do you. When I was part of a worm, I had no idea what light was, or leaves on a tree. When I was a caterpillar, I could see, smell. I had mouth parts and could taste the leaf."

"And then you put the leaf on your back, pretending to be a butterfly."

"I was *better* than a butterfly. The leaves allowed me to turn sunlight into energy. Instead of tearing my essence apart, I made it work for me. The ultimate revenge."

"Ugh, revenge. You were born to be human, all right. No other animal worries about such pettiness. You've been given this gift of awareness, of communication and coherent thought. Why can't you just accept that and live?" Abigail asked.

"You changed from your initial form to your current form so gradually, you don't remember. You went through a time when you couldn't talk, couldn't walk."

"Of course."

"What about me? Today, I can talk and walk when I could not. What could I do tomorrow with all the essence of this area? Mine out this mountain, free myself... Who would I be? What could I do? I can't even answer that."

"What's going on here?" An annoyed voice demanded. Abigail turned and saw the real Daniel standing in a ragged gap in the wall with his arms crossed, a horde of Silver Hillians behind him, all mimicking his pose.

"Don't bother to answer. I can see it plain as day. You wanted her for yourself. You thought you could just be me and take over," Daniel said with a voice edged with iron.

"Don't flatter yourself. I used your template to grow, to come to a greater understanding of this world. Abigail is special beyond your petty grasp on the world and how it works. Even more than you, she provides a means for my mind to form, crystallize and reach far beyond anything I've been since being drawn into this existence," Abyss said.

Daniel charged. With a growl and the stomping of many feet across the throne room, he bore down on his shadowy doppelganger. He punched, thrusting his fist into the other's face, then through. With a small cry, he pulled his hand back as though he'd touched a hot stove. He shook his hand, stalking around in a circle, looking for an opening or a target he liked.

"Daniel, don't!" Abigail said, cutting off his next attack.

"He was trying to steal you."

"I was never yours. Not like that," she countered. "But I don't want you to get hurt. You're my friend. And I'm your friend."

"Friend? I have friends..." Daniel waved his hand at the townsfolk, who all waved back.

"Ah yes, about them... This was amusing, but now you're being troublesome," Abyss said. He reached out a hand, and the throng that led out into the Landing fell like puppets with their strings cut. Streams of black arcane symbols soared through the air toward Abyss. He grew larger. Stygian wings sprouted from his back out to the sides. His head grew broader, sprouting an array of haphazard horns on the top and sides. He grew a second pair of arms which lengthened and inflated with muscle.

Seeing what was happening, Abigail tried to pull some of the streamers of tally marks to herself, but only managed to absorb a small fraction. Unable to quell his growth, she opted for gathering what she could from other sources before it got a chance. The black slipped from the bone wall, slithering along the floor, up one stocking foot with a strange, spastic energy.

Farther out, she saw the miners, the bear, a swarm of smaller things that Daniel had gathered on his trip up the mountain, the remainder of the townsfolk who didn't fit on the ramp into the room. In the office, she spotted Mother and Father and the engineers. They looked different from the miners. Abyss had bonded with them in a more focused way. It was always learning. She had to do the same.

Well played. Abyss said in her head again.

Do you mean me? Or are you patting yourself on the back? Abigail wondered. Abyss laughed in her head and before her in its independent physical form.

"No! Those were mine!" Daniel objected. He reached out his hands dramatically as though to draw up Abyss from the walls around them. "Hey!"

"She beat you to that lot. I'll beat you to the next," Abyss taunted. In moments, the air filled with crisscrossing black streamers of tally marks. Abigail thought of Peter Smalls and feared for her parents. If Daniel or Abyss drew from them, that might be the end.

I would never! Daniel objected as though shocked she would think he would harm any Beckett. *We need to team up against this... Whatever it is.*

How do we do that? A voice disguised as Abigail's asked.

Don't listen to it! Abyss is trying to trick you!

If it can hear our thoughts, send thoughts to our heads,

how can we come up with a plan without it knowing?

That is something of a conundrum, isn't it, children? Thank you for absorbing so much of me. I can feel so much more deeply now. I see much farther.

If it gains power from being in our bodies, using our brains, what do we get? Daniel asked. It was a fine question. Abigail considered the possible answers. She could summon the Abyss material to her, and so could Daniel, as far as she could see. She could push and pull it even as the others tried to claim it. That was something. It was the only thing keeping her parents alive, as alive as they were, at any rate. She tried not to think about that. It would distract her, pull her down.

What can *we do with all this power? This dark motivator that animates the dead, reshapes living tissue...*

CHAPTER THIRTY-FIVE

As a shield for her inner thoughts, Abigail began to sing again in her mind, recalling the song about trees she had sung before to a similar end. It wasn't very long, and she began to cycle through it over and again, making up a few new verses about the trees pushing back and helping themselves save the forest rather than relying on the good will of people.

It's true, she thought beneath the song. *We have no one to turn to. No one is going to come save us. We've got to find a way. Where's Martin?* She wondered, searching, but all she could see was bone warped into a castle, encompassing part of the offices, but not the stamp mills or storage silos. *Or the slag heaps... There's got to be something...* She kept searching, testing her connection to the various groups Abyss had made of the people.

The miners, she could sense, but their minds were blank. She pulled on their dark bodies and a few of them collapsed, just as had the townsfolk when the energy was withdrawn from them. She kept searching. Her mind alit on the office workers, the engineers and her parents. They whirled and spun, around and around, stuck in patterns, barely able to break free long enough to look up. How they had managed to throw the office furniture out to distract Abyss was a mystery. To Abigail, they felt like water flowing down a drain. Were they already too far gone to ever be themselves again? She turned away.

There! She found Thomson, the merest portion of Abyss in his hands, as she had been weeks before. Could she whisper to him as Abyss had done with her? She leaned with her mind toward him, willed him to hear her. In return she got flashes of silver ore being crushed by the stamp mills, vast vats heated to smelting temperatures, fire, and crates like the ones on the wagon when they went to face the bear.

The bear! A flutter ran through her, fright and disgust and pity, but then confusion, pain. She was connected to the creature, amazed that it persisted, even with Abyss' help. *I'm so sorry this happened to you. None of us deserved this, but least of all you, sleeping there in that cave with your young...*

The moaning response from the creature reverberated through the bone castle, making her knees shake. *I cannot give your life back, so many lives have been lost... I can't fix things for you, but together, perhaps, we can stop all this.* She thought the creature, uplifted in its own way by Abyss' presence, understood.

The ramp at the entrance rose, slamming shut, leaving Abigail, Daniel, and Abyss alone within the bone castle's confines, and everyone outside separated from the conflict. She sensed Thomson moving around the Landing, doing something near the stamp mills, and sent the bear over, moving slowly, showing itself to be docile.

"Choose!" Abyss finally cried out. "You choose between us! Who shall be your king? The bandit child, carrying nothing but failure? Or the eternal being who will elevate you to Empress of the Cosmos?" Abigail's focus shifted back to her own person. Abyss, massive, multi-limbed, bore down on her. Daniel, crisscrossed in black bands, but his face revealed, harsher, no longer the friend who saved her and Martin in the alley, or skipped rocks with them on the lake, or...

"Well, Abigail? Is it me, or this monstrosity from under the earth? We can win against it, together, tear it apart and take its power, make our own rules from here out," Daniel said, an edge to his voice that matched the harder expression.

"Do you two think you're the only options? This is my parents all over again. Mother wanting me to find some rich man to take care of me instead of letting me grow and find my own life. Father thinking Mother knew best and allowing her to take away my chance to go to school, to study as I pleased? Making me sneak around to learn from my brother's books?" She railed, keeping their attention on her while the others worked outside. She tried not to think on them, but felt her focus slip as the bear cried out, its paw aflame from a misstep near the smelters.

What's that? What's going on out there? Abyss asked. Now she could hear its thoughts. She peered deeper, seeing its plans, of a world turned to shadow and crawling with "refined" gray creatures, most of which looked nothing like any people she'd ever seen. And she saw men and women fighting back, silver and gold, inert to its power, pushing it back, injuring it with a power even greater than sunlight.

"What are we doing?" Martin asked Thomson. After Abigail had vanished inside the bone structure, leaving them outside with the hordes of gray creatures, Thomson had lain, stunned, wounded, perhaps, for long minutes. Finally, he had risen and begun hobbling around the Landing, gathering tools from the fallen miners and breaking open the door to the explosives depot with a pick.

"Grab some of... some of everything, I suppose. I'm not completely certain how the pieces go together, but we're going to need to figure it out," Thomson said, gesturing past the ruined wood panel.

"We're going to experiment with explosives? Isn't that

excessively dangerous? Aren't things bad enough without blowing ourselves to kingdom come?"

"I thought you were the adventurous one? It's no time to sit down and have a knit. Moments like these call for action, or all will be lost! Crivvens!" Thomson's eyes widened as he looked over Martin's shoulder. When he turned to see what the man spied, he nearly passed out.

The great bear, vast raw, weeping patches of flesh on its flanks and chest, tatters of fur dragging on the ground, and no sign of her cubs, ambled slowly toward them. Thomson raised the pick, but when the bear stopped, staring at him, and then looking toward the stamps, and above, the smelters, calmly, slowly, he lowered the tool.

"I think she means to aid us."

"'Aid us?' How?" Martin asked. With a great paw, the bear righted a mine cart, one digit on the side, delicately as brushing a lover's hair from their face.

"I believe either your sister has some control over the creature, or Abyss has left it far more intelligent than the average bear," Thomson noted. "And its strength is clear. Let us get to work."

In the ensuing minutes, the trio prepared Abigail's plan, assembling materials from around the Landing. Huddled under a coat, Michael Beckett crept out into the open, directing his son in the deployment of the dynamite and detonators.

Time's sand had slipped through the hourglass. Abigail played her last card. She had found a weakness in the bone castle, a series of seams she exploited to create a second ramp while she verbally sparred with the Abyss and Daniel. Now, she let it drop, breaking the top of the castle open and leaving it to fall back against the cliff above the offices. Light streamed into the space. Daniel and Abyss both threw arms up before their faces, screaming. Abigail took her chance and ran up the ramp. Before Abigail got halfway up, Abyss' screams turned to laughter.

"Did you really think I would leave myself so vulnerable? Are you so foolish? Or have you made your choice? Leaving the weak mortal to perish in the sun's abhorrent rays?" Abyss demanded. Abigail gave her best girly giggle, something which she had little practice in and the sound gave her a shiver of disquiet. But she ran up the bone ramp, onto the sparse grass and scree at the top of the cliff, toward the upper access shaft and the crane. Abyss gave chase.

"You're still running? Have you seen me now? I am more powerful than any pathetic creature on this planet! I have greater strength, greater speed, greater intellect!" Meanwhile, Daniel huddled in the shade of the remaining castle wall, smoking, moaning.

"I suppose we'll see!" Abigail taunted, continuing to run. A rush of black wind sped past her on the left, coming to a stop at the edge of the shaft. She stopped, some meters away, pretending to be winded, bending over and placing her hands on her knees. While she gasped, she signaled Thomson and the bear.

Go!

A second later, a massive explosion of rapid fire detonations, starting deep within the shaft, shook the earth. Particulates of ore and soil flew up out of the narrow shaft like shot from a shotgun, spraying Abyss with thousands of silver bullets. The creature shrieked like a terrible wind storm, ragged, pained, enraged.

The ground around the opening began to crumble. Wings

flapped, but they were shredded by the blast of silver and Abyss lost altitude with every flap. It flitted down toward the pit. It lunged forward, clawing at the earth, but every clump came away, splitting under its claws, granting no purchase.

At first, Abigail was transfixed, but her plan was not complete. This was no easily trapped animal. A pit was not enough. She mounted the crane, looking over the controls and testing out different mechanisms. Looking down over the side, she saw the carts on the tier below, full of liquid silver, awaiting her. Nodding to herself, focusing all her intellect, she swung the hook into place to lift the first cart. Aim was key here. Usually, as it was relayed to her, there was someone with a hook on a pole to aid the operator in moving what in essence was a great fishing pole and line into place to lift the cart by a ring suspended above it on a metal frame. Finally, she caught the edge of the frame, if not the ring.

"Good enough," she said through gritted teeth, cranking on a wheel, which, through a massive gearbox, afforded her the mechanical advantage to lift the cart. She just cleared the upper level when an ebon hand reached out of the pit. With a grunt, she shifted gears, using a crank to turn the turret, swinging the cart toward the hole. A wheel of the cart caught one of the support beams of the crane, tipping and spilling the silver into the near side of the pit. Abyss shrieked again, the hand slipped back, but not out of sight.

As quickly as she could, more used to the functioning of the machine now, Abigail dropped the cart and reached for a second. A pole reached out from the shadow of the cliff, trying to aid her, but it was too short. Finally, it lunged forward. For a brief moment, she saw a gray form and a coat fluttering to the tracks beneath the cart. *Father.* The hook sank home, right into the ring, but then the pole dropped, its wielder falling to dust on the breeze as Peter Smalls had.

"No! Noo!" She screamed. Tears in her eyes, muscles screaming at the abuse, Abigail cranked the cart up over the lip of the cliff, above the protruding timber she'd struck the first time. She spotted the tips of horns breaching sunlight again. "This is all your fault!" She screamed, hitting the release on the hook, dropping the cart right onto Abyss' head. A tide of silver splashed out, over the reaching hand, over the horns. Abyss shrieked one final time as it fell. For long seconds, the scream pierced Abigail's brain, drilling into her psyche. Images of terror and torture flashed through her mind, promises from the plummeting creature.

The shriek ended with a crash of metal on stone. Abigail sent the last message and leapt from the crane. She ran toward the woods as fast as she could, taking refuge in the nightmare shadows that had haunted her for so long. As she came around to the far side of a massive sequoia, the shock wave rolled out. A second round of detonations.

Dust rode a sudden burst of air, and then silence reigned for long seconds, broken only by a growing creak of metal. Abigail peered around the tree just in time to watch the crane itself tip into the hole, long arm snapping against the far side and folding back over the hole to be swallowed, hopefully, she thought, for eternity.

She let out a long, cleansing breath and wept, sinking to the ground. Father was gone. So many were dead. She reached out along her connection, but felt nothing. Even the streaks and veins of Abyss deep below seemed to have vanished from her mind's eye. That was for the best, she was certain.

After long minutes, Professor Thomson and Martin appeared over the lip of the cliff, ambling slowly toward her.

The Voice of Silver Hill
ISSUED EVERY SUNDAY
by
C. Valente and S. McGuire

* * *

Terms of Subscription:

One copy, one year........................45 cents
One copy, six months........................23 cents
Single copies........................1 cent
Contact purveryors for advertising rates.

The Silver°

Vol XIX - No. 49 · SILVER HILL, NEVADA

FIRE RAGES ACROSS

SILVER HILL- Last week, a ruckus incited by the Swindon Gang, now headed by Daniel Swindon resulted in fire gutting The Rusty Pick, a favorite watering hole along Main Street, Silver Hill's first and finest tavern. Volunteers barely got the blaze under control before another fire along the riverside strip of warehouses drew firefighters to form a second brigade, drawing directly from the river. Three warehouses were damaged, with one being in such terrible condition that there's already talk of felling it in order to simply rebuild. We do not yet have an accounting of what goods, or lives, might have been lost.

NOTICE.

WE, THE UNDERSIGNED, HEREBY give notice that the co-partnership existing under the firm name of King & Feynman, is this day dissolved by mutual consent. All bills owing to said firm to be paid to S. King, and all liabilities of said firm settled by same.

AURORA- While our sister city has been out of contact for some time, now, observers on the high plains, managing our sheep and cattle, report three separate fires sending up great plumes of smoke. At least one of these seems to continue to rage at last update.
Is this simply a co-incidence? Or is it more serious? We ahve had many troubling days, of late, and one must wonder what has caused Aurora to cut communications.

K. VONNEGUT

ATTORNEY AND COUNSELOR AT LAW

RENO, NEVADA

Will practice in all the Courts of thie State.

Having paid especial attention to the practice before the United States Land Office for nine years, respectfully tenders his services for that branch of business. Will take necessary steps to secure the selection of lands by the State and obtain patents for the same for parties with or without their being present.

Voice f Hill

Weather

No snow yet, but it's just a matter of time! Keep warm and gather fuel for those fires!

SUNDAY, NOVEMBER 29, 1874 • 1 cent

SILVER HILL VALLEY!!

THE LANDING- Observers in town also noted yet another great explosion from up on the mountain. Between this series of unexpected detonations of late and the keeping of workers on site for extended periods, also unexpected, one is forced to wonder what this new project really entails and how well it is going. Silver Hill needs it citizens back, and they no doubt need rest. I urge the Becketts to send a courier directly to this office or the Sheriff's office explaining the current situation.

* * *

NOTICE.

BOVA LEATHERWORKING

Is Moving to the Great State of California!

In order to advance his business and expand his clientelle, Mr. Bova will be working from a new shop in San Diego. He will still be available for requests and orders through the Post.

* * *

HAWKS- While no doubt faring better than we, our friend across the mountain have reported more creatures of their own coming down from the forest. Descriptions are unclear, but apparently they include more chimerical animals and an Pauite wickiup, of all things. This reporter is stunned byt he frankly bizarre nature of these events, and will keep the citizenry informed as to further developments.

* * *

Great Auction Sale

J. TOLKIEN

I WILL SELL AT AUCTION, to the highest bidder, FOR CASH, until out of stock.

Household Furniture

Walnut Chamber Sets,
Bedsteads and Bedding,
Tables and Chairs,
Washstands and Bureaus,
Cookstoves and Crockery, etc

* * *

CHAPTER THIRTY-SIX

Smoke still drifted on the air below in lazy blankets, stacked and obscuring the tightly packed houses along the river that Abigail had called home town all her life. So much of it was in ruin, there was talk of abandoning the town. She had no doubt some would, and wished she could summon some rousing speech persuading those present to remain.

Certainly Professor Thomson, while bandaged up and walking with his traditional limp only slightly worsened, and Sam Clemens avowed to never share the events of their stay in Silver Hill, would go about their lives, however affected by the rise and fall of Abyss in this small mining town. They would go back east, one to Connecticut, the other to Scotland.

But where would she and Martin go? How long would their parents' money hold out? Neither of them were terribly equipped for normal life. Even less so given their injuries in the fight against Abyss.

Father Gerrold, his flock diminished, but all present in the church as one of the last undamaged buildings after fires claimed so much in the aftermath of the final battle, stood before the altar.

"We gathered here every week for nearly two decades, raising our voices and our hearts to God to keep us safe and forgive us our sins. We have seen births, christenings, deaths in our time together, but I think that we can all agree the message God has for us now is to move on from this place, this cursed valley. And so while there are more fathers and mothers and brothers and sisters on their final journey to meet out Maker than in any previous tragedy of Silver Hill, this should be the last such tragedy. I cannot give every one of them the individual funeral they deserve, but take this as a funeral for the town itself, all its lost citizens. I urge you all to gather what you may and join me in a great exodus, fleeing from this place which God has deemed as inaccessible as Eden after the fall of Adam and Eve.

"Worry not, fear not, for He shall guide us all on our journeys, whether we go west or east, north or south. May he lead us to peace and prosperity, safety and happiness in new lands." The priest concluded his speech and waved his hand in the sign of the cross, blessing the tattered remains of his congregation. "Return to your homes, you that still have them, and assemble your households to caravan to the train station. The church shall pay your fares and we shall part, brothers and sisters under His guidance."

"Father?" Abigail asked. "Is that it, then? Is there no hope for what my parents have built? No reclamation?"

"I'm sorry, Abigail. Look around. The town is in ruins, the mine is too dangerous to work, and without it, the garden we have built will wither and die. It is best to go while we can." Abigail nodded. It made sense. The estate was in top shape, but the rest of the town already looked like it had been abandoned. And no, it could not survive without her parents' mine. Could she? Without it, without them?

“May I say a few words before the congregation breaks up?”

“Please, my child. I think that would be appropriate and welcome.”

“People of Silver Hill! My parents came here, individually, on their own, and their meeting, hard work amongst the stone and earth, brought you all here, as well. It is sad that we must move on, but I wanted to thank each of you for participating in the dream Mother and Father had for not just themselves, but for this community."

"I know many of you blame them for recent events, and I cannot hold that against you, though I don't think it comes down to them, but a strange and dangerous world. I have discussed my family's holdings, and while the buildings and large equipment hold no value to pass on to others, we do have money in the local banks and in Carson City which we will make available to you to aid in relocation. My brother and I will make these funds available, in coin, dust, and paper money, to each of you as you leave this dream behind for the outside world once again."

"That's very generous of you, Abigail, and I for one am impressed that in this time, having lost as much as anyone here, and more than many, in your parents, you have the spirit to think of others and put that money to the betterment of our community, though it be cast upon the winds," Father Gerrold said. A few townsfolk cheered. A few grumbled. Most just continued toward the doors, heads down.

"I know these past weeks have been harrowing. You, our visitors, our guests," Abigail said, sitting in the parlor for the first time, for the last time, "and our helpers here at the only home we've ever known." She looked around at Liza and the other faces who were like aunts and uncles to herself and Martin as well as to Mr. Clemens, Professor Thomson, and Aunt Helen and Rupert.

"The town is done for. A few farmers may stay, eking out an existence in the high plains and softer hills of the range hereabouts, and to them, I wish the best of luck, but without the mine, Silver Hill as it has grown up alongside us cannot persist. Thus, we must leave behind the only place we've called home, and many of our possessions, though our personal belongings have been sent ahead to our Aunt's home back East."

"Liza, Michel, Humbert and the rest, you have served us well, kept us fed and out of harm's way for so long. Take with you whatever you may from this place, or stay, if that is truly your desire. We have little claim on this place, and now way to sell it, at any rate. Thank you for all your service." At this, Liza rose, tears welling in her eyes, and clasped hands with Abigail. The younger woman smiled warmly and shrugged off convention, embracing her maid for the last time. The servants shuffled out now, leaving the Becketts and their guests.

"There is... one more thing. I know we have agreed not to... discuss the matters of Silver Hill, the mine, and the... events of this autumn again, even amongst ourselves, but..." Abigail hesitated.

"What is it, child? No, I'm sorry, young lady? None could go through these events still a child, I think," Mr. Clemens said.

"I know why you came here," Abigail said cryptically, "all of you, and it's not for the reasons you may be aware of."

"Oh?" Professor Thomson said.

"What do you mean, Abigail?" Helen put the question clearer. Abigail moved to the fireplace, where the final fire of her time here burned away, low, but merry, staving off the chill of imminent winter.

"This creature I've come to call 'Abyss' lay in the earth for... well, if its account is to be believed, since the creation of the Earth itself, seeded there as was the silver itself fathomless times ago." She turned back to look at those gathered, relishing the heat of the fire pressing into her flesh. They nodded, waiting for her point. She could feel the filamentous tendrils of the creature, stretched all through her body, writhe a bit at the heat, making it all the more delicious.

"It has been wearing away, being freed little by little, and infecting creatures, maybe people, for centuries, at least. More to the point, it made its way into oaks, amongst other flora and fauna. Oak galls that were made into ink, and later the black material the inkmakers found most suitable to the task."

"Ahh..." Professor Thomson nodded again. "It is your conjecture that we were drawn here, pardon the pun, it was unintentional, by Abyss via the ink in the letters you and your brother sent out?" This time, Abigail nodded. Clemens and Thomson peered at their own hands. "But I cannot see the marks you described, nor can I see any in you."

"I think that the mixing process, or perhaps being part of a plant for so long may have changed it. It seemed that its powers of observation and understanding were augmented by the creatures it inhabited along the way."

"An interesting thought, but what does it mean for us now? Will we be pulled, like magnets, by some invisible force, motivated by the dark motivators, one might say, to do or go to places we don't personally wish, influenced by this Abyss?" Clemens asked, a mix of annoyance and fear in his voice.

"I don't know. That's why I brought the subject up to you, to make you aware. And..."

"And?" The focus on Abigail was intense. She blushed.

"And during the Battle of the Landing, there was a lot of this material flying around, back and forth, being pulled from the miners and assorted creatures, townsfolk, even the nearby trees and the great castle of bone Abyss had build. *I* could pull it to me, and send it away."

"You think to free us of this infestation?" Thomson asked.

"If I can, if you will it."

"I wouldn't want to put any undue pressure on you, my dear. If there's any danger-."

"I don't think there is, Professor," Abigail said, "But I'm also not sure if I can do it. I can't see the marks in you, anymore, either. It could be something that happened when Abyss was spread through many bodies, strong, and active, or because I had enough in me." She held out a hand to Thomson. He stepped forward and took hers in a firm handshake position. She closed her eyes, reaching out. It was there, fragmented, thin and enervated, but she couldn't quite reach it. It was like reaching under a bureau and just touching a lost item with fingertips such that it rocked back.

"I'm sorry, it *is* there, but so weak, I hope it cannot do further harm with the main body dispersed."

"Thank you for trying." Thomson stepped back. Clemens extended his hand.

"I'm sorry you all got drawn into this mess. You needn't have been endangered but for our interference," Martin said.

"Nonsense, son, there's no way either of you could have known," Thomson said. "It is an extraordinary thing, this Abyss. If not for its maniacal obsession with spreading, it would be amazing to study and learn from such a being as claims to have existed since before the Earth itself? This entire framework of reality? It boggles the mind."

Abigail was unsuccessful with Clemens, in a similar way.

"Worry not, young lady. As you say, it does not seem to harm us for now, and won't unless someone goes unearthing more of this creature. Then, I suppose we'll all see one another again," Clemens joked. They all laughed uneasily.

"We should start moving toward the station. There are not an overabundance of tickets to be had, seeing how the town is clearing out. They might well shut down the station itself soon," Liza reminded them. Abigail closed the grate before the fire and they all gathered their things while their former servants, released, bustled about gathering what valuables they perhaps had been eyeing for years.

"I'm sorry you didn't get to perform your experiments in the number three shaft, Professor," Abigail said on the platform, her brother at her shoulder and Mr. Clemens standing by.

"And your equipment..." Martin said. "If Swindon hadn't-"

"Let us not dwell upon the immutable past, son. My equipment, while unique, is replaceable, able to be recreated, if not easily. You spoke about moving on, Abigail. You would be a grand asset to me in that project, and I'm sure others. You could come and be my assistant, receive your degree at the same time."

"Professor! I... I don't know what to say," Abigail said.

"Let me know at your earliest convenience. I shall await correspondence from you at any rate. I'm sure I'll have some puzzles for you to solve with regards to the next iteration of the sensing and recording devices," Thomson said. Abigail looked at Martin. "Ah yes, you probably wish to remain together. Of course you're welcome as well, Martin. You acquitted yourself well in this ordeal and don't deserve the rewards yet bestowed upon you by Fate. Come to Scotland, perhaps study in some other arena, or with your sister." Martin winced at this.

"I really don't know what I'm going to do now. I know that Abigail is far smarter than me, and will go onto different things."

"Martin..."

"No, I know it's true. You're driven, intelligent, and able. It is inevitable that our paths would diverge soon enough, even without Abyss and all of this. I just don't know where my path lies, though it seems clear where you should go." Abigail took his hand, holding it tight, imagining for a moment she might never let go. Father was gone. Mother was... she wasn't sure what would become of Mother. Martin had always been there...

"Nevertheless, Martin, my invitation remains open to both of you. Mr. Clemens. A... you'll forgive me if I hesitate to classify our meeting as a 'pleasure,' given the circumstances." The other man nodded.

"Indeed. You are welcome to my estate in Connecticut. I'm certain that we have as much to discuss as not to discuss."

"We can hold that discussion on the train," Thomsons offered. "Becketts." Thomson tipped his hat and stepped up onto the train.

"Martin, Abigail, I came to Silver Hill on a lark. I was in Carson City visiting friends from my newspaper days and thought a nice jaunt down to a superstition-filled small mining town would give me a lot to think about, grist for the mill as they say. For a couple of extra days of travel, I had hoped to earn myself enough research, enough personal tales of fright that I could pursue Martin's idea about writing terrifying tales as a whole new area of entertainment.

"I went up that mountain expecting some shoddily made monster masks or an abandoned Indian site with stories told around a campfire. I'm not usually so obtuse about getting to my point... What I mean to say is that I'm sorry for not taking your stories seriously, even when you said so in the most serious way."

"We understand, Mr. Clemens. How were you to know?" Martin asked. "They certainly sound unbelievable, flights of dark fancy."

"Indeed, but I should have given you more credit. Certainly your writing shows you to be an intelligent, educated young man."

"And will you be writing those stories when you get back to Connecticut?" Martin asked.

"I don't think I will. I shall never forget my experiences here, but I don't think the world is ready for such bone jarring reality. A story's primary goal is to entertain, but I'm afraid these stories might do real harm to the unprepared reader. Perhaps I will find a milder way to transmit the lessons of these days."

"That could be true. I know we weren't prepared when we stumbled upon it," Abigail said. "I just hope it stays buried for good."

"As a student of life and the lies we all tell each other, I know one thing: the truth will always find its way to the surface. But hopefully that one will take its sweet time. Look how long it took to get free the first time."

"If it *was* the first time," Martin said.

"Martin!" Abigail started, eyes wide. "But you're not wrong. It is certainly possible... I suppose we'll have to do some poking around at other mines around the world. I still have a good idea where the highest concentrations of-" she caught herself. "You know... are."

"That is a task I will leave to you. I have a family and a writing career to get back to. Best of Luck."

"And to you, Mr. Clemens. I'll drop you a line when we get settled in. You can send us copies of all your new works as they come out."

"I'll consider that an advanced order, my young friend." They all chuckled and Mr. Clemens stepped up onto the train. A few moments later, he appeared in the window beside Professor Thomson, already deep in conversation before he sat down.

The Voice of Silver Hill
ISSUED EVERY SUNDAY
by
C. Valente and S. McGuire

★ ★ ★

Terms of Subscription:

One copy, one year..........45 cents
One copy, six months..........23 cents
Single copies..........1 cent
contact purveyors for advertising rates.

The Silver°

Vol XIX - No. 50 • SILVER HILL, NEVADA

FINAL MINE CLOSED!

SILVER HILL- Nearly one third of the town has succumbed to fire, though the known blazes have been extinguished. The main currently worked shafts, eight and nine, suffered catastrophic failures in recent days due to a series of fires and accidents. Some are even claiming unprecedented seismic activity as the earth itself has shaken a number of times of late.

As a matter of record, the buildings confirmed lost are The Rusty Pick Saloon, Pertwee's General Store, the post office, fully seven warehouses owned by the Becketts and various others along the river, Vogel's Barber Shop, and a large number of private homes and bunkhouses.

Due to a lack of basic resources and no doubt, incoming shipments, we highly recommend relocation for all Silver Hillians. No response has been gotten from numerous attempts to contact the Becketts. It is feared the adults are deceased and we are left with no leadership to rebuild the town or the mine.

I know a few diehard stalwarts will insist on watching the sun set upon Silver Hill until their last breaths, and we wish those hearties well. May the water run clean and the beasts remain free of whatever has sent the rest of us running.

ANNOUNCEMENT

HAWKS- Sheriff Tennant reports being forced to fire on anyone coming down the mountain on the east side. Too many of those appearing at Hawks township of late have been seriously ill with some unnamed plague or acting in wild and vicious manners. Do not, repeat, DO NOT evacuate due east. Take the train or head up to Carson City for your first step to a new start.

Voice f Hill

Weather

The wind always blows, and the sun always shines, even when we can't see it. May your travels be safe.

SUNDAY, DECEMBER 6, 1874 • 1 cent

EDITION
EVACUATE NOW!

ANNOUNCEMENT

SILVER HILL-Despite the loss of Sheriff Hornsby, Deputy Colin Liu and Father Gerrold are organizing an evacuation committee for the distribution of remaining wealth to surviving Silver Hillians and escorts to the train station beginning Tuesday at ten o'clock in the morning at the sheriff's office. No one will be left behind who does not want to stay, nor made to leave if they wish to remain. This is strictly a service to the community.

AURORA- Our final update on our sister city suggests that she fared no better in this last season of strange and dangerous events. There is no communication via telegraph, and no messengers have been welcomed. The view from the high pastures continues to show only ongoing fires.

ANNOUNCEMENT

FINALLY, this is a sad day for all along the river valley. We here at The Voice of Silver Hill have enjoyed two decades of gathering and distributing important information, opinions, and advertisements for a fuller, more cohesive Silver Hill. This is our final issue. As we lay down these words and run the printing press for the last time, we hold up a glass to those who have gone before us and weep for those who will not walk beside us as we seek the next step in our journey. Fare thee well, Silver Hillians, and God Bless.

ON a personal note, The Voice has served this community for nearly twenty years, and in that time, we have met the best and the worst. By far, the former outnumber the latter, and we are grateful for our time here.

✶ FARE THEE ALL WELL ✶

CHAPTER THIRTY-SEVEN

Martin picked up a copy of the local paper, immediately spotting the headlines, “FINAL EDITION! MINE CLOSED! EVACUATION RECOMMENDED!” And wondering if he had made it into the last printing before they shipped the machine off to its new home.

He supposed it didn’t matter too much, as who would see this final issue, anyway? They were just hanging around to let Abigail say her final goodbyes to folks from town who had lined up to board the train and give away wads of money. He understood it, but he didn’t really get why he had to be there. Nobody cared about the Beckett name anymore, certainly not here, and even if they did, they would be spread across the West and of little help to him in getting to the jungles of Africa or even the deserts, for that matter.

The train's rhythmic rocking like waves on the sea and the racket of metal parts clanking between cars set Abigail into a contemplative state. What would life be now? Where *would* she end up going? What about Martin? What about... She hesitated to even think the name, but it was gone, wasn't it? She knew the answer to that as well. Abyss hadn't just given her a view of the formation of the Earth and other planets, but the ability to see, for a time, Abyss itself, buried deep, but biding its time. Other miners would strike that material some day, or dig to build, somewhere in the world. There was so much of it, so many streaks of utter black mixed in amongst deposits of silver and gold and other materials it couldn't inhabit, couldn't move on its own.

This could all happen again someday, and that was

perhaps the most chilling thought of all. She redoubled her resolve to learn as much as she could about the natural philosophy of Thomson's "dark bodies." They would be ready next time. They would have to be.

Martin set down the paper he'd been reading, the last edition from The Voice of Silver Hill. "Doesn't look good for the old river valley. Sounds like Aurora has suffered its own bout of calamity, and enough infected people came down across the mountain that Hawks is shooting on sight."

"That's horrible. Wait, Aurora's just south of Silver Hill, down stream, right on the river. You don't suppose... May I see the paper?" Abigail asked. Martin handed it across the space between seats.

Abigail looked at the words, but her mind was immediately drawn away from their meaning to the ink in which they were laid out. The deep black letters triggered something at the back of her mind. Were they moving, just a little? She shivered and let the paper drop.

"Hey now! That's the final edition. It could be worth something someday. They're not making any more. That's what 'final' means."

"I wouldn't be so sure we won't see more of those," Abigail said, wrapping her arms around herself.

"Let's not bicker," Aunt Helen said, patting Rupert in her lap. "It's going to be a long trip back east, and we've got a lot to figure out. I don't have room for you at present, but we'll get by. We're all the family we have, now."

Special Thanks

I would like to extend special thanks to my Patreon supporters who have been there for me, reading the sloppy early drafts of my science fiction series and my fantasy series as well.

Especially amongst these are Cynthia, who has given me great feedback on a number of books; Ethan, a great friend who was the first to sign up when I started my Patreon journey; and Marilyn, who has a generous and supportive soul and for some reason likes what I write.

Other Patrons are not to be forgotten, as they have helped me reach this milestone in my writing journey:

Kristin, Grady, Byron, Nancy, and Christine, who are all friends and family from across my life.

Of course, I also wouldn't be here without my team at Ascendent, especially Wally for giving my writing a home, and Dan with whom I hope to spend more days laughing and chatting while people walk by wondering what's wrong with us all at various festivals and cons.

Last, but not least, thanks to Kat Howard, whose suggestions and edits made the Weight of Darkness that much better and helped me refine my vision.

Thanks to you all, and to you, the reader, who have chosen my story from a seeming infinite sea of words.

www.ingramcontent.com/pod-product-compliance
Lightning Source LLC
Chambersburg PA
CBHW030422310726
48979CB00009B/1580/J